All Bones and Lies is Anne Fine's fifth novel. Her first was the critically acclaimed *The Killjoy*. *Taking the Devil's Advice* and *Telling Liddy* have both been adapted for radio. She is also a distinguished writer for young people, and has won the Carnegie Medal twice, the Whitbread Children's Award twice, the *Guardian* Children's Literature Award and a Smarties Prize. An adaptation of her novel *Goggle-Eyes* has been shown by the BBC, and Twentieth-Century Fox filmed her novel *Madame Doubtfire* as *Mrs Doubtfire*, starring Robin Williams. Her books have been translated into twenty-six languages and she has recently been appointed Children's Laureate. Anne Fine has two grown-up daughters and lives in County Durham.

D1427092

Also by Anne Fine

THE KILLJOY
TAKING THE DEVIL'S ADVICE
IN COLD DOMAIN
TELLING LIDDY

and published by Black Swan

ALL BONES AND LIES

Anne Fine

BLACK SWAN

ALL BONES AND LIES
A BLACK SWAN BOOK : 0 552 99898 2

Originally published in Great Britain by Bantam Press,
a division of Transworld Publishers

PRINTING HISTORY
Bantam Press edition published 2001
Black Swan edition published 2002

3 5 7 9 10 8 6 4 2

Set in 12½/14½pt Garamond 3 by
Falcon Oast Graphic Art Ltd.

Black Swan Books are published by Transworld Publishers,
61–63 Uxbridge Road, London W5 5SA
a division of The Random House Group Ltd,
in Australia by Random House Australia (Pty) Ltd,
20 Alfred Street, Milsons Point, Sydney, NSW 2061, Australia,
in New Zealand by Random House New Zealand Ltd,
18 Poland Road, Glenfield, Auckland 10, New Zealand
and in South Africa by Random House (Pty) Ltd,
Endulini, 5a Jubilee Road, Parktown 2193, South Africa.

The Random House Group Limited supports The Forest Stewardship
Council (FSC®), the leading international forest certification organisation.
Our books carrying the FSC label are printed on FSC® certified paper.
FSC is the only forest certification scheme endorsed by the leading
environmental organisations, including Greenpeace. Our
paper procurement policy can be found at
www.randomhouse.co.uk/environment

MIX
Paper from
responsible sources
FSC® C018072

Printed and bound in Great Britain by Clays Ltd, St Ives PLC

For Geoff W.,
and in memoriam
A.R.W.

1

COLIN STOOD IN THE KITCHEN DOORWAY, WONDERING
how others managed when it came to this. His fingers
tightened round the saucer, causing the cup to rattle
horribly as, once again, from the bedroom, came that
rising, two-note bird call.

'Co-*lin*.'

A crow. A vulture, even, pecking away at the scraps of
him before he was even dead.

'Co-*lin*!'

She didn't usually start calling quite so quickly. How
long had he been standing there? Long enough to imagine
himself creeping out to the woodshed and fetching a
hatchet, then phoning the police to explain. 'I'm sorry,
but it reached the stage where I knew, if I heard her calling "Co-*lin*" one more time . . .' They'd understand. They
probably came across this sort of thing all the time.
Regretfully, though, they'd have to remind him that
wheels of justice would still have to turn. Better to—

No. He'd not admit there was anything 'better' about
it. But, laying aside all thought of hatchets, he crossed the
hall and took the stairs slowly, noticing with interest that,

even though his hands had steadied, the tea kept slopping.

'You've taken your time. It'll be cold.'

'It's your own fault for choosing to sit upstairs.'

'I like it here. It's easier on my poor leg.'

'Open your letter,' he told her, to steer her off that grisly topic. 'After all, it took long enough to reach you.'

She flapped the thick cream envelope at him as if he hadn't been the one to notice it stuck in the gap between the rusting umbrella stand and the wall, and bring it up to her. 'I know it'll only be more trouble.'

He set the teacup on the wobbly table beside her chair. More trouble, indeed! You'd think, from the way she said it, she lived in war-torn Kuzubukhstan, or on some city street with drug dealers and pimps for neighbours, and gunfights and screeching whores for evening entertainment. You'd never think she lived in an enviably spacious old house in pretty West Priding, and no one had ever crossed her, and nothing serious had ever gone wrong. 'Why your lady mum so miserable, anyway?' Mr Stastny had asked once, dumping the box of groceries into Colin's arms. And, for the life of him, Colin couldn't answer. Trawl as he might through family history, there was nothing to justify such unsparing self-pity. She was born, just like everyone; had a childhood with some ups, some downs; landed a smart job which took her all over, and, just as that was beginning to prove too much of an effort (and time might, by some, have been thought to be running out), had the good fortune to meet and marry the man who, after fathering the conveniently time-saving twin babies, Colin and Dilys, had done his best for her for a decade more before popping his clogs and leaving her with a quite adequate pension. If, now, she only had one son to brighten her sunset years, it was entirely through choice. It wasn't as if anyone forced her to stop speaking to Dilys.

But she was still Our Lady of the Sorrows. Fascinating, really. It could have been the perfect life, if you translated 'Colin was such a sickly child' into 'I was so lucky to have an excuse not to go back to work', and took 'stuck in this one-eyed hole' to mean 'yes, I've been fortunate enough to live here long enough to get things exactly the way I want them'. Not that she looked at it that way. 'I'm a woman the Fates don't like,' she said sourly and often. And it was a matter of principle to hoard old misfortunes, fetching them out regularly for a brush and a polish.

And welcome in new ones, as she was doing now. 'I do hope it's nothing terrible. I think I would rather live on an island all alone than have any more upsets.'

'Maybe it's good news,' he couldn't resist suggesting, to annoy her. 'Maybe you've won some lottery.'

She gave him a scathing look, then took to examining the smudge of a postmark. 'Does that say Scarborough? What could I possibly have to do with anyone in Scarborough?'

'You could open it and see.'

She lifted a face set like a roughcast wall. 'You wait,' her eyes said. 'Wait till your life has turned so thin and dull you like to savour every little thing that comes your way. Let's hope some snotty bugger comes along and scoffs at *you*.'

'Anyway,' he said, guilt fuelling irritation, 'what's that printed on the front?'

Unwillingly, she admitted, 'It says, "Be properly insured".'

'That'll be it, then. Something to do with insurance.'

'Possibly.'

Oh, for God's sake! He bent down behind the wingback chair, ostensibly to pick up the cardigan that had slid to the floor but really to hide his grimace. What was the *matter* with old people? Why couldn't they simply rip open a letter and read it? Why did they have to mull over the postmark and franking stamp as if they were bloody runes? There ought to be a way of putting a rocket under them when they were being so tiresome. If he arranged his Eurovision Frost-Top Contest a different way, then he could strip them of points each time they——

No. Better to keep the scoring the way everyone was used to seeing it, with points awarded rather than taken off. She was still fretting. 'The insurance renewal can't be due for *months*.' But he wasn't listening. He was pitching his idea to a television commissioning panel. Everyone knew there were far too many old people. All over Europe pension funds couldn't cope and standards of care were atrocious. So every year there'd be a cull. Run like the Eurovision Song Contest (but without the pizzazz), everyone over seventy would be up for grabs, and everyone else would have twenty points ('That's *vingt points*!') to distribute. So if, for example, the old dear next door was forever hobbling around with home-baked cookies and offering to babysit, then naturally, on the Big Night, Mr and Mrs Frayed Parent would award her as many points as they could rake up between them, to keep her alive, and at it. And if, sadly, that meant they had *nul points* left over for their own parents – always a little bit too wrapped up in their own affairs to be helpful – then they'd end up in that year's cull. Simple. And very moral. Because, like the Song Contest, the aim was always to reward the best, and in this case best meant unselfish, useful, loved. Standards in over-seventies would shoot sky high. Entire personalities would change for the better overnight, or pay for it drastically.

The sound of an envelope tearing drew his attention back. He tracked the sense of the letter through her grumbling. 'Overheads! That'll be fancy cream envelopes you can hardly rip open . . . Increasing costs? More fat cats farting through silk, if I know anything about insurance companies . . . Rise in premiums? I knew it! When push comes to shove, it's always bad news for the consumer . . . Barefaced cheek!'

The sudden fall of silence didn't bode very well. But he was well aware she wouldn't take it up with him, and risk letting him in on any of her secrets. Anyone else, he reflected, might ask their only son, 'You can't remember how much I paid for house insurance last year, can you, Colin?' Or even, 'Can you nip down to the breadbin and bring up that big blue envelope?' But not her. She'd wait till he took the dog out, and then she'd be down the stairs like greased lightning, leg or no leg, to see exactly what was meant by 'rise in premiums'.

'Bad news?'

'Nothing that won't keep,' she said cagily, shovelling the letter back in its envelope and pushing it behind the cushion. But there was an air of rising distraction about her. It might, he thought with that sinking sense of coming events casting their shadows before, be worth laying his hands on this letter to find out exactly what was going on.

'Changed your mind over the muffins?' he asked her, to allay suspicion.

'No, thanks. I'm not hungry.'

That was another thing that ought to lose old people points, thought Colin. Pretending they didn't eat. He couldn't for the life of him work out what pleasure could be gleaned from affecting indifference to a treat someone offered to put in front of you, then secretly pigging on bran flakes. He'd checked it out with one of his sister's outgoing friends. 'Is this behaviour *normal*?' Val had, after all, been a qualified and experienced Health Visitor. She ought to know. And her reply had astonished him. 'Well, maybe not *normal*, Colin. But not uncommon. All part and parcel of some vertiginous urge towards the very thing threatening them: in this case, Death. Next time you're there, take a peek at the photos on her walls. I expect you'll find everyone in them is already six feet under.'

And there they all hung still. Aunt Ida. His father. Viv. Tanka the dog. Betty from Swannington. All dead and buried, except for—

'My photo! Where's it gone?'

She barely lifted her head from the loose thread she was tracking through her woolly. 'What photo?'

'That one of me and Teresa Fuller in nursery school, dressed up as two very large ducks.' (No point in harping on about the fact that it was the only one left after his quite unwitting act of sibling suttee, thanks to the bonfire that followed her bust-up with Dilys.)

'I don't remember that one.'

'Of course you do! We were about to be killed by the farmer's wife. I certainly hope that you haven't got rid of it.'

She swatted at him. 'Oh, really, Colin! Do you think I have nothing better to do than keep track of your old photos? Why don't you do something useful? Take Floss and go and get a paper before I go out of my mind.'

Well, look at that. She couldn't wait to get him out of the house so she could scurry down and root through her paperwork. Proof, at the very least, her leg was getting better.

And he'd escape for ten minutes.

'A paper. Right you are. Anything else?'

Wait for it . . .

'Well, while you're there you could just ask Mr Stastny about those special teabags I ordered.'

Bring back the tea. Right.

'And some Golden Churn.'

And butter.

'And if those Crispy Gingers are in again . . .'

Biscuits.

'Just have a little look around. And if there happen to be any nice bananas . . .'

Fruit.

'Oh, and *candles*. If he's got any on the shelves. Just in case.'

Candles.

'But don't go to any trouble.'

'No.'

He rested his hand on the door latch, and waited.

'Oh, and Colin! Before you go, could you just give the room a little squidge of air freshener?'

He picked it up and squirted. 'It's fresh air you need,' he scolded. 'Not more of this stuff.'

But she was already pulling her cardigan round her, ready for the great dash to the breadbin.

'Don't be so silly, Colin. Fresh air doesn't smell nearly as nice as this.'

Oh, but it *did*. The moment he was out in it he felt his spirits soar. How did the people in Val's profession manage it? Were they *saints*? Some, of course, ended up poisoning their clients, or unhooking vital drips. But most of them presumably chugged on, wiping up messes, seeing frightful sights, and steadily answering the same daft questions ten times in a row. 'So Nurse Tippet's still on holiday, is she?' 'Did Doctor tell you all about my feet?' 'Aren't you terribly young to be properly qualified?' The wonder was, he thought, that every paper wasn't crammed from first to last with details of the trials and appeals of nursing staff who had lost patience. Fully inspirited by fresh wind and sky, Colin made for the corner, hampered only by Flossie's recalcitrant dragging that made him a prey to civilities from neighbours.

'Visiting your poor mother, are you, Colin? I do hope the dear soul's feeling a little bit better.'

'Out shopping for Norah? Splendid! I'm sure she can do with the help. And the company.'

But soon he was round the backs, and feeling a little safer, on home ground. Light years ago he used to go this way every morning, endlessly dawdling, picking bits out of walls, inspecting insects and berries. He knew each crevice, every moss pattern, each rise and fall under his feet. This was the route of his imaginary life. At school, of course, his name had been a byword for clumsiness and failure. 'Lost your match?' 'Yup! Colled it up totally.' 'Whoops! Done a Col. Spilled it.' But it was a very different Colin who scuffed his way past these overhanging hedges twice a day for years and years: a sturdy, popular Colin who led the gang, rescued the drowning toddler, and showed the firemen the only safe way out of the building. Was that why that record of Dilys's had haunted him all through his teens? Del and the Stompers. 'Look fancy, have fun, act fearless'? Even back then he must have realized he could scarcely have fallen much further short. Not that he'd had the best start, what with their mother constantly bragging to everyone about what a monstrously ugly baby he had been, and pinning his sticky-out ears back against his head while she wondered aloud about the risks of operations. As for 'have fun', the words were never used inside their house without a slick of sarcasm. French exam? 'Have fun!' Unheated pool? 'Have fun!' The very concept filled his mother with suspicion. Even when other people floated the fat, bright, ballooning prospect of it within his or Dilys's reach, she'd try to shoot it down. 'I expect that the beach will be *heaving*.' 'Don't you think, with this rain, it'll probably be cancelled?' 'By the time you get there it'll be time to come home again.' Under this barrage, only someone as tough as his sister could fail to grow up fearing the worst. So Colin had hidden behind his twin, terrified of anything new – of parties, strangers, introductions even. Sometimes it got so bad it reached the stage where every single word he knew he ought to be saying sounded so ludicrous sitting waiting in his brain that he became incapable of spitting out even the basics like 'please' and 'thank you' without turning as red as a radish. 'Look fancy, have fun, act fearless!' It was so foreign to him, it was unforgettable. He would have done a whole lot better to have lit on a song more his own style. 'Look drab, feel grey, don't risk it.' That would have done him nicely, fitted him perfectly, and maybe he could have grown up and forgotten it.

Red alert! He could hear leaf-scrabbling on the far side of the hedge.

'Colin, dear. Is that you?'

For God's sake! How did the grizzled frumps manage it? Spectacles thick as bottle bottoms, yet they could spot him creeping past a privet hedge. He came to a halt by a balding patch of greenery and pawed the ground in his anguish, knowing there was no escape.

'You don't happen to be popping along to Mr Stastny's, do you?'

More bloody shopping. This one had had him down for skivvy since he was five years old. Already she was rooting in her purse. What would it be this time? Cod liver oil? Sanatogen? Support stockings?

'Rizla papers, dear. Just the one packet.'

'*Rizla* papers?'

She gave him a reproving look. 'For art class, dear. Snowflakes on my little collage.'

Another? She must have thousands of the things. She had been taking the same old art class for years and years.

And wearing the same green turban. (His mother called it The Bogey.)

'Oh, and if he's got any cornplasters . . .'

Too loud. She had been heard over the other hedge.

'Is that Colin off to the shop, Elsie? Would you mind asking him if he'd bring me back twenty Kensitas?'

'Did you catch that, Colin?'

'And a *Telegraph*. If it's not too much trouble.'

'No trouble, no.'

'And I happen to know Larry and June over the wall would appreciate a nice fresh white loaf. He was only this minute complaining that their breadbin was empty.'

Bread. Yes. 'Anything else?'

But, orders given, the hoar-heads had happily gone back to fretting over Mr Al-Khatib's peach rot.

'Yes, *very* nasty.'

'Most disappointing.'

'It does seem to me, Ahmed, that this entire back strip of yours has become little more than a grow-bag for garden diseases.'

He left them at it and fled along the alley towards Mr Stastny's, all hope of idle musing driven from his brain by his snowballing list. It was like being back at secondary school, when he used to mutter his way between the hedges, rehearsing the names of the elements, the virtues of vitamins, or the causes of wars and revolutions. Now it was teabags, two *Telegraph*s, butter, biscuits, bananas, candles, cornplasters, cigarettes, bread . . . What had he forgotten?

Oh, yes. Rizla papers.

Mr Stastny seemed equally taken with this part of the order. 'You got some nice stuff, Colin?'

He toyed with the idea of getting a bit of a reputation locally, and then confessed. 'They're for Mrs McKay's new collage.' Mr Stastny vanished into the back in search of one item or another, and Colin sank on the old person's chair and stared around glumly. How long had he been shopping in this dingy hole? Thirty-five years. Longer! And nothing had changed, except that, instead of pushing past him to the front, or speaking over him, now the rude crumble-brains simply snaffled him as he crept past their back gardens to hand in their orders. He couldn't *stand* old people. He was at the end of his tether with them. Dilys was right. The moment he got back to the house he was going to—

Mr Stastny rattled back through the bead curtain. 'No cornplasters. Only brown bread. And here's your mother's tea.' He jammed it all in. 'One bag will do you, won't it?'

Scarcely a question. More a restatement of the shop's policy of thrift. Colin set off, past Warburton's Funeral Emporium 'poised to assist' on the corner, and back down the alley. There'd been no change to speak of from his note, and he knew perfectly well from long experience just what a chore it was going to be, prising the loot for his purchases out of the fuddy-duddies. And so it proved. 'That's eighty pence I owe you, is it, Colin?' said Mr Manson, with no sign of any hand movement towards his trouser pocket. Prising the loaf from him, June Royston asked, 'I don't suppose you have change for a twenty, dear? Shall I bring it along later?' And Mrs McKay's energetic rootings in her purse proved, as ever, quite fruitless. It wasn't, thought Colin, as if any of them even had the excuse of being poor. As Dilys was forever pointing out with reference to their own mother, ever since old-age pensioners had been turned into sacred cows, most had been swilling in it. But try to winkle a coin or two out of them in return for a brown loaf and you'd soon see their fighting spirit. What were they planning to do with it, anyway? Buy yachts? Winter in Val d'Isère? Live for a thousand years?

In fact, the sole advantage of their seeming immortality was that they had at least all stayed alive long enough to relieve him of the shopping. Flexing his fingers to work back the blood flow, Colin crept past the last of the garden ends, dragging Flossie in his wake. His mother kept on at him. 'You'll be old one day too, Colin. It'll happen to you.' But he didn't believe it. He couldn't imagine a world in which he was hobbling around on a Zimmer frame, frittering away his pension on new hips and peppermints, and engaging the neighbours in mad conversations. 'I see you're escaping the worst of our couch grass epidemic, William.' 'Indeed, yes, Edmund. You see, I live by a simple axiom. Never let it see a Saturday.'

How did they do it, he wondered. Even the ones who could barely cut up their own grub could still think of something to say – his touchstone of ability. 'Sizeable rascals, aren't they, your chrysanthemums?' 'Yes. They're from Manderley's. Mind you, I did get a lovely crop of thistles out of that grass seed he sold me.' What must they think of him, slinking past with his head down, desperately hoping he wouldn't be noticed?

But at least he was safe at his own gate. Well, nearly

safe. Now all he had to do was run upstairs with the paper, mutter something she couldn't quite catch, and slip out again while she was momentarily distracted with whichever idiocy of the day they had chosen to headline. She'd just assume that he was letting Flossie in, or Flossie out. So if he could get the side door unbolted without a rattle and not catch his head on the old goblin next door's windchimes, he could escape for a further few minutes and reward himself for all his good deeds with a quiet five minutes with Suzie in the woodshed.

Strange that he'd lighted on his father's favourite. He tugged the magazine out from beneath the chisels, and it fell open, as it had from the start, at one of her pages. Suzie. Nineteen. It was her poolside party, and she'd been given one too many birthday cocktails. Suzie liked animals, her favourite colour was pink, and her hobbies were dancing and skating. There was a nice line drawing over the page of her doing a twirl on the ice rink with her skirt lifted to show everything. But (obviously like his father) Colin much preferred the drawing of her toppling tipsily into the pool. It was the way that cosy rounded bottom seemed to be quivering, as if, with some special and hitherto untried effort of will, she might be able to regain her footing – a hopeless quest dynamically, since her head, though unseen, was about to hit the water. But still, it gave him pleasure to think about how those pretty buttocks might be, first trembling in anticipation, then clenched in shock. Also, he rather liked the way the artist hadn't cared what would become of the cocktail. Off flew the glass, cherries spinning. And the way it was careering

22

over the water, it was bound to end up shattered in wicked splinters against the steps. But Colin wasn't bothered, certainly not now, and even less afterwards, when he was reaching behind the cans of flat white emulsion to find the rusty old tobacco tin in which (also, he suspected, like his father) he neatly burned the insalubrious evidence of his desire.

He loved the woodshed. And it wasn't just the feeling of peace afforded him by such moments. It was the place itself – dark, cobwebby and hidden. From as far back as Colin could remember, simply to lift the brambles that tumbled protectively over the blistering paintwork and step inside was to feel the world stilling around him. Part of it was the silence, obviously. But mostly what he loved about the shed was the sense that he had inside it of being himself and real, not just some person others had invented and taken to criticizing for being things like careless, or awkward, or even, more outlandishly, something like 'heavy on his shoes'. Inside the shed he'd sit in peace, and feelings, like tiny beansprouts, would burgeon inside him. It was, for example, sitting quietly in the woodshed that he first came to realize he missed his father. (Till then, in the terror of triggering further outbursts from Dilys, any grief of his own had been totally neglected.) It was here that he wept as he burned the teenage diary that had made him the butt of such merciless teasing (though it was now a mystery to him how he could have believed that arid decoy he'd planted so carefully under the lining paper of his sock drawer would ever have fooled prying eyes).

And it was here he cast his spells.

There'd been enough of those over the years. Colin cast spells for every reason under the sun. Spells to avert attention. Spells to silence people. Even, in bad times, spells not to wake in the morning. All through his childhood he had walked around laden with pebbles and foreign coins and fragments of coloured glass. Even through adolescence he'd kept his passion for talismanic objects. He could spend hours shunting shells and feathers into significant patterns, and cobbling phrases into impressive incantatory rites. He'd have kept owls and ravens if his mother had let him. And if Dilys had not been allergic to feathers.

He blew one away now, with the pale, spectral ashes from the tobacco tin. Better get back. And, considering what his mother could be like, it hadn't been at all a bad visit. A snatch of routine grumbling about the tea, a few squawks of resentment at having, like every other homeowner on the planet, to cough up a bit more for her annual insurance. And that was about it. A doddle, really. He could have done a whole lot worse. She could have had one of her migraines. Or fallen into one of her virulent allergies against one or another of her neighbours, tiring him out with her self-righteous bleating. No, it had been a good visit. And that was an excellent joke she had told him about the Welshman on the hill. It couldn't be easy, being stuck in an armchair staring at suppurating bits of yourself. No, he'd go in and make them both a nice cup of coffee.

When he got up there, she was busy on the phone. 'Really? No, I didn't know that . . . Well, I must say, that *does* sound better . . . Much cheaper, yes. Good heavens!

And you're quite positive that there's no trouble with the refund?' She took the cup without so much as acknowledging his presence in the room. 'Yes. Yes, I think I will. It sounds as if it would be mad not to consider it.'

At last she hung up, and looked at him smugly.

'What are you plotting?' he asked suspiciously.

'Guess how much Dolly pays for house insurance. Guess!' She didn't wait for an answer. 'She pays half what I pay. *Half!* Can you believe it?'

'Perhaps it's some fly-by-night company.'

'Frampton Commercial? Fly-by-night?'

That was him put in his place. Shrugging, he tried to look indifferent, but she wasn't watching. She was struggling with the phone again.

'Who are you ringing now?'

'Directory Inquiries.'

'It costs,' he reminded her.

Hastily, she hung up. 'I'll get the number from Dolly later.'

'You ought to think twice before switching companies,' he warned, adding spitefully, 'Especially at your age.'

She made a face and asked, 'Did you get all the shopping?' clearly hoping for the chance to console herself either with criticism of any substitutions he might have made, or with scorn at his failures. Stung, he said, 'Yes,' and scowled.

'Something wrong?'

'No.'

'You look like the man sent to empty the bath with a teaspoon.'

'I'm all right.'

And then, of course, it was open season on him. Astonishing how expressive a face could be that could hold two weeks' rain in its wrinkles. 'Oh, yes. *You're* all right,' the look said. '*You're* not hobbled half to death with a bad leg, and nothing and no one to amuse you except some mardy visitor who slips out of the room each chance he gets.'

And it was true. He wasn't making any effort to entertain her. She must have been at least as bored as this back in the days when he and Dilys were tiny, and she was sharing out their fuzzy-felt shapes, and praising their wooden block towers, and itching to snatch the pastry cutters away from their fingers to make the tarts better and faster. She might not have been all that pleasant through their childhood. (The sunny temperament was foreign to her. A closed book.) But she was *there*. She hadn't hopped it off to the south of France with a lover, like Val's mum, or got herself some hot-shot, high-flying career like those women forever nattering about nannies on the telly. Or even simply vanished (which must have been a bit of a temptation, given the way she always spoke of their father).

Fair's fair. She'd put in the years. So if it fell to him to offer her a soothing game of gin rummy . . .

'Want to play cards?'

She still looked sour. 'Why? Is it so very tiresome, having to spend a bit of time with an old lady once in a blue moon?'

'Once in a blue *moon*?'

She backtracked, in her way. 'I'll give you this, you come a lot more often than your sister.'

26

'Well, thanks for nothing.'

She shrugged. 'Oh, if it's *gratitude* you're after . . .'

And that was him, wrong-footed totally. 'I'll just check that Floss isn't stuck in the kitchen.'

'Yes, slip off again. I know you're bored rigid. It's been written all over your face from the moment you got here.'

He picked up the tray. If she hadn't peevishly turned her face away she would have seen the creamy thick envelope – 'Be Properly Insured' – slip from beside her cushion into the folds of the newspaper tucked between the cups and the milk jug. He wasn't going to mention it. Let her thrash about looking for it, then fret at the thought that he might be downstairs already ploughing his way through its contents.

'I won't be long.'

'Don't hurry back on my account. I'm used to sitting alone for hours.'

Christ! he begged, shutting the door behind him. Please don't let me *ever* grow old. Don't let me *ever* act this way in front of my own children. Then, cheered beyond measure by the realization that he'd never have any, he went down to the kitchen and read the paper from start to finish before slipping back to the woodshed to put one spell on her, and another, for good measure, on her favourite hydrangea.

2

'FRAMPTON COMMERCIAL?' DILYS SHRUGGED. 'NOTHING wrong with them. They've been going for years. Part of the Stanger chain.'

'Is that good?'

'Solid.' She tipped the steaming pasta into the colander. 'What's all this got to do with you, anyhow?'

'I'm just interested.'

'In Mother's house insurance? Why?'

'It worries me. I think she might have reached the stage where she starts making mistakes.'

His sister rolled her eyes. 'Oh, don't you worry about her. She's always been cute as mischief about money.'

'Always has been. Might not be any more.'

She reached across him for the grater. 'What does it matter? She'll probably leave it to some cat home, anyway.'

'It matters that it's insured properly. You can't just walk away from a place like Holly House. If it burns down, it'll have to be rebuilt strictly to specification.'

'Colin, you sound exactly like your *job*.'

'What's wrong with that?' he said, filled with the

daring that came from knowing his sister wasn't in a fighting mood. Only despondency could have propelled Dilys into the kitchen, just as only bad blood with Perdita could have prompted the decision to invite him in the first place.

Reminded, and hearing footsteps overhead, he nodded upwards. 'Will she be joining us?' Dilys made a face but didn't answer, so he set for three, leaving the cutlery for the third place lying so casually that, *in extremis*, it could be taken for a pile of miscounted extras he'd forgotten to pick up and return to the kitchen. Dilys dumped the salad bowl equidistant from all three chairs. Was that a clue? Trawling for evidence, he asked, 'How are her alterations going, anyway? Is that decrepit little workman of hers anywhere near finishing?'

'He's on the last bedroom, so she can move back to-morrow.' His sister suffered one of her very brief tussles with discretion. 'And I must say, I won't be sorry. If there's one thing I can't stand it's people who are prepared to exhaust themselves and others simply to save a few pennies.'

The door swung open. There stood Perdita, a pillar of ice. 'Excuse me?'

You had to hand it to Dilys. For quick wits, only Mother could beat her. 'Colin and I were just discussing how much fuss Norah's making over this rise in her insurance premiums.'

Perdita's eyes rolled. 'Oh, God! Not her again. All you two ever seem to talk about is your mother.'

Was it really true? Last time he'd called by, hoping he'd summon the courage to wriggle out of some bank-sponsored event to which Dilys had just sent him a spare invitation, his sister had been regaling Perdita with tales of how, to frighten Colin out of bed-wetting, Mother had painted his name on a trunk and kept starting to pack it, telling him he'd be taking it with him to the orphanage.

Perdita's response had been startling. Turning to Colin, she'd asked him sharply, 'And what about your father? How come he didn't slap your mother hard, and tell you it was all nonsense? Or was he just a wuss, like you?'

Colin sat silent, all too aware he might have been a little more successful in finding her response offensive, rather than disquieting, if it had not raised such a clear echo of Val on the same sofa: 'There's no such thing as one bad parent in a marriage, Colin. They always come in pairs. The bad one. And the other bad one, who just sits quietly and lets it happen.'

Unnerving, even to recall. And, now he came to think of it, only an hour later, at the grim event itself ('New Portraits for a New Age'), Dilys had slid all too quickly from the general subject of portraiture into her memories of their school photos on the landing: 'You were all right, Col. She just walked past yours without even looking. But every time she went past mine she shook her head and made this little clucking noise. Don't you remember? Half disbelief and half contempt. Imagine! Twenty times a day! No wonder I can barely stand to look in a mirror!'

So he could see how Perdita could end up accusing the two of them of spending their entire waking lives carping on about their mother. But Dilys clearly wasn't going to give an inch.

'On the contrary,' she countered. 'Up till that moment

we were actually discussing' – she barely faltered – 'Colin's work.'

'Really?' Out of spite, Perdita turned her quite evident disbelief onto the weaker witness. 'Go on, then, Colin. Don't let me interrupt.'

Oh, God. Back came that terror from childhood that, if he let her down, Dilys would slap him. Spitting words out at all in such a poisonous atmosphere was tricky enough. To lie was beyond him. He would have to tell them something about his week.

'I went to listen to a singing house.'

Even Dilys had trouble pretending she was halfway through hearing this one. And Perdita was startled fresh out of peevishness. 'A singing house? What on earth's that?'

'We have a lot of them,' said Colin. 'They cause a good deal of trouble. We're forever being called out.'

'To houses that *sing*?'

'Well, hum, really,' he admitted. 'But it usually sounds far more like singing, so that's what we call it. It can drive people mad.'

Perdita was making a pretty fast comeback on the spite front. 'Must do, if they're prepared to call out people like you.'

He knew it was curiosity, rather than a favour returned, that made Dilys break in and rescue him. 'Where does it come from, this singing? Is it power lines?'

'Sometimes there aren't any. And it's nothing inside. We can spend hours traipsing round with fancy monitoring equipment, following cables and drains. But nothing fits. The house just keeps on singing.'

'So what happens?'

'The owners go mad. Or move.'

'Really,' said Perdita. 'Who would have thought that being an Environmental Health Officer could be so exciting?'

She hadn't even bothered to pretend it wasn't sarcasm. But, still, he was too cowardly not to respond. 'Mostly it isn't,' he admitted. 'Mostly it's just smells, noise and germs.'

She looked down her thin nose at him rather as if he personally embodied this unsavoury trinity, and, not for the first time, Colin found himself wondering just how it was that his sister, who, scathing and insensitive as she was, had never been malicious, could spend so much time in the company of such disagreeable people. Was it some mere continuation of that perverse principle of boyfriend recruitment whereby, if the young man concerned didn't annoy Mother mightily, he held no charms for Dilys? Now, it was women friends she picked up with a passion, and dropped just as quickly. He'd never thought that it was sexual. He didn't even think she 'swung both ways'. He just thought that she hadn't changed since she was four and terrorized the playgroup. 'Today, only people with yellow ribbons are allowed in the sandpit. And that's just Tessa and *me*.' Did his sister get lonely between her great enthusiasms? He suspected not. Rather, that the one thing the two of them had both inherited from Mother was that they were happier – well, less on edge, at least – in their own company. He was straightforward about it. And Dilys had this strange, exhausting – not to say down-right unpleasant – way of disguising her preference to herself and to others. For, of course, if you're continually in the habit of dumping friends, after a bit you're bound to find that all that's still available is the dregs. Of all the companions his sister had chewed up and spat out over the years, the only truly kind one – indeed, the only one with any heart at all – had been dear Val, now spotted only as an occasional flash of friendly headlights and a brief backwards wave in his blemished rear-view mirror.

Never mind, he consoled himself. At least she's on her way out. Gone tomorrow. He sat down with relief where Dilys ordered him, and forked his way through his *Tortolini Portoli* with his head down, eyes darting to the clock as things got worse. To him, it was obvious Perdita was hoping to stage some last dramatic clash, larded with brilliantly wrought valedictory insults and (now the last bedroom was safely finished) crowned with a massive door slam. Presumably gratitude for things like a fortnight's free bed and board was not really her style, and she, too, would prefer to head for the clean break that marked the end of almost all his sister's friendships. But it was equally clear that Dilys, an experienced combatant herself, was out to thwart her. Time and again Perdita steered the conversation into dangerous waters. And time and again a look of bland distraction crossed his sister's face as she affected not to listen, then rose to go back into the kitchen, returning with one or another of a seemingly endless parade of bottles and jars, and a more neutral topic.

But even Dilys couldn't pretend anyone took capers with coffee. So she sat glowering over her spinney of condiments as Perdita moved in sideways on yet another attack.

'About these visits to your mother, Colin . . .'

'Yes?' he said warily.

'How often do you go? Every night, is it?'

He tried the sort of careless little laugh that means, 'Oh, really! Nothing like that.' But it came out as a half-witted splutter.

'Every two or three days?'

He took a deep breath. Oh, how he hated being forced to lie. 'Nowhere near that much.'

'But once a week, at least?'

Inside his head, he heard an urbane man admit with dignity, 'Yes, now I come to think, it probably does tend to average out at once a week or so, given the shopping.' Over the table, his stab at this pretence was barely audible. 'I suppose so.'

Perdita said gaily to Dilys, 'You told me he went practically every day!'

Dilys ignored her, and Colin sat tight, knowing full well which side it was safer to stay on.

'But Dilys *never* visits?'

Silence. Dilys was watching Perdita watching her. Colin dived in. 'That's different.' His stomach churned. He'd realized he'd be paying heavily for this impromptu lunch. Pasta had never agreed with him. But he hadn't guessed it would mean playing the rabbit in the snare. 'That's very different. I haven't broken off with Mother.'

'But you could, easily. Dilys says she's just as rude and horrible to you.'

He made a face. He could have said, 'Oh, that's just her quaint way of remembering you're family.' But it was obvious where Perdita was headed. Wiser to keep quiet.

'So why do you keep going?'

She leaned over the table, waiting for an answer. Alarmed, Colin turned to Dilys, but she pretended to be absorbed in picking the price stickers off her stockade of bottles. He tried to run through his options without panicking. 'Because she's there'? 'Because I don't have much else to do'? 'Because the neighbours would notice if I stopped'? But the sense of traps proliferating round him froze his poor brain, and, like a fool, he found himself practically offering to Perdita, handle first, the weapon with which she could move in and stab his sister. 'I suppose, if I'm honest, I'd rather go and be insulted than not go, and feel guilty.'

'Guilty?'

How lightly she said it. And how heavily the word hung in the air.

'Well, not *guilty*, exactly . . .'

'Guilty is what you said.'

'Yes, but—'

'Oh, I know!' Perdita's eyes shone. 'You think it's *different* for Dilys. That's what you said, isn't it? But don't you think, Colin' – and here she rested her thin arms on the table and leaned towards him as if the two of them were out together at some intimate candle-lit restaurant, not sitting over the dishes of a meal prepared by, and shared with, the person under discussion – 'don't you sometimes think Dilys might be being just that tiny bit *selfish*, leaving it all to you?'

He stared at her, fearing that any moment his sister might snap out of feigned indifference and lift her end of the table, sending everything flying, just as she'd done once, out of pure temper, when she and Val—

And there was his answer! He had a flash of memory of sitting at this very table, being alternately lauded by Val ('I think it's very *nice* of Colin to go round so often') and scorned by his sister ('It isn't "nice" of him. It's simply *wet*. He's just a fool in a bad habit, and she doesn't deserve it').

'I'm just a fool in a bad habit.'

'Nonsense,' said Dilys, startling both of them. 'You won't admit it, but you keep going to see the old bag because you love her.'

His cheeks caught fire. Dilys gave him one of those odious I-know-you-better-than-you-know-yourself smiles that she'd inherited from Mother. And he sat seething, hobbled by the usual inability to come out with the words rattling in his head. If he'd been anyone else, he could have shot her such a caustic look and said, 'Oh, smart move, Dil! Decide *you've* had enough, and never mind that she was acting no worse than usual, just flounce out on your high horse. Don't let it bother you that I might have to do more to make up. Just tell yourself that I keep going because I love her, then everything's fine – for *you*.'

But the painfully timid will always spend their lives in two completely different parallel worlds: the invisible, missing one, in which the things they want to say tumble out easily, the world in which everything's different; and the one that they're stuck in, where everyone round them chooses to take their nervous nods and craven smiles for simple acquiescence. It seemed to Colin that, ever since nursery school, people had cheerfully taken it upon themselves to interpret his inability to speak up for himself as compliance with what suited them. 'You *like* the green balloon, don't you, Colin?' 'You don't mind waiting, do you?' 'Colin, I take it that this month's schedule raises no problems for you?' If Dilys took even a forkful of interest in anyone around her, she would by now have realized that silence didn't always imply consent. It could imply a whole load of other things as well. Fury. Frustration. Resentment. And contempt.

Mercifully, his sister had stopped smirking at her own percipience, and reverted to her usual jackboot style. 'Well, anyway, you ought to stop letting her jerk you around like this. I don't see why you have to do her shopping. She's more than capable of phoning an order in to Mr Stastny. He still delivers, doesn't he? What you ought to do is tell her the council's sending you on a course for the next few weeks, and you can't come.'

'Yes,' he said weakly. 'Perhaps I should.'

'No perhaps about it. You're as soft as shite. You're an idiot, Colin.'

He tried to defend himself. '*Somebody* has to go round every now and again to check that she hasn't been robbed or murdered, or sold double glazing.'

But she was unstoppable. 'No, I honestly don't know why you keep visiting. It isn't as if she's grateful. From what you say, she doesn't even enjoy your company very much. So why bother? Why don't you just wait till the next time she says or does something really mean – it won't be long – then stalk out and leave her to it?'

'Like you did?'

Not even a blush. 'Yes, like I did.'

The answer seemed obvious. 'Because she's old and

frail, that's why.' But one thing he'd learned from all the conflicts associated with his job was that, the milder the rebuke, the hotter it stoked the fire. So he took revenge by wiping his greasy fingers on the frills of his seat pad and saying pathetically, 'Maybe next time I will.'

She snorted. And Colin kept his head down rather than intercept the look he knew was passing between the two of them. Colin? Stick up for himself? Oh, I don't think so! And maybe he was a bit feeble. But that was better than being a harpy like Dilys. Or coolly disdainful, like Perdita. Frankly, he was glad this new friend of his sister's had lasted no longer than any of the others. And at least his presence at the wake was serving some purpose. The two of them had temporarily sunk their differences, to pick on him.

'I reckon Colin will still be saying, "maybe next time" this time next year.'

'He'll still be saying it outside Warburton's Funeral Emporium.'

'*And* in the Chapel of Rest.'

'*And* at the graveside.'

Unwisely, he retorted, 'At least you won't be there to have to hear it.'

'Oh, I'll be there.'

Instantly, he was all suspicion. 'You've always said before you wouldn't bother.'

'I've changed my mind,' his sister said complacently. 'That's allowed, isn't it? In fact, I think it would be nice to come.'

'Why?'

Out slid the grin he remembered so well from

childhood. 'Can't you guess, Col? So I can dance on her grave.'

That really got him. What right had Dilys even to come to Mother's funeral, let alone dance on the grave? It wasn't as if it was she who had spent hour after brain-rotting hour in the last years fixing taps, filling the larder, or sitting in that bleak, bum-numbing chair, listening to gripes about family and neighbours. No, that had all been his job. If anybody in the world was going to dance on Norah's grave, it ought to be him. But he wasn't going to bother to say so. For one thing, it sounded too childish for words, and he'd already spent half of yesterday listening to the Lees and the Haksars hurling infantile insults at one another over their mutual wall, just as they had apparently been heaving rotten food into one another's back yard. 'I can have both your restaurants closed down,' he'd warned them when he'd had enough. Pity he couldn't shut his sister up as easily.

But she had bored herself now. She was on her feet. 'Come along, Perdita, or we'll be late.'

This was a trick he'd seen her use so often on others, he took it as a slap in the face that she was trying it on him. He felt like trumping her. Instead of answering, 'Oh, are you going out?' he could miss out all the middle stages and come straight out with, 'Well, since it turns out that you're going the other way, I won't bother to wait for you.' That should embarrass her.

But instead, picking up his jacket, he simply muttered, 'Thanks for the lunch.'

'*De nada*,' chirruped Perdita, irritating him even more with her pretension than her indifference. He closed the door behind him and stood on the front stoop, wondering where to go. Back to his flat? No, far too boring. And nothing on telly till later. To Mel's, to borrow Tammy? How could he? He'd been round there twice this week already, and though Mel might not exactly narrow her eyes at him and say, 'Oh, Col, do get a life,' she'd definitely think it.

A walk round the park on his own? Sad. Very sad.

Leaving him only one option. But at the bottom of the steps he made a point of turning left, not right, so if the two of them were at the window, arm in arm again, placing bets, they'd never guess that, not only was he going to spend half of Saturday at Mother's as usual, but his life was so empty he was going there early.

Colin scowled at the hydrangea as he walked up the path. ('It's *glorious*, isn't it?' his mother was warbling down from the upstairs window. 'It was lovely before, but since your last visit it's come on wonderfully.') His irritation at the failure of his spell turned to suspicion. She was too cheerful by far. And since her principal pleasure always stemmed from the discomfiture of others, it made him nervous.

He edged through the door to meet her hobbling down the stairs. 'Don't leave the shopping there. Someone might trip over it.'

Who? *Who?* He was about to start the counter-attack ('Sorry. I hadn't realized you had other guests') when his eye fell on the brown envelope propped in the letter rack to attract his attention. *Frampton Commercial*. Well, there was at least one non-confrontational subject for the afternoon: her undimmed consumer skills. And credit, to be fair, where it was due. Anything she could still do for herself was one more thing he didn't have to do for her. And Dilys had given them the thumbs-up. So he made the effort to reward her for her competence with a touch of civility. 'They came up trumps, then, your Frampton Commercial?'

'Tickety-boo! I'm as happy as two babies in a bath. Do you realize I've saved more than a third of the annual premium?'

'Over a third?'

'It's a lot, isn't it? I'd no idea that I'd been overpaying all these years. I'm quite delighted with myself. I'm not quite the stupid old woman everyone thinks I am.'

'Nobody thinks you're stupid.'

'Oh yes, you do. Don't try to hide it.'

He pushed the shopping under the hall table, making an effort not to kick it. Let it defrost there. Let it *rot*. Where did old people learn this knack of making it impossible to keep a conversation pleasant? And why was it so difficult not to fight back? 'I expect there'll be some problem with the amount of your coverage . . .'

And look! He'd lost! 'That's where you're wrong, Mr Smartypants! With this company, my coverage is exactly the same. Better, in fact, because . . .' And all the way up the stairs she tormented him with the new policy's advantages in the matters of Coastal Erosion ('You're eighty miles from the sea here!'), Damage from Riots ('In West *Priding*?'), and Escapes of Oil ('I think you'll find, Mother, you're on gas'). Hoping this persecution of him was not to be the theme of the whole afternoon, he trailed her up

41

to her bedroom, where she limped noisily to her armchair by the window. 'So, all in all, I'm quite a chump for not changing years ago.'

She sank in the cushions. And with the light full on her face, she looked horribly old. It suddenly seemed so unsuitable to him, so very wrong, that she should have to think about things like insurance at all.

'Not necessarily,' he offered generously. 'The good terms might be quite recent. Or a loss leader, or something.'

The turtle eye opened and glared. 'Oh, that's right. Tell me the premiums are going to shoot up again, now that poor Muggins has signed on.'

'That isn't what I said.'

But his concession had won him a truce. Instead of pursuing her malevolent interpretation of his remark, she gazed at the house opposite. 'See that new porch? They were fools enough to buy it from Manderley's. Piece of old tat. It's been leaking from the first day – just like those cut-price welly boots he sold me.'

A trace of a memory surfaced from his last visit. 'Did I tell you that Mrs Deary got a lovely crop of thistles out of that grass seed he sold her?'

'*Did* she?' Now he had given her a gift indeed. She was delighted with him. He didn't dare break the spell by offering to go down and get the tea for which he was gasping, now Dil's leaden-brand pasta had started its long, distending run through his poor gut. He simply anchored his feet more comfortably against the comatose Floss and let the soothing flow of his mother's words wash over him. 'I suppose you know your pack of villains are threatening to have our drains up again? That'll be the third time in eighteen months. Scandalous! Everyone at that end of the backs is writing, silly buggers. I've told them it's a waste of time, what with one half of you being simple and the other half crooked. Look how unhelpful you all were when that devil next door started persecuting me with his windchimes. Oh, and I don't expect Mr Carter up the other end will come out of hospital again, unless it's feet first. I can't say I hold out much hope for Mrs Al-Khatib, either, given the size of that lump of hers.'

Colin was shocked into speech. 'You've never *seen* it!'

'No, but Elsie has.' A tremor ran down her cheek. 'Elsie sees *everything*. I must say, I'm very careful to put on my winter stockings when I go past the Emporium. Nosy witch.'

'You're getting about all right, then?'

'I manage.'

And certainly, thought Colin, you had to hand it to her. Somehow she managed. Maybe he was too quick to get impatient. If making a simple pot of tea took him a good half-hour, and carrying it anywhere became too awkward, and having to empty his bladder afterwards became some great fumbling effort in itself and not just something he did unthinkingly on the way to his next task, then maybe he too . . .

'Let's see how that leg's doing,' he said, dropping to his knees in front of her on the carpet. She slapped him away. 'No, thanks! It's only just getting better. I don't want your grubby fingers poking at it.' And clambering, embarrassed, to his feet, he had another of his blinding visions about his father's famous 'accident'. Dazzled by oncoming headlights, indeed! Sick of having his hands slapped away, more like. Sick of being humiliated. Sick of her viperish tongue. It was obvious even the police officer bringing the bad news didn't for one moment believe the tale he was telling. But people were kind, and what was the point in stirring things up unnecessarily? Her horror had been unfeigned, her sense of outrage at her loss deep and real. She must have spoken about their father practically every day (as often as not in scathing terms, but that was the way of her). And it couldn't have been easy raising a daughter as awkward as Dilys. Or even a son as unforthcoming as himself.

He made another effort.

'So, apart from winning the Comparative Shopper of the Year Award, what else have you been doing?'

She said with relish, 'It's really got to you, hasn't it, this insurance business? You can't let go of it for a moment.'

Stop it! he longed to shout at her. Stop making things so *impossible*.

'I was just interested.'

But to the person whose only tool is a hammer, everything looks like a nail. 'Interested in finding fault!'

Affecting deafness, he escaped to his shopping bag. 'Oh, goody!' she said with unaffected glee as he dropped the great slab of papers he was in the habit of bringing her onto the wobbly little table at her side. Instantly, she started pulling them into sections and dropping half of them in the bin.

'Don't do that,' he complained. 'It's like visiting someone in a fundamentalist sect. "Thou shalt not read *Sports* or *Appointments*."'

'Moan, moan,' she chided. But the newspapers had done the trick. She was already feeling in her pockets for one of the many pairs of spectacles she hoarded around the house. Enjoying the silence, he picked the *Business* and the *Foreign News* out of the bin, then promptly fell in a depression, realizing he didn't want to read them either. Already his world, like hers, was narrowing. He'd noticed it first with Chad, a country for which his school had raised thousands of pounds during his sixth-form year. Colin had signed up for a Sponsored Silence, behaved through the fortnight almost exactly as usual, and, but for his crippling inability to ask people to sponsor him, would have raised a lot of money. For some years afterwards, he'd taken quite an interest in Chad, devouring everything the newspapers had to offer about that benighted land. Then gradually a feeling of *déjà vu* crept into his reading, as drought and famine and hardship wheeled past his eyes again and again. He took, first to scanning, then skipping. And somehow, before he even realized what was happening, he'd given up on Chad. Africa in general followed. Then the Middle East. Already the lights were going out all over Europe. And, were it not for the fact that news from America so often doubled as Entertainment, he would have given up on there as well.

And in this, he admitted, he was his mother's son. How often had he heard her, over the years, declaring, 'I can't be bothered with the ozone layer any more.' (Or recycling. Or the teachers.) Secretly he'd sympathize, knowing that he, too, was halfway to hell in the handbasket of indifference, and, like her, soon the only things that he'd be

45

stopping at as he flicked through the pages would be gossip and murders, scandals and divorces. In fact, she'd have wider interests than his own, because she kept up with interest rates and enjoyed the obituaries.

And this, he thought, digging a lump of chewed slipper out from the small of his back to settle more comfortably with the Arts section she'd discarded, was why she still liked him to come, and why, when he was there, he only toyed with the idea of running her through with one of his father's old chisels. There was a balance between them. His visits to her passed in a fine mix of mutual condescension and respect. She had a fathomless contempt for his naïvety and weakness. And he could only despise her lifelong failure to put her talents to good use. But he respected her untiring courage and impregnable cynicism, and she was continually impressed by his flashes of mutiny. As a child, Colin had never dared even to try to stick up for himself. But one day, as she was working herself into a froth about one of his adolescent shortcomings, he'd somehow come out with a crosspatch remark and brought her up short. It was a revelation. From that day on, at least with her, he was a different person. Unlike with the spells, where regular failure had tended to augment rather than diminish his sense of her supremacy, his caustic moments were good for both his spirits and hers, as now when, handing back the slipper, he said, 'I see you're still favouring Flossie as your personal designer.'

'They might be old, these slippers, but they're comfortable.'

'Perhaps it'll catch on, this natty notion of keeping them on your feet with elastic bands.'

'Perhaps you should mind your own business.' But it was in a companionable silence that she read on, making it clear from a few tart utterances about 'the disadvantaged' that, by her, the expression was taken to be entirely synonymous with 'wastrels', and, just as he was thinking of making quietly for the door to put the kettle on at last, raising her head to make a series of observations about child prostitution in Salford that left him in no doubt that, in her book, the war on this evil could most usefully begin with the speedy and permanent dispatch of its victims. Cunningly without giving him a moment in which he might get the suggestion in ahead, she rounded off this peroration with a plaintive, 'And I don't know *when* I'm going to be offered a cup of tea . . .'

He put down his unread paper. 'Biscuits or teacakes? I bought both.'

'I'm sorry. I've simply no appetite.'

Notwithstanding his pasta ballast, he took the downstairs run at speed, determined not to have to hear how long it was since she'd forced nourishment between her lips. As he rushed by the letter rack, he had the presence of mind to snatch up the envelope from Frampton Commercial and, under cover of his kitchen clatter, take a quick look. It all seemed perfectly reasonable. The conditions were unexceptionable, the exclusions customary. (If the policy had been a coin, Colin would have bitten it.) Feeling the smug good son who spreads his safety net beneath his mother's increasingly enfeebled wings, he was about to stuff the printed sheets back in their envelope when he finally noticed it, up in the top left-hand corner, dwarfed by the reel of numbers trailing halfway across the page to try to create the impression that everyone in the world had some sort of policy with Frampton Commercial.

The amount of the coverage. It was next to nothing.

He stared. Had some computer glitch sucked the noughts up a line, to fatten the policy number? Surely there must be some mistake.

He rushed up the stairs, stabbing the policy with a finger. 'The house must be insured for more than this!'

She glanced up. 'Oh, so you're nosing through my letters now?'

The prudent man in him was far too exercised to be derailed. 'Listen,' he told her. 'This won't do! You couldn't rebuild the woodshed with this sort of money. What can you be thinking of? With coverage this low, you might as well be totally uninsured!'

She turned back to her paper, saying indifferently, 'It's as much as it's ever been. I've never had a problem.'

'You've never had a bloody fire!'

'I hope I won't,' she said, in a tone that implied he was threatening to build one on her carpet. 'And, if I do, I hope I'm safely burnt to death in it and don't have to listen to the likes of you moaning on and on about insurance afterwards.'

'You won't,' he said. 'Because one or another of us is, right this minute, going to phone this Frampton Commercial company to quadruple the coverage.'

He stood there, waiting for the argument to start. 'How dare you! It's my business. This is my house. Don't think that you can – bleh, bleh . . .' But she was already back to reading the paper. He waited a little longer, at a loss, but nothing happened. Should he make for the door? Perhaps then she'd pounce, with one of her dangerous little last-minute slingshots. 'And, by the way . . .' He gave it a go. But still his mother didn't say a word. Colin stopped in the doorway, unsettled. How was he supposed to wrap himself safely in the mantle of martyrdom if she was this complaisant, this indifferent? Surely she couldn't be about to let him get away with reading her mail, scolding her roundly, and being responsible for a rise in her premiums?

Of course she couldn't. No. She'd have revenge. He'd pay for it later. But still he felt uneasy. And even more so when, as he was still staring, baffled, at her bent grey head, she dragged her attention back from the unsavoury details of the rape case she was devouring just long enough to say, with only mild irritation, 'Don't stand there watching your boots mildew. Go and fetch that tea.'

His unease deepened. Surely the bedrock of his confidence had always been her sheer predictability, his absolute assurance that she would never miss a chance to put a member of her family in the wrong? Look at the times his father had fetched up in the doghouse for anniversaries forgotten, or birthdays missed. Look at the weeks of small snubbings ignored by hard-boiled Dilys when, year after year, she'd dared to sail home from guide camp without the statutory present. (A world away from Colin, in whom their mother's daggered silences fuelled inarticulacy till it turned to blinking dumbness, and honed his clumsiness till he was barely capable of getting through a doorway in his own home without a hip bruise or a damaged shoulder.)

All right, the glory days were over. But still . . . But still . . .

What was the *matter* with her? Was she *ill*?

All the way down the stairs he was as firm with himself as he could be. Rubbish, he kept telling himself. There's nothing wrong with Mother. She's just saving herself up to eviscerate me later.

And yet it wasn't convincing. Not her style. He was so rattled he found himself fumbling as he jotted down policy details. (If she didn't make the call he'd be doing it for her.) Stooping to pick up his pencil for the second time, he caught his sleeve against the old toast rack that served as a letter holder, and, reaching out to steady it, knocked it so forcibly that everything in it cascaded to the floor.

Including a photo of Perdita.

Colin peered closer. There was no mistaking it. Those eyes. That hair. He picked it up, sighing, and put it, separately, in his pocket. What mysteries his mother weaved around herself. You'd think, to find yourself enmeshed in them, that it was she, and not he, who kept all those little piles of weird things in the woodshed.

By the time he came back with the tea, his curiosity had triumphed over caution. He chose his words carefully, determined not to let drop his own connection with Perdita and spark off the usual disquisition on his sister's faults. 'So how come this drop-dead redhead is risking her death lying about on your floor tiles?'

Immersed in her sexual horoscope, she only muttered, 'What are you wittering about now?' He held the photo

50

so close she couldn't help looking. 'Oh, *her*. That's Dolly's Perdita.'

To glean more, he affected idiocy. 'What, Dolly from Canasta Club?'

She nodded, scowling. 'Look at her! Tarty carroty hair. She must fling her mascara on with a tablespoon.'

'So why keep a photo of her on your hall floor?'

'Don't be a twerp. It must have—' She interrupted herself. 'Is it Saturday?' Forgetting she was already in the right glasses, she flapped her wrist towards Colin. 'Quick! Tell me what it says.'

He glanced at his own watch. 'Just a little after four.'

'Oh, drat! I've missed it. Now I am really going to be in Dolly's Book of Sinners. Her precious Perdita was on television this afternoon.'

'Is that why she sent the photo? So you'd recognize her? What's she doing on telly anyway?'

'Spouting about property values in the Rift Valley.'

'The Rift Valley? Are you *sure*?'

She shook her head. 'Rift . . . Ribble . . .' (Even his mother didn't dare add, 'What's the difference?') 'And *Weekend Round-up* will be over now.' She glared. 'I'll simply have to tell Dolly you made me miss it.'

Less from a sense of helpfulness than in self-defence, he suggested, 'Why don't you tell her what you'd end up telling her anyway? That her daughter looked lovely, and it was a pity the bit with her in it was over so quickly.'

Oh, they both knew their telly. Her eyes narrowed as she appraised this advice without finding any flaw. 'Do you think I'd get away with it?' He was in the middle of replying, 'I don't see why not,' when the phone made them both jump. You had to hand it to her, Colin thought. She certainly had pluck. Still eyeing Colin closely, she lifted the handset. 'Dolly? . . . Yes. Yes, I did . . . Yes, *wonderful*. I thought she looked tip-top . . . Yes, *didn't* she?' There was a longish pause, during which he could see his mother visibly growing in confidence as she listened. Indeed, it was almost with a hint of cockiness that, at the end, she added, taking an obviously quite unnecessary risk, 'My only complaint, dear, was that they could have given her just a little more time.' Another long and satisfying pause gave Colin reason to think his mother must be home and dry. 'Yes, dear. Yes, *absolutely*. Yes, I will. Of course you must. She'll be *waiting*.'

She put the phone down and her eyes were gleaming.

He shook his head in wonder. 'I expect your performance was even better than hers.'

For a moment, his mother looked baffled. 'Whose?' Then wires touched. 'Oh, you mean *Perdita*.' She tossed her head in what he realized, but for her corded, sagging neck and sunken face, would have been rather a flirtatious manner. 'And why not, Colin? After all, what is there left for me at my age, except bones and lies?'

3

HALFWAY THROUGH THURSDAY MORNING CLARRIE TURNED from the relentlessly flashing telephone and told him, 'That sister of yours is downstairs. Wants to have a word.'

'Oh, *Christ*!' He was up to his elbows in messages about the Lees and the Haksars. 'Tell her—' But then he saw that, not for the first time, the freshly glossed fingernail had landed on Speaker, not on Secrecy, and, in his panic at Clarrie's blunder, he unintentionally compounded his own. 'Oh, *bugger*!'

He hurried down to find Dilys wiping the floor with Arif from Accounts about the errors in her direct debits. Hastily he steered her away. 'You can do all this by post, you know.'

'Don't think I haven't tried. Four times. If Tor Bank ran this way, we'd have no customers.'

Thinking to placate her, he offered, 'Cup of coffee?'

'Not here, thanks. No.'

Still fearing that she might have overheard his howls of horror earlier, he led her next door to The Little Bakery, and, in a misguided stab at being companionable, allowed her to buy him one of their notoriously indigestible cakes.

To stop her nagging him to eat it, he tried to distract her with an update on their mother's ongoing War of the Windchimes; but, unnerved by the steady drumming of her fingers on the small table top, he soon dried up and switched to the tale of the insurance.

At once, Dilys was entranced. 'You're *joking*. Only *that*? For Holly House! Why, these days you'd need that sort of coverage for a chicken coop!'

'Maybe that's what she told them it was. I must say, I'm astonished that no one's ever come round to check.'

She waved her last forkful of cake. 'No reason why they should. No skin off their nose, after all.'

She ought to know. Her bank seemed to dabble in everything. 'But I thought all these things were index-linked.'

'Mostly they are. But if she signed on some time back in the stone age, she could have been hugely under-insured before all that started.'

'It's all fixed now,' he assured her. 'I posted the confirmation myself.'

'What should *I* care?' said Dilys, sounding so like their mother that he was, first startled, then deeply irritated. He'd really won the mad goat in the raffle, hadn't he? All right for these two to chirrup their unconcern, practically in concert. Neither had that much to lose. Dilys was already out of things – was even by now, in all probability, struck from the will. And he sensed that his mother was quite far enough along the track of not caring much about anything any more to be ready to act helpless the moment it suited. But *someone* had to take responsibility. For him, there was no choice but to keep fretting. His mother's levels of insurance cover were not a matter for flippancy. He, after all, was the one who would have to face his conscience – and the bloody neighbours – if Norah fetched up strapped to a chair, drugged stupid in front of a blaring telly, simply because her savings had been snaffled by the council to repair her timber cladding and replace her carved casements. Easy for Dilys to sit there, smug with indifference. She hadn't spent half of yesterday facing a barrage of unpleasant innuendo. 'Listen,' he'd said a dozen times. 'This is absolutely nothing to do with ensuring there'll be plenty left for me to inherit.' But how could his mother turn up the chance of hovering, bent-backed, over her fading cheque book for all the world as if her only son were bullying her into paying his gambling debts, not sensibly suggesting she scale up her premiums. 'I'll pay for it *myself*,' he told her more than once. 'Just so long as we get it all sorted out properly.' But she was adamant. 'No, no. I wouldn't dream of having you a penny out of pocket over some poor old lady on her last legs.' Leave it, he told himself a dozen times through the long, grinding afternoon. For once in a lifetime, be brave. Take a chance. And instantly the alternatives paraded in front of him. If he were lucky, just sleepless nights and half a heart attack each time he heard a fire engine tear past his own drab flat in the direction of West Priding. And if he weren't? A heap of rubble, years of argument with his own colleagues about possible economies in the rebuilding, and Mother living in his own back room.

It didn't bear thinking about. And mercifully he was distracted from the nightmare vision by Dilys flicking at his plate. 'Buck up and eat, Col. We're not all council drones with endless tea breaks. Some of us have to get back to our desks.'

At the mere mention of desks, he felt another stab of panic. To try to make a little headway on the cake front, he set his sister off on the first topic to come to mind. 'So how is Perdita? Safely gone?'

'Thank God! And I can't say how glad I was to see the back of her. She was so *sneaky*.'

Sneaky? That pricked his interest. After all, what could be sneakier than insinuating yourself into a strange house inside an envelope? Manfully struggling with what appeared to be, on dissolution, nothing but a mouthful of whipped oil, he was still hoping to break in with news of the curious materialization of Perdita's photograph on Mother's hall floor when his sister not only kept on as if his thoughts were perfectly audible, but also as if they were grist to her mill. 'Do you know, the bloody woman gets *everywhere*. Last week she even fetched up on *Weekend Round-up*.'

'I knew that,' Colin admitted.

'How? Did you see her?'

Lamely he shook his head.

'Well, she was *terrible*. Vain enough to get her hair done at Tatiana's, but all she did was mumble a few inanities over and over.'

Anything, even risking an argument, was better than taking another mouthful of cake. 'Really? That doesn't sound at all like Perdita.'

Rumbled, his sister felt obliged to backtrack. 'Well, all right, I suppose she sounded sensible enough. *If* you're as obsessed as she is with property values . . .'

Forcing words out of his mouth still held a good deal more attraction than forcing cake in. 'I didn't know she was in property. I always thought she worked on all that arty sponsorship stuff, with you.'

'That was only to keep her busy while they were over-staffed in Insurance Services. Now she's moved over and carving out empires in Estates.' His sister's principle of never denigrating a fellow female professional took another hard knock, Colin noticed, as she finished dismissively, 'No, Perdita's really just a glorified estate agent now. And Marjorie says—'

'Marjorie?'

Again Dilys tapped the side of his plate. 'Do get a move on, Col. I haven't got all day.'

'I'm eating as fast as I can,' he responded pettishly. 'I do have to *chew*.' And along with this echo of the squabbles of childhood came yet another reminder of everything he'd left abandoned on his desk: the report that the youngest Haksar boy had crept over the wall to jam a wedge of carrot deep in Mr Lee's extractor fan; an account of the father's response when confronted – 'Boys will be boys. A mere prank.' On the top of these lay a litter of irate messages passed on by Shirley at Switchboard that he'd been trying to sift into piles according to gravity: threats, punch-ups, complaints of laxatives fed to the Haksars' cat. From Colin's point of view, of course, this childish feud could not become *Vendetta!* fast enough. That, after all, would move it from its current file in Public Health into some overflowing police in-tray, and he himself could once again lean back against that great dependable stone wall, 'I'm afraid that it's out of my hands now. Sorry,' and get back to his report on the safety of balconies.

He had stopped listening. Surfacing temporarily from his midden of anxiety, he realized that, apart from registering the steady drip into his sister's monologue of this new woman's name — Marjorie, was it? — he'd not been following at all. So he was startled when, once again as if she'd been sitting across the cramped café table monitoring his own inner voice, Dilys finished up roundly, 'and Marjorie agrees with me that any day now it'll be a police matter.'

He tried a bit of fishing. 'Really? A police matter?'

'Well, yes. You can't, after all, keep worming yourself into the houses of all your mother's elderly Canasta Club companions without a few eyebrows being raised. Sooner or later someone is bound to complain. You know how these things work. "Perdita Moran? Now where have I heard that before? Didn't some old lady phone in last week about a woman of that name practically offering to carry her off to the old folk's home?" They'll make a few inquiries, and then, because of the embarrassment, Tor Bank will have to move her back to Insurance. Or on to Home Loans, or Arrears.' She beamed with satisfaction. 'No fat commissions there! And I won't have her back in Corporate Sponsorship. Absolutely not.' Reminded by this reference to her own little enclave, she dug in her bag. 'Here. Invitation for Wednesday, in case we're a little thin on the ground.'

He tried not to accept it. 'Actually, Wednesday's going to be rather diff—'

But, leaving less of a tip on the table than he would

ever have dared, she was already halfway to the door. 'So we'll meet at the bank at seven? Then we can walk down to Stemple Street together.'

And she was gone. Mournfully he pocketed the invitation without even looking at it, and sat wondering if he dare risk the stares of other customers to wrap the remains of his cake in his napkin, so he and Tammy could feed it to Timothy Duckling.

But, as he might easily have guessed at the start, in the end he just stabbed it to death and then left it.

Did his family have nothing better to do than pester him at work? It was only next morning when Shirley tapped on the fortified screen designed to protect her from frenzied citizenry, and said accusingly through the little patch of holes drilled in the glass, 'You've been unplugging that little machine of yours again, haven't you, Mr Riley?'

His face flared. 'No.'

'And don't think I haven't guessed what you've done to your mobile.'

Rain from his waterproof spattered his Slaughterhouse Inspection Rota as he pawed the ground, waiting.

At last she favoured him with the bad news. 'I'm afraid it's your mother again.'

He couldn't help the shudder. 'Any clues?'

'No. She said it'll keep till you get there tonight.'

'Tonight? I'm not going tonight.'

'*She* thinks you are.'

Oh, God! This was a poser he could never crack. Could she really no longer be bothered to remember which evening he'd mentioned (in which case what difference did it make, today or tomorrow, except that, being a whole day later, tomorrow really ought to be preferable)? Or was it, as he suspected, some subtle variation on the old, old theme, 'Whatever Norah wants, she gets'? Perhaps tonight suited her better. (He must glance at the television listings and see if he could rumble her.) And though, in the past, she would have felt robust enough to come out fighting ('No, Colin. I distinctly remember Monday was what you suggested') maybe more recently she'd decided she was too old for that kind of effort, and, as the first stage of some sort of home-based psychic retirement, had begun to take advantage of his skills at obstructing the council's cripplingly expensive state-of-the-art voicemail by leaving her more disquieting directives with the long-suffering Shirley.

Effective, either way. For as soon as the dog warden had finished grousing about the inadequacies of her new van, to Holly House is where he went.

She met him on the doorstep. 'Devils are queuing up to spit at me, and I blame you!'

For one mad moment he reviewed his spells. But then he saw that what she was flapping at him was another of the envelopes from Frampton Commercial.

'Oh, yes?' he said, manoeuvring past her with a few staples he'd stopped off to pick up on the way. 'And why is that, then?'

'This new insurance company you forced me to join—'

'I didn't force you to—'

'Now they want some stupid safety thing. This is entirely your fault. If you would only keep your nose out of my affairs, I could get on like a house on fire.'

'Perhaps a house on fire is why—'

'Don't you be smart with me! If you hadn't bullied me into raising those premiums, I'd have been left in peace and quiet.'

He tried to defend himself. 'It can't be anything to do with that. I only posted the paperwork the day before yesterday.'

'Don't try and wriggle out of it!' She flapped the letter in his face again. 'This is your fault!'

'*What?*' he said, losing patience. 'Don't *hit* me with it. Tell me what it *says*.'

'It doesn't *say* anything. It *demands*.'

'*What?*'

She wasn't wearing glasses, so her dramatic reading was for effect. 'It demands "A Certificate of—"' Oh, how her lip curled! '"Approved Electrical Installation"!'

'Really?'

Her scornful look turned personal. 'I don't know why you, of all people, pretend to be surprised. I should have thought this sort of persecution of helpless homeowners was right up your alley.'

He paid her back by playing Bait the Taxpayer. 'Oh, no. Safety's quite different. We have a special officer for that.'

'Well, he'd better not visit this house. I won't be discouraging him from sticking his wet fingers in my plugs.' He took advantage of her settling into a state of mere baleful quiescence to wriggle past. She trailed him through to the kitchen and gazed disparagingly at his purchases. 'I certainly hope you haven't bought any more butter. I'm up to the gunwales in it. And what on earth is that very nasty-looking affair?'

He picked up the packaged gourmet meal he'd thrown in for a treat. 'This is our supper.'

'I don't feel at all like eating.'

'You'll like this. We had it once before and you said you thought it was delicious.'

Her look gave him clearly to understand that she couldn't have meant it. Again he stamped down resentment. This was the bit he hated most about his dealings with her. Not only did she have the knack of poisoning the minutes he was trying to get through, she also somehow seemed to manage to spread the misery back over jollier occasions when he'd thought he'd done rather well. 'No problem,' he snapped. 'I can easily take it home with me.' But part of the trouble, of course, was that, although she acted like an ungrateful child, she had an adult's self-command. 'Maybe that's best,' she retorted. And down, down sank his spirits. He hated being skewered this way over food. It meant either a couple of hours of sitting with his stomach audibly complaining, or sitting forlornly at the table spooning his luxury meal into his mouth while she affected to busy herself round the kitchen, somehow managing to create the impression that clattering pans about was the only way in which she could charitably disguise his greed.

'Let's see the letter, then.'

She passed it over. He ran a practised eye down the paragraphs, taking a professional interest in the skilled way Frampton Commercial had managed to make out that each and every one of their costly and inconvenient demands was for their clients' benefit, not their own. She'd never lend it to him, and he'd never ask; but he'd have loved a copy. At least a dozen of these weaselly worded phrases might usefully be introduced into his own department's raft of unwelcome communications. He tried to commit one or two of the most general to memory. '. . . responding to heightened public concerns about safety . . .' '. . . with our ever-increasing awareness of the responsible policyholder's commitment to the environment . . .' And why couldn't Priding Borough Council, too, 'proudly restratify security hierarchies to empower renewed client confidence'?

She was getting impatient now. 'This is the sort of drivel your lot write. Surely you can work out what it means.'

At least it couldn't mean another bout of workmen, he thought with relief. After the unravelling of the mystery of the exploding attic lightbulbs, she'd had the infestations of men in boots, the little heaps of plaster everywhere, the streaks of ill-matched paint spilling down to each wall light. Mess and expense and fuss. Tea breaks. Endless supplies of shortbread fingers and cries of, 'Can I just use your phone to check something with the suppliers?' The horror of all her querulous grousing about that was so fresh in his mind that any matter of certification must be a formality.

'You'll just have to ask that Mr Herbert of yours to come back and sign you one of these Approved Whatsit things.'

Her mouth looked like a burst slipper. Was she going to *cry*? 'It's only paperwork,' he assured her hastily. 'I can't for the life of me see it costing more than a tenner.'

She shot him a harsh look. 'Try not to be sillier than you look! Do you really think I'd be fool enough to drag you round here if things were that simple?'

Now he felt close to tears himself. 'How should *I* know?' he wanted to bellow at her. 'How should I have the *faintest* idea any longer what you can and can't do? You've spent so long aping helplessness whenever it suits you that now I'm quite *lost*.' And it was true. He didn't know – he couldn't even *guess* – if she had truly lost her grip to the extent that Frampton Commercial's smarmy letter (which, credit where it was due, went on to explain in the plainest of words the procedures she should follow) had rattled her enough to phone him at work.

'So what's the problem?' he asked, and was appalled to see the rheumy eyes redden and fill. Pretend it's *work*, he told himself, trying to stem panic. After all, didn't he meet this little human tragedy every day – old people overwhelmed? He put his arm round the trembling shoulders, and asked more gently, 'What *is* it? *Tell* me.'

He knew she was tempted because she didn't spit out the usual, 'I wouldn't walk from here to the door knob to tell you anything.' Turning her back, she only tugged at a cupboard door and hauled out a baking tray in a deafening clatter. 'Here. Put your fancy gourmet supper on this. How do you want the oven, Mr Smart-Set? Hot or medium?'

He tried again. 'Whatever it is, I might be able to advise you.'

'Oh, yes? A penny for *your* thoughts, and you'd have to give change.'

He fingered the wrapping round his special supper.

This is my chance, he thought. I could just do it now. 'Look,' I could say, as calmly as if she were just one more ratty restaurateur heaving foodstuffs over a back fence. 'I really don't have to stay and listen to this rudeness. I've tried to be helpful. But since your only response is to insult me, you can sort it out yourself.'

Then he could go.

Go. What a ring the word had to it. *Go!* Be finished for ever with sulks and insults. There was no point in offering advice in any case. She went her own way as a matter of principle, and, in her accounts to the neighbours, his efforts to help or explain things were always somehow transmuted into things like, 'Colin's been frightening me to *death* about the boiler (or the old gas fire, or the new alarm).' Dilys is right, he told himself. No one should be expected, for love or duty or anything else, to have to put up with having their very sense of self being chipped away minute by minute. The trouble was, of course, that Mother's self-absorption had been permitted to grow unchecked, till there was no room left for any true awareness of others. Like everyone else, she had her ready filecard of pat phrases: 'Teachers? They're only in it for the holidays.' 'Vote that lot in and they'll be as bad as the others.' But, with her, even the nearest and dearest weren't exempt. 'No, Dolly only stops by as often as she does because she likes to get away from that grisly husband of hers.' 'Oh, Colin only visits because I'm handy for a free cup of tea on his way home from the office.'

But still, she seemed to have an instinct for how far she could push her luck. He heard a marshy sniff. Now that wasn't like her. And, as she was always saying, people born round don't have the choice of dying square. So . . .

'Hot oven, please,' he said, pulling the outer wrapping off his star purchase.

She stabbed a fork through the cellophane cover as if it were Priding Borough Council lurking underneath, not Fifine's Fancy Beef and Celeriac Maribou with Tomato Truffle stuffing. He pulled a chair out and collapsed on it. 'And, while it's heating up, you can explain why the idea of getting Mr Herbert to sign a piece of paper has put you in such a tizzy.'

The nearest she ever came to remorse was capitulation. 'Well, that's just it. Old Goody Two-Shoes Herbert won't sign.'

'Of course he will. His men worked here for *weeks*.'

'That's where you're wrong. He won't.'

'Why not?'

'Because of the cable entry.'

'The cable entry?'

'Don't *you* start on about it! The very words have me in hives. It seems my wiring can't just come in the front way like everyone else's. Oh, no, it has to come down the backs. So it runs under the lawn, and nobody's bothered to look at it since it was put there. Holy Joe Herbert has made it perfectly clear he can't sign my certificate until I'm upgraded.'

'If this cabling's so ancient, why on earth didn't the fellow have the sense to get his men to replace it while they were here?'

She slapped on her innocent face, then, clearly deciding it wasn't worth the effort, told the truth. 'I wouldn't let them.'

'Why on earth not?'

'Don't snap at *me*! If I'd taken every stitch of advice I was offered, I'd be in a madhouse.'

He said, in as conciliatory a fashion as he could manage, 'Sick of the mess?'

'Sick? Those men of his tore through this house like a bagful of cats tipped down a mousehole. I'm not going to let the clumsy tykes loose on the garden. I'd be left standing on a blasted heath.'

'Nonsense,' he reassured her. 'These days they can track cables underground.'

'I don't know whose side you're on.'

'I'm on yours.'

'Well, it certainly doesn't sound like it. Lord knows, my life has been no crystal stair, but I hardly expected that both of my children would turn against me.'

'Dilys didn't turn against you,' Colin rehearsed the ancient litany. 'She's simply staying away until she gets an apology.'

'I'd sooner be blown to flinders than say I'm sorry that I spoke the truth.'

'It wasn't the truth. Dilys didn't get her job by wearing skirts as short as life. She doesn't keep it by wearing blouses so thin you can spit through them onto her bosom. And she didn't get that promotion by acting the sassy slut on that course in Wolverhampton.'

She larded her face with the usual outrage. 'I never said any of that!'

'Oh yes, you did.' In desperation, he turned the oven up from hot to fierce. 'Don't forget that I *heard* you. I was *there*.'

'Well, you can get boils on your bottom!' She took to a virulent clattering of pots and dishes that lasted well past the time his supper was scorched on the top, if not heated through the middle. Forlornly, he picked at the warm clag round the edges. It was horrible. The filling tasted peculiarly metallic, and the topping could have been carpet underlay after a boiler leak. He took advantage of the fact her back was turned to twist Frampton Commercial's letter round on the table. *How* had they managed to make that business of annual fire extinguisher inspections sound like a favour? 'Nice?' she asked over her shoulder, moving on from clashing pots to trimming a fresh metal scouring pad to ram down the mouse hole at the back of the larder. 'Very tasty,' he told her, pushing his plate as far away as possible. But obviously the mantle of conviction was not round his shoulders, for, swivelling round from the sink, she reached to pick up, not just his abandoned plate, but also the carton in which a huge slab of Fifine's Celeriac and Truffle Whatsit still lay, congealing.

Scraping the hideously expensive leftovers straight into Flossie's bowl, her only real revenge on him for his statutory and practised defence of his sister was to announce with satisfaction: 'I suppose I shall have to let her have it – though it will almost certainly make her sick.'

4

COLIN SHOWED UP AT TOR HOUSE DEAD ON TIME. IT WAS Dilys who sent a series of busy-busy messages down through Security, and finally stepped out of the lift into Reception still acting as if, without her last twenty minutes of full attention, the entire glassy edifice might well have crumbled.

'Sorry,' she said, dropping a last few envelopes into the tray on the front desk.

'I don't mind at all if we're late.'

Still puffed with office importance, she missed his mild tease. Otherwise, he might have thought that it was in retaliation that she said, glancing at her watch, 'It's very nearly half past. We'll have to go the quick way, down Bridge Row.'

'No!'

But she'd already started off. He had to follow. Fine till they reached the corner, but the minute the wide expanse of street swung into view, he broke out in the usual sweat and his heart started thudding. He hated Bridge Row. He hadn't once walked down on either side since – since that morning – without feeling faint. How could it possibly matter if the two of them were five minutes late for some stupid gallery opening? Just because Dilys's bank had sponsored the exhibition didn't mean that the doors couldn't open without her. It was typical of his sister's cast-iron self-importance that she would ride over his known susceptibility, his absolute distress, to get there on time.

And odd that she felt nothing. Not a pang. It was, after all, she who had saved the baby. The way she walked down the street now, you would have thought all she had reached up to catch that eerie, steel-blue morning was a ball. You'd never think that while he was standing like a dummy pointing at the rainbow, and wondering slightly at that strange, isolated *thwack!*, she'd been the one to turn towards the ashen-faced driver stopping on a six-pence, the crumpled pram, and seen that little mound of snow-white tracery hurtling towards them out of the sky, trailing ribbons and blanket. Shouldering him aside so forcibly that he'd stumbled, she'd raised her arms as if in supplication, and, with the most flawless precision and even a little twirl on her toes to lessen the impact, accepted a pink and perfect flying baby into her hands.

'Blimey!' That's what she'd said. 'Blimey!' Traffic had stopped, shoppers had frozen in their tracks, and everyone had stared at her as if she were Christ in the middle of a miracle. And she had said nothing but, 'Blimey!'

And that's when it came to him first, this sickening vision of the tiny fuzzed head splatted like yolk on the pavement, the blood-streaked shawl, the chubby legs twisted like something dragged from a toy cupboard and chewed by a dog: what he'd have been looking at if this impossible sister of his hadn't been there. What would quite definitely have happened if that extraordinary, precious moment had been left to him.

Now, over two years later, the merest thought of it still made him so nauseous he could barely stand. Everyone else had got over it. Even the local paper's interest in 'The Flying Baby' now amounted to mere anniversary reminders. His sister and the young mother were down to occasional 'been so busy' flowered notelets. The baby herself was now a toddler. (Last time he'd taken her out, she'd stared at a fir cone lying underneath a tree and asked it gravely, 'Are you here all by yourself?') And only Colin still sometimes felt as shaken and unnerved as if his world were once again listing on its axis, as it had then, with the sheer *accidentalness* of things, the blinding *chance*.

That's why he'd visited the first time, desperate to find another person who might understand this sense of horror of his that would not fade. Naturally he'd turned to Mel. He'd wanted to ask her, 'Isn't the thought of what so nearly happened to your baby driving you *mad*? Are you *haunted*, like I am?' But as he'd stood at her door, unable to spit out even the first civilities, she'd slickly transferred the hairdryer in her hand to an armpit, her comb to between her teeth, and slipped off the safety chain. 'Come in, then. Though you'll have to wait till I've finished my hair.'

The carrycot was in the corner. Was the flying baby inside? He didn't dare go over to look. He just stood on the edge of the swirly green carpet till, irritated, the leaning naiad lashed to the worrisomely overloaded double plug waved him down on one end of the leaking sofa and switched off the dryer. 'All right. I'm ready. You can start.'

It struck him as an odd beginning to a conversation. But who was he to cavil at another's inability to string words together in the usual way? Anyhow, it made it easier for him to stumble through his most peculiar question. 'What I want to know is, are you still bothered by – by the sheer *split-secondness* of it?'

She looked at him, not blankly, more as if wondering if she'd heard him right. He tried to struggle through it another way. 'What I mean is, it's almost as if she—' He pointed to the carrycot. 'As if she—'

'*Tammy*,' she said, quite sharply.

'Yes, Tammy. As if she should have—' He was really floundering now. But he so wanted to get it said, he tried again. 'As if, really, she shouldn't be—' He couldn't finish that one, either. 'As if it was all so *unlikely* – that catching – that it shouldn't really—'

'Shouldn't have *happened*, do you mean? That really my Tammy ought to be *dead*?'

He nodded, horrified. It seemed even worse as cold words than as nightmares. But, to his astonishment, she simply drew her cheap cardigan more tightly round her shoulders and spoke slowly and clearly to the dustpan and brush that were propped against the fender.

'I think we were just very, very lucky. I suppose you could say Fate smiled on us. I am so grateful that dear Dilys happened to be there, and that—' She broke off. 'Why aren't you taking notes? Have you got some tape-recorder running?'

'Sorry?'

And then he'd realized. She hadn't recognized his face. She thought he was just one more reporter. 'No!' he said, shocked into the nearest he came to fluency with people he didn't know. 'You've got it all wrong. I'm *real*. I'm asking a real question.'

'A *real* question?'

'Yes.'

'Do I think Tammy really should have died?'

Again, he nodded. Again, she stared at the dustpan. But, this time, a real person answered. 'I worried about that. I kept thinking weird things like, "I bet they try again," though I didn't have the faintest idea who I was thinking about, and anyway I don't believe in—' She stopped. 'Who *are* you?'

'I'm Dilys's brother,' he said, desperate for her not to distract herself, not to stop trying to explain. 'You've met me. I was there.' Truth compelled him to add, 'And if it had been me, I would have dropped her.' He sensed her terror. 'No!' he said. 'I didn't mean it that way. I meant that I'd have—' Oh, God. How did people who hadn't gone to the same school as him say, 'Colled it up totally'? 'I'd have been caught off guard.' He risked a glance. 'It mattered so much, and I would definitely have botched it.'

She gave him the longest look. Then, 'Perhaps,' she said gently, 'if you were to pick her up and hold her . . . ?'

And he had wondered, as he scooped the snuffling lump out of the carrycot, if this was how she'd worked her own exorcism. Or if she'd simply guessed that it might work on him, holding those solid little wool-wrapped struggles and watching the fierce sneezes that didn't even make a dent in sleep. He was still gazing, rapt, at the veined lids that barely hid the rolling business of dreams behind, when the door opened.

'Another visitor, eh, Mel?'

Colin, the target of a thousand playground tauntings, couldn't be fooled by the easy way the young man chose to lean against the frame of the door he'd rather insolently left open wide. What was the accent? Czech? Romanian? He wasn't sure which was the stranger's more intimidating feature: the powerful, almost oiled shoulders, or the dark, brooding eyes. But Colin had played his bit part in this scene often enough to get his lines out pat. 'I'm from Environmental Health.' He reached for his card, the gesture, as always, designed more to reassure the suspicious third party than encourage any contact in the future. 'There's a bit of a problem elsewhere in the building, so I'm just checking round.'

The scowl was instant, the tone bellicose. 'Who is bloody complaining?'

'I'm afraid I'm not at liberty to say.'

'Well, what they bloody complaining *about*?'

'It isn't a problem with this flat,' Colin said hastily. And then his eye fell on the gas fire. No point in going through the proper channels. The baby could be dead before morning. 'Except that we will, of course, be fitting you with a brand new gas fire, at no expense at all to yourselves, later this afternoon.' Now he would have to go all the way back to the office to beg Old Hetherley to take a couple of his men off Tanner Street and send them round here. And then he'd have to fiddle the paperwork – and probably end up paying for the whole damn thing himself.

Never mind. He might not be able to catch infants in flight, but he could save them from carbon monoxide poisoning. Sagely, he stuffed his card back in his pocket before shifting the baby round on his lap, then handing her back. 'Thank you,' said Mel, though whether it was because he'd given her back her baby or promised her a gas fire, he couldn't tell.

And it still wasn't clear as he watched her face later. She sat impassively, cross-legged on the sofa while Hetherley's crack force tutted and grumbled their way through a simple replacement fitting and reline of flue. 'Where's your "unfit" tape, then?' Tubs Arnold kept demanding. 'You didn't ought to have peeled that off. That's quite illegal.' At first he thought that Mel was simply being smart, keeping her mouth shut. (As one of the council's tenants, she could hardly, thought Colin with a stab of embarrassment, have thought this prompt service was standard.) But then he realized she was barely listening. Men could peel back her threadbare carpet, chip at her fire surround to make it bigger, and even spill grease on her tired little fire stool, and she, in some whole other world, paid no attention. She was hardly there.

At least by the time they'd checked the sealant and packed up their mess, she had come back to earth enough to agree he could come round next day with the last of the paperwork. Tubs Arnold pounced. '*What* paperwork? We had it straight from Mr Hetherley that this was a Special that got lost in *pro forma*. He said all the rest of the ink-slinging's been signed, sealed and knotted.'

But evil sprites of billing had not prevailed. Mel had her gas fire. Tammy had her life. And Colin was soon in the habit of popping in every now and again to see the child he now considered that he, too, had saved. He'd have his excuses at the ready. 'Bit of an on-going noise problem in your block. I thought I'd just—' But she'd simply step back to let him in, and make him a coffee while he cuddled the baby. There'd been no sightings of the challenging young man, and Mel's indifference to footsteps outside on the walkway, and even the odd drunken rattling at her door, gave him to understand there was no need to assume he'd be back in a hurry. Over the last few months it had become a friendship, of a sort. Comforting (though it hadn't helped at all with this business of going down Bridge Row). But he hadn't told Dilys, for fear of the teasing he knew would follow. 'Found a tart with a heart, have you, Colin?' And neither, he couldn't help noticing, could Mel herself have got round to mentioning his visits to Dilys. Otherwise, why would his sister keep trying to bring him up to date with snippets from the flowered notelets, as she was doing now? 'Did I tell you little Tammy has started at playgroup?'

In the wash of relief from getting round the corner into Stemple Street, he put a foot wrong. 'It isn't playgroup, exactly. More a supervised Mother and Toddler session.'

She broke her stride. 'How do you know that?'

'Council,' he said hastily, and, when her look of astonishment didn't fade, improvised, 'Cooper was inspecting them last week for "sufficient parking", and they pointed The Flying Baby out to him.'

'Really?' She seemed quite proud. 'That's splendid. Absolutely splendid. *Excellent!*' Her enthusiasm for the notion of little Tammy at Mother and Toddler sessions seemed only to grow, until he realized she'd lost interest in that and was speaking of the display in the Stemple Street Gallery. There, staring at them through the freshly washed window, was a giant gold and blue crotch, fashioned from patchwork. 'Oh, that is striking. Very, very striking.'

Turning to seek out acquaintances, she caught him making one of his 'I-can't-see-people-wanting-something-like-that-on-the-walls-of-their-living-room' faces, and told him sharply, 'I hope you're not going to start acting like Mother in front of my colleagues,' before abandoning him to hurry up the steps after a couple who were vanishing through the swing doors. Too dispirited even to consider legging it, he trailed up after her into a world in which he knew no one, and was quite sure he wouldn't like the artwork. If you could call it that. At times like these, their mother shot unnervingly high in his esteem. For years she'd been saying it: 'The whole lot's rubbish – though I don't suppose they could do better if they tried.' He'd put his time in, trying to dismiss her views, dogging strangers round galleries as they gave each exhibit a fair shot. 'That's interesting.' 'It's very clever, isn't it?' 'I like the colours.' Sometimes he eavesdropped on the Know-It-Alls. 'See how the blues speak to the greens!' 'I'm getting Modigliani through these brush-strokes.' '*Now* talk to me about the curse of line!' No luck there, either. He'd even had a stab at seeking revelation out of the mouths of babes and sucklings. But whenever he'd managed to inch close enough to those small milling herds of arm-punchers and hair-pullers, all that he'd ever heard were squawks of things like, 'Give me back my

77

Mars bar!' Or sniggering whispers: 'Didn't one of Gary's old dads have a beard like that snatch hair?'

No, there would have to be a second great Enlightenment before he'd come to think that this display of giant patchwork crotches was any more than money thrown away by Dilys's bank. And if it came from Tor Bank's fund for Goodwill in the Community, they would, in his opinion, have done a whole lot better to have invested in a serious upgrading of the Market Street lavatories. Surely the people of Priding would far rather have a nice clean plaque staring down at them from a tiled wall as they reached for their own private parts than some grubby knitted crotch staring at them as—

'Colin?'

He swung round. Perdita!

She wasted no effort on any greeting for him. 'Is your sister here?'

He nodded.

'With – *Marjorie*?'

She didn't say it nicely, so he kept his expression blank. All he dared offer was, 'She left me on the steps,' and burnished as this might have been with the virtue of neutrality, even to him it sounded pathetic. More to ratchet himself up in his own esteem than to try to raise himself in Perdita's, he forced himself to nod towards the nearest greying crotch. 'I don't think much of that.'

Perdita sighed. 'Oh, haven't we seen it all far, *far* too often? But there's your sister for you. The world moves on, but she still gets excited by a few dregs of Reservation Art and a free drink for every no-hoper in Priding.'

Did she mean him? Bitch. And what on earth was

bloody Reservation Art? He turned to squint at the bedraggled knotted thing. Could he have misunderstood? Was it a *wigwam*? Oh, how he loathed these ghastly events of Dilys's. The trouble with the arts was that they were forever knocking you sideways and taking your breath away. Look at that exhibition Tor had sponsored called Shapes of the Century. He'd stood in front of all those brightly patterned eggs, and – whoomph! – out of the past like a swipe from a sock stuffed with wet sand had come this memory of his Easter gift to his mother – the eggshell he'd wax-stippled and dipped, and dipped and wax-stippled, along with the daintiest of them for an hour each Friday, before the bell rang. Miss Dassanayake had teased his grim determination and his rigidly protruding tongue.

'Stop *fretting*, Colin. Eggshells are tougher than you think. You're not going to break it.'

And, miracle! He hadn't. No, he had carried it home, wrapped carefully in cotton wool in its box, and on Easter morning he had held it out to her.

Even to a child primed to think that absence of criticism is a positive response, she'd seemed lukewarm. At first he'd put it down to the possibility she hadn't realized he'd decorated the egg himself. Then he'd wondered if, as so often, he'd somehow picked up the wrong end of the stick, and (though his classmates had sat with almost equally furrowed brows and fixed concentration) decorating eggs was really easy. It only became clear just how indifferent to his gift his mother had been when Dilys's failure to produce so much as a home-made card for the occasion had triggered, not wrath, but the infinitely more dangerous dark grievance: 'Oh, I can see your sister doesn't care any more than *this* for my feelings!'

He'd seen his mother curl her fingers. He'd even heard the little *crack!* But only as he saw the patterned shell scattering across the carpet had he truly believed it. And when, standing all those years later in front of the display case, the recollection had flooded back and, on impulse, he'd pushed through the crush to find his sister and check ('Can what I remember be *true?* Can that really have *happened?*'), he'd found her beached in the corner with a crowd of Tor acolytes, unwittingly capping his story: 'So I spent *weeks* on a painting to win this little Minnie Mouse camera. Weeks and weeks and *weeks*. It was practically a *Brueghel* by the time that I'd finished it. And when I finally carried it through to show her, before I sent it in, guess what she said!'

Only one's own humiliations are burned in memory. So Colin had had to stand, glass in hand, with the rest of them, waiting, until she'd finally come out with it.

'She said' – and Dilys could still catch it perfectly, that overloaded, almost-too-busy-even-to-say-this tone that had echoed down their childhood – ' "That's very nice, dear. Have you just done that while Mummy's been having to rush around all by herself, setting the table?" '

Small wonder neither of the two of them ever picked up a paintbrush again! Still shuddering, Colin came back to present torments to find the crush around himself and Perdita had been shunting a very much younger and better-looking man close to their elbows, and Perdita's smile had accordingly switched up to full beam. 'I certainly hope you missed my last telly appearance, Colin.

I was terrible. *Terrible!*' The silvered nails on the thin fingers flashed and the startling eyes rolled in humorous self-deprecation. 'Well, *did* you happen to catch it?'

'No,' he said, happy to lose her attention to the stranger. But no one could stop him continuing to stand pretending to be part of a contented trio instead of the gooseberry he soon proved. In the end, Perdita and her new acquaintance moved off on the excuse of getting drinks, and he was left with the unenviable choice of either feigning further interest in the dispiriting grey growths on the wall or seeking other company. His sister was very close now. From her expression of rapt interest and frequent nods, he took her to be talking to someone much higher up in the bank than herself. And then he realized this was Marjorie. How odd it was to watch someone he knew so well deploying her charm on a stranger. With him, her technique was the simple *splat!* – that, and the pick-and-mix Colin, whereby every now and again she chose another sort of brother who suited her better, and he was supposed to be that. And it had always been risky – not to say downright dangerous – to fail to pick up the signs that a metamorphosis would be timely and advisable. It hadn't been an issue back in nursery, where Dilys had treated him as if he were as much of a stranger as all the other children. But by the time the two of them reached primary school, she'd realized his birth-day acted as the best possible early-warning system for hers, and would whip up great storms of attention around him for two weeks every year, while ignoring him the rest of it. Through teenage she had made him so invisible, you would have thought that she'd been at his spell book. But in their twenties she had brought him back to life as Colin Dogsbody, to help her sudden fancies with their removals – in and out. (And he'd put up with it, till one of her neighbours leaned over the hedge one day to ask him about his prices, somehow furnishing him with the impetus he'd been needing to claim he was busy each time in the future.) Once in their thirties, he'd been transmogrified again. Was it to do with his hair loss? In any event, the lag of twenty minutes between his birth and hers had somehow magically become extended until, in front of men friends in particular, he'd even heard her say, without a blush, things like, 'Shall we chat to Old Colin?' or, 'Meet my Big Brother'.

She wouldn't thank him for stepping in to play even this part while she was busy with new prey. She was dressed in her hunting gear. One of the things he'd realized ages ago about his sister was that she had outfits, not just for things like cycling or decorating, but for deep inner purposes. At that last lunch with Perdita, she'd been in the funereal Wronged Woman gown he'd seen so often. Today she wore Fringes of Art, but along with the velvet breeks and buckled shoes came the intriguing ask-me-where-I-got-it waistcoat – her moderate little touch of Vamp. This Marjorie, on the other hand, could not have looked more dowdy. Stompy shoes. Corduroy skirt. And a sensible woollen top with the obligatory toss-around bright scarf to signal the distinction between work-time and leisure. A baffling choice of new friend, unless you took contrast with Perdita to be part of the attraction. It pricked his interest, certainly; but still it was purely by accident that, as the group to his left pushed out to let in yet another braying member, he was shunted so close that Marjorie's attention shifted to him for a moment over his sister's shoulder.

Curious, Dilys turned. Her face fell. 'Oh, it's you.' There was the longest pause, in which Colin's inability to think of anything sensible to say made him feel like an idiot. In the end, Dilys cracked. 'Well, let me introduce you.' Another good long pause. 'Colin, this is Marjorie, one of Tor Grand Insurance's most experienced actuaries. And Marjorie, this is Colin. He's in Environmental Health.'

He'd been demoted, then. He wasn't even a brother now. 'Pleased to meet you,' he mumbled, secure in the knowledge that, even without his sister's ferocious warning glare, he was unlikely to have managed to come out with his surname.

Another grisly silence gripped the three of them, till Dilys said meaningfully, 'Colin, didn't you mention you wanted a chat with Perdita? She's over there.' 'Oh, right,' he said, as if a thing like 'chatting' sat quite as high in his basket of social skills as in that of the next man. Obediently, he scuttled off, then edged round the clumps of people the other way, reckoning he'd done his bit to bump up the numbers for her bank, and was free to go home and watch telly. That comedy his mother recommended began at nine, and if he walked briskly and left his shower till morning, he could—

'Colin!'

She'd trapped him *again*. 'Hello, Perdita.' Her new acquaintance had vanished, so clearly, till she found a substitute, he was to be her social stooge. 'Well,' she said, eyes tracking busily round the room. 'And what have you been up to since last we met?'

'Talking to Dilys.'

She looked at him as if he were an imbecile.

'Visiting Mother,' he tried again hastily. (It was all he could think of, except for pursuing Chisholm Farmholdings about their runaway slurry.)

'And how is the dear old lady?'

She said it with such warmth, sincerity almost, that he assumed she must have spotted yet another freewheeling male appraising her over his shoulder. Cheered by the prospect of rescue, he offered, 'She's doing very well.'

'Not finding that big house a bit too much for her?'

Oh, ho! he thought. What had his sister said? 'A glorified estate agent'? Well, Perdita wouldn't have much luck winkling her way into Holly House. Or Mother out of it. She'd made that clear enough: 'No, I'd sooner be fat in the fire than sit in a circle with a pack of old biddies.' Any suggestion that four airy double bedrooms might now be one or two too many always met with short shrift. Why, only last week when, staggering across the hall under the weight of Flossie's bag of dogmeal, poor Mr Stastny had been ill-advised enough to offer conversationally, 'You could fit a good few homeless into this house, Mrs Riley,' she'd given him the most crushing look and batted back, 'Yes, and so I will, Mr Stastny, the day I see them spilling out of *your* front door . . .'

And she'd not tipped him.

If she could stick up for herself, he could support her. 'I think Mum's happy where she is.'

'Your mother? *Happy?*' The laugh that followed came

84

out practically as a snort. Deeply resenting Perdita's careless venting of intimacies gleaned at a time that was now firmly over, he came as close as he dared to being rude back: 'And that, of course, will save us from having to deal with one or two grasping and unpleasant characters.'

He was amazed that someone with curls could look so menacing. Instantly, he tried to pretend estate agents were the last people on his mind. 'You see, if she went into a home, we would have to have tenants.'

It was obvious how very keen she was from how casually she offered it. 'But you could always *sell* . . .'

He shook his head, having, as usual, a good deal less trouble inventing the excuse than getting the words out. 'No, no. Some special Trust thing, I'm afraid. Holly House has to stay in the family.'

'Really? I don't remember Dilys ever mentioning it. And, I must say, I've never heard of anything like that with—'

People like you, she meant, though, still in client-seeking mode, she knew better than to say so.

'I know. Daft, isn't it?'

'So who *is* going to get it?'

'What?'

'The *house*.'

'Oh.' Tiresome woman. When would she ever let up? He gazed round, stumped, before he realized that it didn't matter what he said. The only thing that was important was stopping her going round, off her own greedy commission-grubbing bat, to try to charm Norah. He knew exactly what would happen then. She'd get her foot in the door. 'Mrs Riley, I think you know my mother from

Canasta Club. Yes, that's right. *Dolly*. Indeed, I believe that she recently sent you my photo.' Inside, the temptation to believe that she'd gain ground by spilling little Dilys beans would overwhelm her. And Norah would listen. Oh, yes. Norah would listen. She'd take the chance to gather all the ammunition she could, and have him in the trench for months on end. 'You never mentioned that your sister said—' 'You could have told me that—' 'I'm very hurt that you've let Dilys go round telling everyone—' It would be grim, each predatory onslaught lasting for hours and only ending with the obligatory tragic sigh: 'I might be old and feeble, but who'd have thought I'd ever reach the stage when my own daughter sent a perfect stranger round to try to prise me out of house and home!'

No. Better for Perdita to drop the whole idea of seeing any For Sale signs at Holly House.

'Who's going to get it? *I* am.'

'The whole *caboodle*?'

The envy in her eyes confirmed how very valuable his mother's home must have become. He spread his hands. 'Who else? What with things between Mother and Dilys being as they are . . .'

'So it'll still be sold, then, in the end. Trust or no Trust.' (He could tell from her tone that she hadn't bought that one.)

Flustered, he asked, 'How's that?'

'Because *you'll* be the end of the line, that's for certain.'

If she'd not said it so offensively – as if he were some mutant slobbering in her face – he would have let the whole thing go. But her disparagement maddened him. He tried his own limp version of one of his mother's Mr

Stastny-crushing looks; but not only did it fail – really, those eyes were quite extraordinary, it was like trying to stare down a snake – but his own colour rose, and with it the ghosts of a million similar petty humiliations. And only a fury fuelled with all of these, he realized later, could so have sprung him out of his true timid self that, just for once, he managed to toss, not just his caution, but his inarticulacy to the winds, along with the lie he threw over his shoulder.

'Well, that's just where you're wrong, Perdita! You see, I already have one child. And her mother and I are still very much in love and about to have another.'

5

HIS FLAT SEEMED DOUBLY EMPTY FOR THE LACK OF THEM. HE gazed around at every dull surface, each silent appliance. 'Wife, eh?' he practically heard his oven muttering. 'Perhaps now at last we'll get into some interesting cooking.' 'Child?' yearned the table. 'Excellent! Clear off these boring old papers and bring on the plasticine and poster paints.'

Wife and child . . .

Can household goods conspire? The phone that stayed silent all evening. The over-hot water steaming from his showerhead (more than enough for two). The extra pillow on the far side of the bed he only changed to keep his patterned laundry in step. Even the gift that fell from his breakfast cereal seemed to rebuke him. 'So where's this child, then? Go on. Tell me that.'

Putting the car in gear, he tried to shove the whole thing out of mind. Still, best to warn his mother before the little rumours began to seep back. After all, Priding was tiny. It would be easy enough, next time she started carping on about someone in Canasta Club, for him simply to leap in, 'Oh, people can be impossible! Do you know, last week I met a woman at a private view who was so pushy, I all but ended up telling her I was married with children.'

Then it would be a toss-up. He might get pilloried for the private view. 'Hob-nobbing now, are we? I hope that our cat can still run up your alley.' Or it might turn personal. 'I'd like to meet the beanbrain who'd marry *you*.' But chances were he'd be lucky. 'That's right,' she'd tell him. 'Fend the trollops off. Stay as you are, then you can walk in your own front door Lord, and out the back Master.'

Or he could simply put things straight by marrying Melanie. Go round and lay his cards directly on the table. 'Someone's about to tell my mother I have a family. Would you and Tammy oblige me? If we got cracking, we could have another child by early spring.'

And he was off again. The files before him vanished, and he was on his knees on her disgusting carpet. 'Mel,' he was saying, 'Please, Mel—'

She'd look down, baffled. He'd take her hand in his and point to Tammy. 'I could take you both out of here. I know I'm no great catch, but I am clean and sane, and drab as it is, my flat is nicer than this place. You could do worse.'

Except he didn't love her. Not at all. He found her rather strange indifference, her willowy passivity – really, if he were honest, her ability simply to take and take – rather off-putting. No, it was Tammy he adored. Tammy, whose life he'd saved. Who, but for him—

A call across the office fetched him back. 'That's Cleansing again, Mr Riley. Still wanting to know if you're going to be able to fit in that landfill.'

He'd better. Forty thousand suffocated chickens. And as he ground the last available council vehicle out from behind the egregiously poorly parked Mice'n'Maggots van, he had to admit to himself that it was becoming a problem, this business of living in a dream world. Not that it hadn't started as far back as the sandpit and the swings with Stol, who lived behind the rain tub, and, inasmuch as he had any physical characteristics at all, preferred to stay standing. Stol had no family. But he did have his story, and for a long time was the most important person in Colin's life. Indeed, looking back, Colin realized he must have felt the same way about Stol as Christians feel about Christ – that he was close and vivid and utterly real, a strong and gentle presence who knew his feelings and his thoughts, with whom there were no barriers. Stol was so real, in fact, that when Miss Dassanayake showed up in school one morning with the slides of a recent class outing, for a moment Colin had been disappointed, he remembered, that his friend didn't happen to be in any of the photos.

But, he thought, braking for yet another set of Highways' homicidally ill-timed lights, his Tammy wasn't like that. She was *real*. How sad it was that, just to get a toddler, you had to have a wife. He didn't want one. The whole idea of anyone ever again spreading her tentacles over every part of him – the place he lived, his routines, his emotions – filled him with dread. And it was not the dread of the unknown. Back then when they were in the other building, he'd been as close to Helen Letherington as people seemed to think you needed to be before you got married. He'd been as astonished as anyone the day she'd told him she wasn't going to see him any more. More so, in fact, since everyone else had probably assumed it was some incompatibility that caused the relationship to founder, and only Colin knew that there was none. The two of them had met. She'd managed his shyness skilfully enough for them to get on reasonably well in public and even better in private. He'd dared to think his future was assured. And then, in one baffling evening – 'Colin, I am so *sorry*. But it's like living with some shell you've left behind to pretend to be a person' – *kaput!* It was over.

He never wanted that again. No. Better to stick with the daydreams. Then all that happened when the bubble burst was that he had to risk the council van's suspension along a half a mile of rutted track and pick his way past hosts of scavengers, to see what some anti-social chicken dumper had left to fester in a rancid pit.

The stench was awful, but it hadn't deterred the real professionals, two of whom seemed to be making a valiant job of lifting a full-sized wardrobe out of the stinking heaps of feathered corpses. He couldn't bring himself to offer help, although he knew that, in his virulent yellow plastic safety jacket and tough rubber boots, he was far better equipped than either of them to paddle in drifts of rotting carrion. But guilt, as ever, told on him, to the extent that, on his way back up the dirt track, he stopped to purchase a rather fine brass umbrella holder from a man with a heap of *trouvailles* at the entrance.

He might have known his mother wouldn't like it. 'Why should I want that?'

'It's just like yours. But better.'

She stepped back smartly. 'I like mine.'

He twisted the patterned brass cylinder full circle, to show her. 'But, look. Rust-free!'

She played the old card. 'No, thanks. It was your father who bought me mine.'

He dumped his on the doorstep and, scraping the last of the chicken bones off his boots onto her lobelias, went for revenge. 'Have you thought any more about replacing that cable?'

'If you've come to torment me, then you can turn straight round and go back to your rats and your rubbish.'

'I was just passing by.'

'Go on, then. *Do* that.'

Honours now even, he felt free to ask, 'Well, aren't you even going to give me a cup of tea?'

She looked a bit shifty. Then, 'All right,' she agreed. 'But since you're in those workboots, could you just take a peek at that dratted drain?'

It was the conciliatory tone that made him suspicious. He set off back down the path, but the moment he sensed she'd vanished he turned and kicked off his council footwear. Chasing her silently across the stone hall into the kitchen, he caught her clearing the table of a huge swathe of paperwork.

'So,' he confronted her sternly. 'What's all this?'

The look she gave him would have cracked a stone. 'None of your business, Mr Nosy Parker.'

But he had read the words Tor Grand Insurance upside down. 'You're never switching companies *again*.'

'I'll do what I like,' she said, disappearing into the larder with her arms full of papers.

'But there's no *point*,' he wailed after her. 'Wherever one lot goes on this sort of safety certificate business, the others always end up following.' Though he was speaking to the larder door, he still kept on. 'You'll change, then, in a month or so, exactly the same thing will happen. You'll get another letter.' Out she came, glowering horribly. But he was determined to finish. 'You might just as well give in now and let Mr Herbert's men do their worst and give you your signed piece of paper.'

She started the tuneless hum that meant, 'Don't for a moment think I might be listening.' Should he play one last dirty card and remind her that Dilys now worked for the great octopus of Tor? No. Simply couldn't face it. Turning to Floss, he said, exasperated, 'Walkies?' But she just spread her body flatter on the floor. Even more irritated, he strode back across the hall and snatched up his umbrella holder. 'I'll put this in the dustbin.' Out of sheer spite, on his way down the side path he reached up to give the windchimes a hefty smack and set the war between his mother and next door straight back on track before diving in the woodshed. There, he rammed home the bolt his father had had the foresight to switch from the outside to the inside, and, in search of distraction and comfort, reached under the chisels. But before he'd even managed to give his sweet bouncing girl a fighting chance to soothe his spirits, he'd realized that it wouldn't work. He was too rattled. And anyway, the added guilt of seeing Suzie in work hours always made things so much more difficult. It wasn't worth the candle.

Candle . . .

Time for a spell. Lifting the old varnished box out from its hiding place behind the ancient mangle, he sifted through. What did he need? A few of the pretty things, more for their comfort than their efficacy. The spiral stone, perhaps. The chipped medallion. A handful of shells. And the beetles, all three of them, glossy, black and perfect, and, for all he knew, dead for a thousand years before he'd found them in that hollow stone down by the quarry. He wrote his incantation backwards with the silver-tipped pen from the spine of his father's last diary, repeating it over and over under his breath as he shoved the torn scraps of paper deep in the twisty shell. Setting the candle in the very centre of everything, he spread his hands and began as usual: *'Something from inside, something from outside* . . .' In moments the spell took off, the sheer word-spinning command of it startling that tiny part of him he'd had to leave alert for calls or for footsteps. When else had everything ever spun along so well? No words said wrongly, no charm water spilled, no candles tipping over. When else had that silent, watching custodian out of self had such a strong sense that, with a bit of luck, this time, this time . . .

So what went wrong? Was it the rustle in the ivy outside? That, after all, could have been Floss, nosing around in repentance. Or the way that the candlelight swam in the shadows? Perhaps, he thought after, it was simply the nastiness of what he was wishing another poor soul on the planet that made him, at the very last – and he could sense it, it was about to be the *perfect spell* – lose his nerve utterly, and let that shadow vigilant who watched for danger break in to stop things in their tracks, and twist the force of magic round.

'Blimey!'

This echo of his sister brought Tammy instantly to mind. And he felt shame. How could he go and shuffle in Mel's doorway, holding the indispensable bag of fruit and this week's excuse, the lovely bright alphabet letters, when scarcely an hour before he'd been hunched over a trestle top, playing at wizards? What on earth was the matter with him? Raw with the sense of his own lack of dignity, he raised the candle to the twisty shell and punished himself with its heat on his fingers. The spell words floated down, spluttering ashes, and, still disquieted, he stirred the mess into his father's work bench. Had it been haste? Or panic? Hard to tell. But still it had been a very strange thing to end up wishing his mother.

Light and Life.

Still in his socks, he took the opportunity to climb in the larder window and examine the paperwork she'd stuffed in the breadbin. You had to hand it to her generation, he decided; they'd had a proper education. None of the botchalike Clarries in the office could have made nearly so good a job of jotting notes on the application forms he found himself holding. At the bottom of Prudent Secure's notes, she'd summarized: 'practices in review'. (Clarrie would have spelt it 'practises'.) On Heft Insurance, 'nothing definite – changes in pipeline – girl *very* shifty'. And on good old Tor Grand's, it was 'no plans at present – but no guarantee'. Inspecting the envelopes, he noticed with interest that she'd been more efficient than Clarrie ever would at getting the forms sent to her first class. Even playing the Old Lady card, that was impressive.

She'd only filled in one. Tor Grand. He ran his eyes over the printed name that, in as much as it mirrored his own, still echoed of catcalls down drab school corridors. He almost heard the snort she'd have given as her pen sailed over the contemptible Ms to circle the full-bodied Mrs. He read the old address that still, at heart, he felt belonged to him as well. If there had been a section labelled Medical, he probably would have read that too, but Tor Grand's only interest was in the house: its age, its size, proximity to the neighbours. On it went, all filled in perfectly, over the page to details of claims under previous dispensations, where she gave the lie to his fears of her gathering vagueness by recalling some pre-neolithic disaster with the boiler. Here, in fact, was the ideal application form. No sections hopelessly left blank. No crossings-out. No claggy contoured heaps of whitener over which the poorly schooled likes of Clarrie hauled their pens time and again, leaving errors like spoor. If only all those halfwits in Personnel – whoops! 'Human Resources' – had had the sense to let department heads like his own recruit from the elderly, then his out-tray would be empty now, not threatening avalanche.

And then he saw it, nestling so innocently amongst the Have You Evers: *Have special conditions of any sort, or any form of specific certification, ever been requested in respect of insurance for this property?*

She'd answered, *No.*

No need to panic. Maybe she wouldn't even send the application in. After all, unless Frampton Commercial shared her first company's easy-going attitude towards the refund, she might decide she'd prefer to get the cable entry done.

Then, fat chance, he told himself, and sank, exhausted, on the breadbin. Ranked jars of pickled onions eyed him mournfully. What should he do? Carry on battling? Or simply let the whole thing go, and pray that, out of the gamut of ills a house was heir to, it was a jet plane through the roof that got it first. Anything else would almost certainly provoke the usual suspicious investigation of a Johnny-come-lately. One routine phone call to the last insurer and, sure as he never saw a banker on a bike, her claim would come back stamped 'Invalid'.

So it was into battle. Christ! Old people were *exhausting*. Look at him. This visit alone he'd played four roles already – recycler, spurned benefactor, sorcerer, spy. And now he had to turn insurance adviser yet again. Sighing, he slid the application form back in its envelope and dropped it into its hiding place, along with the others. Then he climbed out of the window, and, slapping the windchimes again purely for the hell of it, walked in to accuse her of concealment and criminal misrepresentation.

She slipped her own attack in first. 'You've got a ghost up every sleeve. Where have you been?'

He lost his nerve. 'I was just looking for a bradawl in the woodshed.'

'Don't you go stealing my tools, or I'll soon have your name crossed off my Christmas card list.'

He took the tray she was carrying, and though she hardly went up the stairs like a spring lamb, he could tell she was finding it harder and harder to pretend she was limping. 'Is your leg better?' he asked, with deep suspicion. Affecting not to hear him, she fought back. 'I don't know what's the matter with me. I feel limp as a piece of chewed string.' He plunged in as close to the business worrying him as he dared. 'Listen,' he lied. 'I don't know what all those papers lying on the table were, but really, you'd be mad to switch companies a second time and have to go through this whole performance again in a few months.' He laid his precious September fortnight on the line. 'I could take time off work and be around while Mr Herbert's men are doing it.'

'Oh, wouldn't you be everybody's star attraction!'

'I could make sure—'

'No. Why should I suffer a boiling of mess and noise just so your bum's on plush after the will's read?'

'This has nothing to do with the property's value. It's to do with *insuring* it.'

'I think that's my business.'

'You won't be so quick to say that when your insurance company refuses to cough up because you never mentioned any special condition.' Ignoring her look of suspicion, he waggled his finger. 'Because that's what your being asked to get this electrical safety thing is, you know. A special condition. And you won't be able to pretend to Tor Grand that you didn't know anything about it.'

'I see you've been snooping through my post again.'

'I'm sure I don't know what you mean.'

'Tor Grand?'

Rumbled.

He spread his hands. 'Well, what the hell am I *supposed* to do? Leave you to make decisions as daft as this? You won't be so happy for me to leave you to it when you're standing in a heap of charred rubble and Tor Grand won't pay you!'

'You've put in your twopennyworth. Don't think for a moment I'll expect any help from *you*.'

To hide his flush of vexation, he bent his head over the teapot. This daft refusal to be *sensible*. This stubborn *rudeness*. How did the rest of the world steer their way round it without feeling homicidal? When old people acted like this, it wasn't even normal life slid into reverse, but something much uglier. Kids on the wasteground next to Mel turned a deaf ear to everything said to them, but all they seemed to want was not to have to call a halt to whichever anti-social game it was they were enjoying. This was more personal and to do with power. 'All right,' she might as well have said out loud. 'So my world's closing in. I can't make sense of that new electronic timer on the water heater. I'm scared to take a car out. And I could no more haul that great heavy old wheelbarrow out of the shed again than cycle to Guadalajara. But there's one thing I still can do. I can still watch you having to gnash your teeth as I do everything my way. And I shall.'

Small wonder granny-bashing was so popular. But even wimps like him could put their fists up in their own weak way. 'I'd no idea you were so confident you had so many other good friends around, ready to offer help in emergencies. Perhaps you'd ask one of them to take the mower for its annual service. And another to fix that hinge on the shutter that you say has been annoying you.'

'If doing me one or two tiny favours is such a trial, I'd rather be six feet under.'

'Sadly, it's not that easy to fold yourself up neatly and disappear,' he said, regretting the words instantly, since it manifestly was. Look at his father. One last kind, wordless pat on Colin's head, one last attempt to show Dil how to tie a proper sheepshank, and he'd slid out the door, never to return – except as a gentle ghost striding through Colin's rich imaginary life, and an occasional dizzying vision of a horizontally revolving skeleton. 'You realize your father would be turning in his grave if—'

He risked a glance to see if his sharp response had triggered dread memory. But she was busy mumbling. 'Lord knows, I didn't expect the rainbow trail to stretch all the way to the horizon. But if I'd had the faintest idea what a cindery path I was going to be asked to tread, I would have wished to have been gathered into glory's arms a long, long while ago.'

He nearly retorted, 'Well, don't for a moment think you'd have been wishing it alone!' Then, fighting the very same surge of self-pity he'd just been despising in her, it struck him that it couldn't only be the two of them. Out there, there must be thousands who shared this feeling. Millions, over the world. After all, just as the last guests at a party never knew when to go, Death never knew when to arrive. Someone, he thought, should have the courage to air this issue properly. On radio, perhaps. Or even telly. A panel discussion, a bit like *The Moral Maze*, but to soften any unpleasantness they could give the programme's name a lighter, maybe even a literary, spin. What was the line from that Hardy poem Mrs Hunter forced him to learn as a punishment for horsing about when Talbot pushed his head through that window? *'Till the Spinner of the Years Said "Now!"'* That might work well. It could be launched at a slot around midnight, when all the real complainers had gone to bed. As it became cult viewing, it would be shifted to a popular hour. Fans would begin to call it *Now!* for short. There'd have to be at least four panel members. Some would be regulars, others one-off guests. And, as the chairman might say winsomely each week during the introduction, 'To be a good deal more blunt than the scissors with which Fate finally snips the thread of life,' they would discuss the stage at which there was really no point any longer. 'Our panel's first case this evening is Mr Eric Fanshawe. Mr Fanshawe has been in a wheelchair for eight years now — I've got that right, haven't I, Eric? It is eight? But now the doctor's put him on such a high dose of steroids that he can no longer — bleh, bleh, bleh.' At the end of each discussion, there'd be a studio audience vote. *Now!?* Or, *Not Yet!?* Nothing would hang on it, of course. But it would give these burgeoning hospital ethical committees food for thought. And, if you added on a national phone-in, you could begin to take the pulse of the country on these matters, and, what with the steadily rising number of elderly, that sort of thing could be ever more useful . . .

'*Colin!*'

'Sorry?'

'Was that a knock?'

'I didn't hear a thing.'

Her look gave him to understand that that proved nothing. 'Go and take a peek.' Dutifully, he stepped over

Flossie and edged closer to the window. 'My God!' It was Perdita on the doorstep. She was wearing the smartest of summer suits and clutching flowers, and spangles of sunlight were dancing all over her. 'Who *is* it?' hissed his mother from her chair. He panicked. 'Elsie.' 'That nosy witch? Don't let her see you.' But it was too late. Stepping back in a pool of bright sunshine in order to look up and appraise the guttering, Perdita had spotted his shadow.

'Hell-ooo!'

'That doesn't sound like Elsie.'

'Well, now I come to take a closer look . . .'

'Oh, really!' In her exasperation she made it to the door well before him, and slammed it in his face. Relieved, he crept back to the window. It didn't take his mother long to get down the stairs, and Perdita was clearly quite happy inspecting the state of the chimneys. He strained to hear, as voices floated upwards. Perdita's vague mention of 'simply passing by . . .' matched by his mother's less airy-fairy 'not really at all convenient . . .' Perdita's gushing '. . . to thank you for taking the trouble of watching my television programme . . .' as she tried to hand over the flowers. His mother's adroit mention of allergies as, fully in practice refusing umbrella holders, she made absolutely no move to accept them. Perdita's sly sidetrack towards the weather '. . . makes one so *dry* . . .' that was greeted with a silence like nerve gas. Oh, how he admired his mother! He'd have been grovelling round the kitchen by now, offering their unwelcome visitor a choice of beverage.

And then, the clincher. Perdita's reference to 'a little chat', and Norah, the sunlight beating on her scalp, murmuring, 'Perhaps another time, when the weather's better . . .' By the time she came back, he was ready to hug her. But she was spitting poison. 'The cheek of it! Up my path, bold as a crab. The little hussy needn't think there's any point sweeping *my* doorstep with her eyelashes.'

'Who was it?' he asked, keen, this time, to do a much better job of allaying suspicion.

'How should *I* know? Some woman with a bucketful of hair trying to dredge up viewers for her telly programme. Really, these people have no sense at all. This house isn't even on cable.' He stared. Had she truly not recognized the face in the photograph? Or was she, as usual, working on the principle that knowledge is power, so best not to share? And what about bloody Perdita? Did she really have him logged down for such a feeble opponent she didn't even give a toss if he was in there, listening, as she started her sales pitch? Or was her greedy head so stuffed with percentages she hadn't even noticed the huge blue council lettering on the side of his van? His head was spinning. Oh, to be back in the haven of his office, with only Clarrie's sporadic howls of technologically related anguish and hourly tranches of embittered messages from Lees and Haksars to disturb and unsettle him. Colin peered out of the window – had she gone? was it safe to leave? – just as his mother appeared at his elbow. 'So who is the pushy little madam pestering now? That black-hearted fiend next door, I hope. With luck, the over-painted little trollop will get her hair caught in his windchimes and fetch the whole noisy boiling down.'

She craned a little further. 'Colin, is that your van cluttering up Ruby's entrance?'

'Parked at the kerb beside her house, do you mean?'

She eyed his vehicle as keenly as Perdita had appraised the guttering. 'You could fit quite a number of black bags in that.'

'Black bags?'

Already she was leading the way into her dressing room. Piled on the narrow unused bed were clothes he hadn't seen for years. 'You're never getting rid of all of these!'

'I shan't be wanting them.'

From the huge heap he lifted a patterned silk jacket Dilys had begged for time and again. ('Mum, it's a Tavernier! And you never even wear it!') A stab of rancour made him drop it back. Why should he worry where the jacket went? If Dilys wanted things, then she should be on hand, doing her bit. 'Some of these things are well worth hanging on to, surely.' He held up a pair of tartan trews he remembered his mother wearing on those very rare occasions she'd agreed to a picnic. 'You could use these for gardening.'

'No.' She was adamant. 'The whole lot's going out.'

'But you'll have nothing left.' He tugged the closet open. 'Look! It's practically *empty*.' He swung the hangers to the sides and played her tune. 'You could at least put back this coat that Father bought you. It's lovely, warm and cheerful—'

'And not a bit of use to me.'

She said it with such bitterness that he was startled. But then again, why shouldn't someone her age feel deep resentment? After all, what sort of sadist had designed the universe so you could burst out of cot and nursery without a thought, leave your home town without a qualm, and make the entire world your oyster, only to find that, in a blink, the process had slid in reverse? Harder to miss the long and grim unravelling: world back to town, town down to room, room closing in to bed, and all the time, ahead of you, kept well in mind, only that final wooden lidded cot. 'Come on,' he urged. 'You have to keep a few smart clothes. You're not dead yet.' Spotting a shoe he remembered, he held it out. 'What about these? You always loved them.'

Furious, she twisted it over, scraping his wrist with the stiletto tip.

No chance she'd wear a heel that high again between now and the grave. 'Oh. I see. Sorry.'

'It doesn't matter.' But now, of course, he had to accept the bags she thrust at him, and shovel in clothes. From time to time over the black rustling he tried to raise a cheerful memory. 'Isn't this what you wore for Aunty Ida's wedding?' She was more than a match for him. 'And wasn't *that* about as lively as a misers' auction! A waste of good crepe de Chine . . .' And that set him thinking. Perhaps he should be offering Mel first root through the bags, in case there was something she could salvage for Tammy. Or for herself, of course. If his mother wanted her closets cleared, that was her business. In fact, it was admirable. After all, most people were stupid enough to waste the first half of their lives gathering all sorts of paraphernalia around them, and the second half wondering where it ought to go after.

She noticed him taking a little more care with the folding and stuffing. 'And don't forget it's for the Lifeboat

Shop. Don't you go offering it round to all your gannet friends.'

He played the old trick, dropping his head over busy hands. So typical that, in the urge to relieve her own feelings, she'd trample on his. She knew he had no friends. Now more determined than ever to give Mel the chance to root through her cast-offs in search of forgotten gems, he shouldered the bags and set off, a disgruntled Santa, down the stairs. Struggling with the catch on the front door, he swung his load against the cherished umbrella stand, sending great showers of rust flying as its bottom fell off and rolled under the coat rack. Oh, God! More bloody trouble. He could, of course, nip back round to the dustbins and swap his new find for her piece of junk. That would save his face – and hers. But then he thought, Oh, bugger it! And that was what he found exhausting – this constant swivelling between his eagerness to ease the details of his mother's life and the desire to think, 'Who gives a *fuck*?' For the eight-millionth time he wished to heaven his twin had only had the decency – the sheer rock-bottom *fairness*, after all – to stay a part of this grim pilgrimage. At least he would have had someone with whom he could share his endless frustrations. It would have been such a comfort to have another person who really knew the house – really knew *her* – to whom he could pose the knotty questions of the hour like, 'Should I try sneaking in the house one evening while she's out at Canasta, and do for that bloody toaster before the bloody thing does for her?' Or, 'Is she being *unreasonable* about this new cable?' Excuses for not pitching in tripped oh, so easily off the tongues of skivers like Dilys. Hard, perhaps,

even for people who didn't find saying practically anything difficult, to stand firm and say 'Bollocks!' He
should tweak one of his television shows round till it
fitted the bill. Call it *Excuses! Excuses!* These family
shirkers could trolley in with all their lame pretexts for
not being any help. 'And then my youngest – that's Teddy
– well, he's only four, so he takes up a lot of time.' 'Not
only is the job demanding but I have to travel a good
deal.' Or, in the case of Dilys, 'I've got this grudge I've
most conveniently managed to whip up into a full-sized
rift.' The studio audience, gleaned from the ranks of toil-
ing mugginses like him, would enjoy giving them short
shrift. Oh, yes! Wouldn't they soon get told, in no un-
certain terms, they weren't the only people in the world
who were entitled to a life.

She'd changed, that was the thing. Lord knows, his
sister had been born with fangs, but she had always had
her loyal side. Why, even after all these years, Colin still
felt the occasional shaft of gratitude to her for never passing on that doctor's casual mention, during one of their
school check-ups, of his 'almost imperceptible spinal
curvature'. (Christ alone knew what Mother would have
made of that, if ever she'd heard of it. Probably strapped
him in some sort of bodice and talked endlessly of his
'deformity' to the neighbours.) A thousand times his sister
had sailed near the wind, slapping on a grin and affecting a
hunched back as she walked past. 'And what was all *that*
about?' Mother had demanded. But she'd never let on.
Where was that sense of loyalty now? Just like their father,
Dilys seemed to have slipped away, leaving him alone and
bereft. Why, sometimes it even seemed that—

'What's got up your back? You look like a hen hatching a grievance.'

'I was just thinking.'

His mother's farewells were perfunctory. Did she suppose that he was coming back after dumping the bags? If so, hard cheese, because there wouldn't be a charity shop in town still open now. He'd just stop by at Mr Stastny's to pick up a bit of fruit. (Daft not to make an appearance, if only to undercut her next few disparaging dismissals of any suggestion he might have been round. 'Seen Colin? No, not for ages. I'm sure he's far too busy with his precious cockroaches and mice droppings to bother visiting his poor old mother.') Then he'd drive back to the office. If Clarrie wasn't standing at the window, buffing her nails, he might be able to get the bags unloaded out of the van and into his own car without her noticing that he, too, wasn't busy on council business in council time.

Then he'd nip off to Mel's. He'd leave her to sort through the stuff in peace while he took Tammy for a walk round the estate. 'Watch out for a rather nice flowery jacket,' he'd call back over his shoulder. 'I seem to remember my sister once saying it was a good one.' He and Tammy would go down to the swings (if they'd been mended yet) or over to see the new saplings (if they'd not yet been uprooted). Or she'd just walk, arms outstretched like a pudgy little ballerina, around the low wall, while he fed their imaginary Timothy Duckling, as usual.

And suddenly a vision came to him, of leading Tammy to a patch of bright marsh marigolds. The stream ran past, bright clouds sailed overhead, and kingfishers flashed. Laughing, she squeezed his fingers in her excitement, and he bent down to drink in her delight at these new wonders. He was about to offer her a glimpse of her first rabbit when yet another set of Highways' bloody awful lights fetched his attention back. Christ, Mel's block of flats looked dreary from this side of the station! And he had never realized quite how close some of those windows were to the vents of Chaffer's Bonemeal. He'd send someone round in the morning to do an inspection and take a few samples. No point in taking chances with the health of a toddler . . .

She met him at the door and flung her little arms around his legs. 'Drawberries!'

Mel took more interest in the bags he dragged behind him. 'What's all that?'

'Clothes.'

'Jumble?'

'Not if I know the owner,' was the closest he dared come to implying he didn't.

Mel's eyes lit up. 'What, take what I want? First picksies?'

He nodded, thrilled to have brought her pleasure with such ease. 'You have a root through. I'll take Tammy round the block.'

'In *this*?'

He turned to look. True enough, in the short time it took to drag his load up the stairs, it had started to tip down. His disappointment was intense. But Tammy saved him. Ripping the fattest bag, she tugged at something blue with strawberry-streaked fingers. Mel hauled her off.

'Col, couldn't you just *take* her somewhere? Just for half an hour or so, while I look through.'

His heart leaped. 'Where?'

She picked at the knot of the first bag. 'I don't know. That café behind the station?' He watched her remembering the times he'd offered that most insalubrious eating place as his excuse for popping by. 'They keep that mangy cat right off the counter now.'

He had a vision of parental bliss. 'All right,' he said, though he was already envisaging accusations of kidnap from neighbouring tables. But he was rescued even from these terrors when her sublime maternal indifference spilled down in a call from her balcony to the car park:

'And if that sodding social worker gets you, just say you're her father.'

Was it the first time she'd ever sat in a highchair? Having no faith in Mel, he drove straight by the chip shop beside the station ('There's Pussy!' shrieked Tammy, pointing) and chose instead the ice-cream parlour on Skelton Road. Tam's short legs strained, pointy-toed, as he swung her up and held her, poised, over the seat. Then she slid in and sat, all eyes, all attention, accepting with her usual gravity the spoon he offered, and formally copying each of his movements as, equally gravely, he spooned his own knickerbocker glory into his mouth.

'Banana,' she informed him — the first word she'd spoken since he'd unstrapped her from the car.

'Banana,' he agreed.

'And drawberry.'

'That's right.'

While she was working her way through the litany of ingredients, he dressed her in a sober navy-blue tunic and Start-Rite shoes, and packed her off to her first private nursery. He was about to start her on Suzuki violin lessons when she broke off from listing the more tooth-rotting foodstuffs to tell him conversationally, 'There do be a ghost under my bed at home.'

He felt a rush of panic. He wanted to be accessible and cordial. But surely he shouldn't be colluding in the notion of the existence of spirits? They weren't, after all, like bananas or strawberries.

But she was staring at him with such trust. He'd have to fudge it.

'Really? A ghost?'

She nodded, solemnly raising a pointy finger.

'One?'

She gave this quite a bit of thought and then, presumably in answer, laid her spoon carefully on the glass table top and raised the matching finger on the other hand.

'Two?'

Again, she nodded.

Totally abandoning his very first principled parental stand, he asked her, curious, 'So what are these ghosts of yours called?'

'Lavender.'

'What, *both* of them?'

With crystal calm she nodded once again, and he could feel his heart bursting with tenderness at this short peep into the untamed landscape of her mind. Without a blink (except when a lump of ice-cream slithered from her spoon onto the table top) she told him, first, how

Lavender could already swing upside down, and then about Lavender's shiny red cotton. Much of the rest of her conversation centred on this cotton, whose arcane attractions proved so lost on Colin that he indulged himself, in between encouraging noises and questions, in sending her, first to a fine secondary school with a host of enriching extra-curricular activities, and then, with a sheaf of impressive examination successes, to a bright modern university to enjoy herself thoroughly whilst still studying enough to earn a creditable degree. He was just walking her up the aisle to her future husband when the solemn little face in front of him crumpled without warning.

At once he panicked. 'Do you want to go home?'

She cheered immediately. 'Go and see the frocks.'

He glanced at his watch. They'd hardly been gone half an hour. But he could drive about a bit on their way back. She wouldn't know the difference. He set off down Tanner Street, determined to avoid the Pickforth Avenue snarl-up, in which he couldn't help envisaging perfect strangers tapping on the car windows and asking him, 'Is that child *yours?*' At the turn to the tyre factory, he was forced into merciless braking by yet another set of Highways' tiresome lights, and, in the distraction of raising himself to check Tam in the mirror, fudged the lane change on Mount Oval and found himself headed straight into West Priding.

And that's when she broke off chatting about the two Lavenders and their beguiling cottons, and told him firmly, 'Need to go.'

He turned off as soon as he could. But in his eagerness

to avoid the streets round his mother's, he clean forgot that George and his men had yet again torn up the corner at Barnham Avenue, sending the traffic back down endless, winding Green Lane instead, past Mr Stastny's.

And it was here that she insisted, 'Need to go *now*.'

Again he levitated in his seat to try to gauge if she were desperate, and saw her worriedly plucking at her knickers between her chubby little stuck-out legs. How could he take her home with panties soaking? She'd be upset, and his credibility as a competent man would hit rock bottom. For heaven's sake, he told himself. The child is *three*. Do what everyone else in the world does. Pull to the side and hold her over the gutter.

Now fully as anxious as she was, he drew up in front of Warburton's Funeral Emporium. 'Poised to assist'.

And why on earth not? Here, after all, was where his mother went whenever she felt the call on her way to Mr Stastny's. She'd bragged to him often enough about her system: look solemn, pretend to sign whichever Book of Condolence was lying open, nip in the Ladies', and then scarper. Slipping the car back in gear, he pulled in through the pillared entrance onto the gravel of the forecourt and, sweeping Tammy into his arms, rushed up the wide faux-marble steps. 'Nearly there, Sweet Pea.' If he'd been in less of a panic, he would, he realized almost instantly, have wasted time agonizing in the foyer; but, as things were, he automatically pushed at the door labelled Gentlemen, and, in the privacy of unaccustomedly scented graciousness, sat Tammy on the spanking clean seat.

There was the sweetest tinkle. Then, in her mother's

voice, she said, '*That's* better!' and pushed him away so she could reassert her dignity by sliding off the seat without his help and pulling up her own knickers.

'Right,' he said, filled with pride at his own resourcefulness. 'And now we'll just take a peek in their little book to say thank you. And then go home.'

The book wasn't little at all. The huge mock leather-lined spread of it lay, lectern-fashion, across the wings of a dispirited-looking fake brass eagle. Colin and Tammy approached hand in hand, both nervous in their own way. It was Tammy who recovered first, lifting both arms to Colin, who obediently swung her up to sit in the crook of his elbow, where she could reach to pat the eagle's bowed head and tell it sadly, 'Never mind.' It appalled him to think she might be worrying that the book was too heavy for the drooping wings. Freshly alive to the horrors of anthropomorphical thinking, he reached for the sham-jewelled pen, and, stretching its imitation gold chain to the limit, leaned over the Book of Condolence, aware of a shadow moving restlessly in the corner, and ready to make a pretence of signing his name and getting on with the bit that appealed to him – the scarper.

But it wasn't the book itself that was laid open to be signed. As he peered closer, he saw, discreetly pinned over it, a sheet of simulated parchment. Across the top, in flowing script, was written *George Henry Besterton*.

And nothing else.

He stared, appalled. Could he be *first*? Had George Henry Besterton only just died, for God's sake? Could that stooped, lurking shade be some close family member already wondering how this presumptuous interloper had

114

had the nerve to stride in the funeral parlour before the beloved body was even cold, and, along with his cheaply dressed, knicker-plucking toddler, muscle his way to the top of the list of legitimate mourners? But surely in that case the forecourt would be busier. This shadow wouldn't be alone. No, he told himself firmly as sense reasserted itself, this can't be the first page. It must be some freshly pinned replacement: the third or fourth, perhaps; even the tenth. It was just his rotten luck that there was someone watching who might draw closer after he had gone and notice that, though he'd been wielding the pen so convincingly over the simulated parchment, in such a formidably illusive environment, even the act of signing could prove false.

He'd have to write something, it was as simple as that. If only they'd left out another sheet as a guide for the unseasoned mourner. Were the bereaved supposed to scrawl a signature? Or was it more usual, as in forms, to use capital letters? And what was supposed to go on the right-hand side? More names? One's role? Friend, father, milkman. Perhaps a home address? Or even, as in war cemeteries and small hotels, some bland but pleasant comment: 'Excellent lavatories.' 'A most imposing eagle.' 'We shall most certainly try to come again.'

While he was standing worrying, Tammy grabbed the pen. He tried to snatch it back, but she gripped tighter, assuming that look he had come to associate with battles with Mel about bedtime and sweeties. And he had seen and heard enough of those over the last few months to know that only the most proficient derailing of her desires would get them out of this impasse now in a decorous fashion.

'That's right,' he whispered. 'There's a clever girl. You hold the pen, and together we'll write your name in the air over the nice paper.'

She hadn't been born yesterday. She was *three*. Down came the pen with a jerk, making a black line on the paper at least half an inch long. 'Oh, Christ!' he muttered, though he had told himself a hundred times that if this angel in his arms belonged to him, he'd never swear in front of her the way that Mel did. To make things worse, the apparition hovering in the shadows was drawing closer, obviously curious. Don't Col this up, he told himself. Stay calm. Act sensibly. Folding his own hand round Tammy's chubby fingers, he stemmed her petulance by guiding the pen across the paper. Tam, they wrote neatly together, using her black line as the upright for the first letter. On the pinned sheet it looked horribly wrong: pert, bare and unfinished. And so, since Tammy was clearly very keen indeed to carry on, and the shade was still watching, Colin once again tightened his hand round the wriggling fingers and pressed on to the end.

Tamina Poppy Gould.

If you stood back and squinted, it didn't look too bad, what with the Gould bit even spreading across to use up a little of the second column.

Right. Duty done. Time to flee. Prising the pen from Tam's fingers, he shoved it in the fake-ivory holder and turned to go.

Whoops! Directly in front of them in light from the mock stained-glass window the shrouded apparition stood. It was a woman in a heavy veil. Up till that moment she'd been the least of his terrors, but that was all over now. Burning with envy for Tammy who, at first sight of the stranger, had twisted to burrow her face in his shoulder, he forced himself to nod politely and smile in what he hoped was a fitting way.

The woman murmured a greeting and reached out to pat the smooth pale hummock of Tammy's knee. 'A pretty child.'

Colin hugged Tam and waited. But the black apparition said nothing more, clearly expecting him to turn away again, to write his own name.

He weighed the dangers. Signing the book could invite tiresome questioning. For all he knew, his mother would pop in first thing in the morning to waft the pen over the page and make use of the facilities. Or Nosy Elsie. Knowing the best place to look for secrets is always in joy or sorrow, a witch like her was probably in the habit of nipping in daily. She'd see his name there and report it back.

But with this shrouded stranger at his side, how could he not write something? Anyone else, he knew, would have been bold enough to sign a false name. Mel's, in its short form, would probably pass muster, and have the added advantage that the last name matched Tam's. But when the moment came for him to bring the pen down on that crackling paper, all of the rule-following bureaucrat in him shot to the fore, and the best he could manage was to append his own name, Colin Aloysius Riley, in a handwriting so shaky as to seem half-illiterate.

His fear that the unmatched surnames might look suspicious was instantly confirmed.

'You don't, I hope, mind my enquiring how the two of you happened to come together?'

Mad to rattle on about Flying Babies and gas fires. So, giving Tam another secret little squeeze, he answered, more in the spirit than with the bones of truth, 'Oh, in the park.'

'Ah, yes. The park.'

Her doubt passed as a ripple of iridescence across the veil as she stood trembling in a shaft of simulated evening light through the mock stained glass. She waved a cadaverous hand. 'How very good of you to—' Even through swathes of black netting the glitter of tears was discernible, and she could manage no more.

Colin shuffled uneasily. From the dark swamp of memory rose half-forgotten horrors of standing, crucified, on the school stage with Mrs Barker bellowing in front of everyone. 'Shyness, indeed! I'll tell you another way of putting it, Colin Riley. Pure, simple, stupid self-regard!' For the first time in his life he felt a glimmer of forgiveness for those great cohorts of torturers who'd ordered him, his whole life long, to make an effort, pull his socks up, spit out the words. Brave of this frail, frail vision to try to make conversation at all. To see a widow stifling tears to try to welcome him, a perfect stranger, was deeply, deeply chastening. If she could summon the fortitude to take up the reins of civility, then so could he.

'I am so sorry,' he told her. And then, because he couldn't think of anything else, he said it again. 'I am so sorry.'

She distracted herself from a fresh wave of grief by peering over his arm at the Book of Condolence.

'Tamina Poppy Gould?'

There was a squirm of terror as Tammy realized this

shrouded visitation knew her name. Taking the small con-vulsive movement for a sob, the woman asked, 'Is the child very upset?' 'Very,' he said, after working through each possibility and deciding that anything short would sound needlessly offensive. And it was scarcely an untruth. The warm, fast-breathing bundle in his arms was clutching his tie so hard he was practically strangled.

The lady in black held out her hand. 'I mustn't keep you.' She walked them to the door as if their company might hold off, for just a few moments longer, terrors of silence and loss. 'Do you have far to go?'

'Only to Tanner Street.'

'Tanner Street!' He watched the bony fingers wave away years. 'When I was little older than Tamina here, I used to walk down Tanner Street to the factory with my father.'

Fearing a detour down that very memory lane that, by common admission, was Planning's worst failure, Colin opted for accuracy. 'Well, more *behind* it, really.'

Can veils look startled? 'What, near those dreadful flats?'

Unwilling to get drawn into a discussion on one of Housing's most egregious blunders, he took advantage of the policy of disguising notorious developments by rechristening them with fanciful names. 'In Chatterton Court.'

It worked. There was a shimmer of relief. Before the fates could think of yet another way to punish him for try-ing to save a small child the indignity of baring her bottom over a gutter, he shifted Tam on his arm and put out his free hand. 'I hope – I really hope—'

Words wouldn't come. The blood rushed to his face,

and in the end all he could do was take her thin hand in his and, appalled by its skeletal nature, fail even to dare to shake it successfully before hurrying down the steps with his still-cringing burden. He almost threw poor Tammy in the car. Flouting the safety precautions proclaimed in needlessly expensive council posters all over Priding, he even drove round the corner before buckling in his small charge, and sitting for a moment while he waited in vain for his hands to stop shaking.

The doorway was knee high in plastic bags. Rather than shift them, it was easier to lift Tam over. He didn't feel that he could follow without an invitation. And none came.

'You didn't take much.'

'I didn't take a *thing*.'

How tense she looked. Had that intimidating young man been visiting again? Or was she what his mother tended to refer to with relish as 'in business'? At any rate, he knew enough, from being Dilys's brother, to tread with care.

'Not even the jacket? It was supposed to be quite good.' He paused. 'A Tavernier.'

If this meant anything to her, she hid it well. In fact, she looked even more ratty, stooping to reassert her importance with her daughter with a bit of unnecessary tucking and buttoning rather than ask about the outing and lay herself open to having to put on a smile while she listened to Tammy, or said thank you to Colin. Sensing his future visits were at risk, he longed to step over the bulging black barrier she'd laid between them, and shut the door.

'Listen,' he'd say. 'I'm sorry I raised your hopes unnecessarily. It doesn't matter, though. They're only clothes.' Instead, he stood helplessly watching her eyes fill as she said petulantly, 'Nothing's right,' then let exasperation overwhelm her: 'Nothing's *ever* right.' Furious, she pulled Tammy off the nearest bag – 'You come away from that! It's not a toy!' – while he watched his missing world unreel in his mind's eye: how he'd step forward and put his arm round her till the tears dried. 'There, there. Don't fret. None of it matters really. It was silly of me to bring the bags round here.' Oh, he knew exactly what he should be doing as he stood, doing nothing.

'I'll take them away again.'

'Yes, do! It was stupid of you to bring them round here in the first place. *Stupid!*'

He only blinked, and, as with mother and sister, found that his sheer passivity had riled her more. 'You've got a cheek, you know! Coming round here to dump your rubbish.'

'It isn't—'

'It is to *me*!' More tears. 'I know you've always been frightened even to *squinny* in my direction. But do I *look* as if I would want to give house room to clothes that could easily have been worn by your *granny*?'

He forced himself not to look away. 'I thought, well, *shawls*, or something . . .'

'*What* shawls? There *aren't* any!'

He hadn't known, of course, because he hadn't cared. It hadn't entered his mind. And that was the cruelty of shyness. The timid spent their hours spinning round things nearly said, steps nearly taken, till they were far too dizzy to see the person right in front of them. No wonder Helen Letherington had walked away. He'd probably done the same to her: said something, offered something, that made it clear he'd always be so taken up with fretting over the next few moments in his own life, he'd never have the time to look at her. Mel's eyes were blazing with such contempt. What did he know about her? Almost nothing. He hadn't even had the courage to ask if that broad-shouldered young man had been Tammy's father. Indeed, he'd barely asked her anything. Now that he thought about it, he realized that, in a score of visits, he hadn't even managed to steer their conversations down enough channels to know if this life of hers was going up or down, that she and her daughter should fetch up stranded in this flimsy-walled hell.

'I'm sorry. I really should have thought.'

'*You? Think?*' She hooked a thumb towards Tammy. 'As far as I can make out, all you ever think about is *her.*'

His felt his face burn. 'Sorry.'

'For Christ's sake, stop *saying* that!'

How could he? It was all he was: just sorry, sorry, sorry! Sorry for his offensive lack of interest in someone whose tea he drank and daughter he adored. And sorry for the half-life a man like him was forced to lead, incapable of breaking through walls of self-consciousness to snatch back the other half of himself that must be out there somewhere – another Flying Baby, another crucial catch missed, so he could never be the Colin who could have dumped four giant bags in front of her and said with confidence, 'Now look, Mel. Unless you strike gold with some fancy wrap or something, then nothing in this lot's going to interest you. They're all Old Lady clothes. But you might find the odd nice bit of material you could cut down or shove in Tammy's dress-ups. And if there's anything you want for friends, or to sell . . .' There was a Colin who could have cheered her up. Not one who'd raise her hopes so high she'd pack him off with her daughter, and then haul one expensive tailored garment after another out of the bags, only to hold them against herself and find her own great-aunt staring back from the mirror.

To be so horribly upset, though? Admittedly, he'd been a halfwit. But—

'Oh, *please* don't cry.' And then he could have bitten off his tongue because, alerted, Tammy froze. From astride her fat glossy black mount she gazed up at her mother, and Colin stood, equally paralysed, waiting for the child's perfect porcelain cheeks to turn pinker, her huge eyes to fill, until, after what seemed a lifetime, she was suddenly, deafeningly, bawling her eyes out.

He kept his head down as he dragged the bags out in the corridor, fully aware that if some residual sense that they weren't hers to lose had not stopped Mel shoving them out earlier, they would conveniently have been nicked by now, and he could have gone straight home. He dragged them all into the lift, and then, remembering it wasn't working, dragged them all out again and bumped them down five flights of stairs as far as the basement. There, in a hidden corner, he ripped them open, rooting through until he found the Tavernier jacket, and one or two other things he suspected that Dilys might slay him if he didn't salvage. And then, abandoning the rest to drunks and glue-sniffers whose evidence of nightly gathering lay all around, drove home through each virulent traffic light, depressed beyond measure at the thought that the only female he'd failed to reduce to tears in a once hopeful day was the one who deserved it: his own bloody mother.

6

HE CAME INTO THE OFFICE TO FIND THE USUAL SILT OF messages. Mrs Moloney still banging on about her invoice, though he had pointed out a dozen times that, even if the card mouldering in her Coronation teapot did happen to bear his particulars, the whole sorry business was a matter for Accounts now. There was a note from Hetherley, deploring the slack way in which some of the orders for last year's gas fires had failed to go through proper channels. He pushed aside till he felt stronger piles of demands from several members of the Lee family that he ring back at once, and, as a penance, forced himself to pick up the letter from Flatts Harries' lawyers reminding him this was the third time in a row his department had flouted their very own procedures. 'You really must try to get it right,' he told Clarrie as sternly as he dared. 'First, warning letter. Then, "Ask you to accept a caution". "Have to decide to prosecute" always comes last.'

She wasn't in the best mood herself. 'I *meant* to send a yellow one. I must have got all mixed up, what with that horrible man going on at me on the phone.'

'What horrible man?'

'You weren't here. It was when you told us you were out on those fire extinguisher inspections.'

It was the dangerous little 'told us' that made him drop the matter, and turn instead to Mr Leonard Turvey's renewed insistence that the specks in his poppadoms had been mouse turds, not cumin.

'Send him a 45/B, and tell him—'

But Clarrie had vanished. As ever in the mornings, she had a host of things to do. Repairs on her nails, and then the full-bodied hair tease. And God knows what else these young women got up to in flocks in the Ladies'. If only she'd thought to leave at least one of the filing cabinets unlocked before making her getaway. Left to shift for himself, he got crosser and crosser, stumbling from one heap of papers to another, shaking pens, scouring the floor for the glint of a paperclip, and finding the coffee jar as empty as last week. Not for the first time he found irritation with one of the women in his life spilling out on the others. How dare Mel put him through the wringer like that, just for failing to pass muster on a matter of dress style? How had his mother got the nerve to treat good advice like a grease spot? And as for that insolent Perdita! Where did she get the idea he was so bloody half-witted she could sell off his inheritance while he was actually standing in it?

From Dilys, obviously. Bitch! Bitch! Bitch! And all the loneliness of the last weeks welled up inside him. Dilys was perfectly within her rights to leave Mother to him. She couldn't be doing with her, and that was her business. And yet . . . And yet . . . She was his *sister*, after all. She was his *twin*. She wasn't supposed to pretend it was nothing to do with her, and she couldn't be bothered. She knew the score better than anyone. Why, it was she who'd first sussed out that Mother's sudden onset of 'travel sickness' masked a very different weakness. 'Travel sickness, indeed! Pure bloody idleness, that's what it is. Getting people to visit you rather than have to stir yourself to visit them. It's like her sitting in front of *Songs of Praise* instead of taking the trouble to stroll along for Vespers. You'll notice she still manages the ride to Canasta Club!'

Yes, it was Dil's support he needed now. It wasn't fair to leave all the decisions dumped on him. He wasn't going to accept it. The least she could do was advise him. He was going to phone her.

By the time he'd remembered just why it was that his console couldn't raise a dial tone, and had re-attached the wires, Clarrie was unenthusiastically wandering back to her own frenetically blinking phone. Embarrassed to be dealing with personal matters while the in-trays were lowering, he spoke in a whisper.

'Dilys, that business I was telling you about—'

'What business? Speak up! What?'

He felt an idiot. 'Those papers in the breadbin. Well, I think Mother might have posted them. When I went round there last night, they weren't there.'

'*So?*'

Pushing aside the note Clarrie was thrusting in front of him, he responded with irritation, '*So*, Dilys, after all my efforts, she may well have sent in that form she deliberately and knowingly filled in untruthfully.'

Dilys was less than helpful. 'Well, you've done your bit. You've warned her. If she's no longer properly insured, then that's her look-out. Nothing to do with you.'

He felt a shaft of loathing for his sister. So easy to come out with this sort of guff when you'd left all responsibility to others. But caution made him take a sideways tack. 'Look, Dilys. This is an application to Tor Bank we're talking about.'

'Tor Grand. It's totally separate.'

'It's in your building. With your name.'

'Maybe so. But it's completely another department.'

'But can't you just ring them? To find out. If she *is* on their books, they could arrange some sort of unofficial "spot-check" on the property, and force her to put in this bloody cable entry.'

'Colin, you're obsessed. If I hear you say the words "cable entry" one more time, I shall come out in hives.'

Had hers and Norah's responses begun to spring from the same box? 'Look, Dil. It's all very well for you and Mother to—'

'No, Colin. I'm sorry, but we at Tor Bank make it a point of principle never to interfere in the affairs of other departments. I'm very sorry if you feel this puts your own interests in any way at risk—'

And that was it. It was that calculated little 'your own interests' that made it clear he might as well stop listening. She knew as well as he that no inheritance on earth could make his current torments worth their while. She'd said as much often enough. 'Honestly, Colin. Anyone sensible would rather be pegged out and eaten alive by driver ants than step in the shadow of her front door.' What did she care if Holly House went up in flames? Or

128

Mother in it? He let her drone on for a moment or two, then interrupted with a fair pretence of matters arising. 'Oh, sorry, Dil. Must go. Clarrie's just dropped an urgent message on my desk.'

'Not half,' warned Clarrie. But he barely heard. Across his mind was sweeping grey rage. That word 'obsession'. What a blunt instrument it was – so glibly, cruelly used by anyone who'd ever wanted an excuse to jump ship. 'Oh, yes. I was married for seven years – for my sins! But after our youngest was born with his brain problem – well, I'm afraid my good wife did become a little bit obsessed, and, you know . . .' 'Yes, yes. We were good friends. But then he developed this obsession with corruption in the construction industry – something to do with the death of his son, I believe. And, if I'm honest, he became a bit of a bore.'

A bit of a bore. That's how his sister saw him. And that's what he was. Worse than a bore, in fact, because at least most people were obsessed with proper issues, and he was now entirely, mind-numbingly taken up with something that (once he'd got rid of that bloody toaster) was never even likely to happen.

He could have one last go at making his mother see sense. But it was clear, even to him, that though she'd spent almost a decade skilfully dumping one tiresome responsibility after another onto his shoulders on the grounds that they were too much for her, somehow in the last months, without his noticing, she had grown into her excuse. Slowly and stealthily, those false assertions had become the truth. She could no longer manage. The woman who had seen off determined beggars in Tangier, muggers in London, and a particularly foul-mouthed gypsy family in the park in West Priding, had reached the stage where merely the thought of glancing from a window to see those cheery, booted thugs of Mr Herbert destroying her lawn could practically drive her into the madhouse. This woman's stuffing had spilled out of her till she had reached the stage where, astute as she was about financial matters, she'd actually prefer to gamble, and, for a week's peace, risk the lot.

How had it come about so fast? There'd been a bit of slippage in her capabilities. Look at the time he'd walked in the gate to find her almost in tears over an overflowing drain. The time he'd found her cowering behind the door. 'Thank God it's you. I thought it was that bloody man selling teatowels back again.' And how could he not have noticed that business of the high-heeled shoes? But there'd been nothing either to justify, or to explain, a slide like this. What on earth could have happened to cause this headlong, almost deliberate, rush towards old age? Admittedly, the business couldn't be easy to face. It must take grit to look with equanimity at not being able to make your own decisions any more, or run your own life. It was everyone's worst nightmare. Perhaps in some strange way she had her wits about her more than most. Maybe, if you were sentient, it was the smartest tack stolidly to ignore the whole ghastly dead-end looming up at you as long as was possible, then, when you got to the stage where there was no choice but to face the unfaceable, pinch your nose, shut your eyes tight, and dive through the wave breaking mercilessly over you as she was doing right now. All her life she'd been brilliant at getting things done with the minimum outlay of effort. It was almost her speciality. Practically her trademark. If hurrying blindly into old age was as good a way of dealing with its rigours as any, then perhaps he should back off and stop trying to confront her.

Unless, of course, this was the old game, played a little harder. What was that Val had said when he was standing up for Mother once against one of Dilys's scornful tirades? All that he'd done was point out how often Norah had said to them over the years, 'Don't either of you let me become a burden. As soon as I become a nuisance, just shove me in a home and don't ruin your own lives.' And Val had rocked with laughter. 'They all say that! It's brilliant, when you come to think. It sounds so generous and understanding – self-sacrificial, even. But peel back the layers and what do you have? Another message entirely: "Don't expect me to make an effort to eat sensibly, stay active, or keep my wits about me. I'm going to run to seed in whatever way suits me. And if you end up pushing my bloody wheelchair ten years longer or ten years sooner, you won't even be able to blame me. After all, haven't I always said, "Don't let me be a nuisance. Just bung me in a home"?'

On Clarrie's phone, another light began to flash.

'Better get at least one of those, don't you think?' he tried suggesting mildly.

She looked quite anxious. 'If it's that horrid Mr Braddle, then I'm transferring him straight to you.'

'Fine,' he said, thinking it a small price to pay for distraction from family matters. But it was only Gloria from Accounts, on the trawl for some nail bond. So no reprieve there. Sighing, he dug in his wallet for the details he'd copied from Mother's policy. The two of them had gone through life yoked together for so long – his weakness to her strength. When the strong weaken, do the weak get strong? He'd come a long way since the days when even to hear her saying 'Sit!' sharply to Flossie would set him wincing. He might not yet, like his sister, be strong enough to pack in bothering at all. But he could summon up the grit to make a short phone call to check what sort of risk she was taking with her assets.

Oh yes. He could, and would.

The voice was the usual sing-song of indifference. 'Tor Grand. How may I help you?'

'Building insurance, please.'

'Commercial or Domestic?'

'Domestic.'

'Bear with me.'

He waited, unthinkingly shredding the note that Clarrie had thrust at him, first into quarters, then into eighths. Back came the cool, bored warble. 'Putting you through.' And he was on to yet another of those inattentive voices, so featureless in tone it took a moment to decode the bit for which he was waiting: 'How may I help you?'

He launched out, thinking if he had only had the sense to put Clarrie on the job, she could have offered just that peculiar mix of confusion and indifference that spoke of pure disinterest. But out it all came passably enough. '. . . bit of a mix-up . . . rather a frail old lady, no longer quite on top of things . . . not quite sure if the application form was ever posted . . . know it's a bit irregular, but thought it best to check . . .'

Out came the ubiquitous chirrup. 'Bear with me.'

It seemed an inordinately long wait before she came back with the query he, personally, would have thought crucial from the start: 'And the name and address, please?'

He was tempted to say, 'Bear with me,' but didn't. Meekly he spooned it out. There was the slightest pause, then back came the voice. 'Is that R-i-l-e-y, or R-e-i-l-l-y?'

Was it his guilt that made him sense a little tightening in the sing-song? Guardedly larding his voice with a faint touch of Clarrie's singularly unfavoured inner-city comprehensive, he dutifully spelled out 'R-i-l-e-y'.

He heard the faintest tapping. Then: 'So this would be a query on behalf of a Mrs Norah Constance Riley?'

Aha! What better proof of posting could you get?

And time to hang up. But once again, under that lilting veneer of indifference, he thought he'd caught that hint of quickened interest. Well disguised, but there. It didn't sound like anyone he knew. But then again, Shirley from Switchboard had a featureless drone for her phone lines that bore no relationship whatsoever to the firm Brummie tones he heard daily across the canteen. So was it possible this seemingly anonymous voice belonged to his old enemy? Could this be bloody Perdita, black-balled already from Home Loans or Arrears, and off once again on her Flying Dutchman travels around the Mighty House of Tor?

Whoever it was had embarked on a matching interest in his own identity. 'And in order to record your inquiry, I'll just need one or two details. You are . . .?'

He absolutely in a million years was not going to offer

anyone who might even possibly be Perdita the satisfaction of thinking she'd rattled him enough to make him hang up. So, thickening the East Priding accent till it could have startled a downtown landlord, he pressed on as boldly as he dared. 'Me? I'm the family solicitor.'

'I'll need your address, of course.'

'Mine?'

My, she was cool. 'To send on the written confirmation—'

That he hadn't even requested! But wouldn't it look suspicious if someone claiming to be within even spitting distance of the legal profession appeared to balk at accepting a little something on paper?

If this was Perdita, then she had him on a hook.

Unless—

Willing onto his cool interrogator a total lack of acquaintance with that bleak part of town to which, in less frayed times, he'd happily banish Perdita out of spite, he doctored the only address he dared proffer. 'Send it to Suite 578, Chatterton Court, please,' and waited, sweating, through another pause. Was he, perhaps, being paranoid? This could, after all, be one of any number of bored women laboriously tapping onto a screen information in which they took absolutely no interest. That stone-bored lilting chirrup was practically universal these days.

'And that would be Priding? Thank you. Bear with me.'

But it could be Perdita, cunningly stepping up the ubiquitous rhythms to set the next trap.

'And a name, of course. Just for the paperwork . . .'

Well, now that he had to face Mel anyway, to explain some strange letter falling on her doormat, he might as well take advantage of her name. 'It's Gould.' And, come to think of it, he could appropriate her first name too. 'Mel Gould.'

If he'd been nurturing one last pathetic hope that, even if this were Perdita asking the questions, he might be able to convince her he wasn't Colin, he'd failed outright. The last query came in a tone of contempt he was sure that he recognized.

'Oh, yes? And that would be *Melvyn*, would it?'

He'd had enough. Even a worm could turn.

'No!' he snapped. 'No, it wouldn't. It's *Melchior*.'

And he slammed down the receiver so hard that he cracked it.

So that was it. Mother had posted the bloody thing. That was quite certain. But what to do now? He could whip round there, of course, straight after work, and give her a rocket. Or he could simply confiscate the toaster, buy her a fire extinguisher and live in fear. And that was the trouble with trying to cope with old people. There were no handbooks, nothing in the way of standardized practices – not even any real consistency to offer guidelines. If you had dealings with them, you spent your whole time in a centrifugal whirl of indecision about what it was reasonable to expect. All over Britain people his age were watching clocks in stuffy rooms, nodding along in unfeigned sympathy with their own grizzled back numbers about what tough luck it was they could no longer get to the shops, what with their shocking bunions. Then they'd go home, pick up the newspaper and find themselves reading about some even more ancient geezer who'd lost both legs in the war and had just done his first parachute jump. The world was full of dutiful sons and daughters who had revamped their whole Saturday to cheer some seventy-year-old through a drab birthday only to find that the reason the Social Club was closed in the first place was because all the Over-Eighties had gone off on safari. Why, children were a doddle by comparison – expected by general agreement to be fully on their feet by two, reading by eight, and mardy from twelve to twenty. Old folk were different, and, as with so many other things, one's attitude towards them was a matter of temperament. The world was, after all, split down the middle on pretty well every other issue to do with people. With the weepy, there were those who thought even more time spent whingeing to professionals was just the ticket, and those who would snarl, 'Oh, for God's sake, snap out of it!' With the unemployed, those who would shower them with consolatory hand-outs were roughly matched in number with those who would cheerfully starve them of comforts till they took the trouble to work up some sort of a saleable skill. With this old people business, who was to say whether the hard or the soft line was better? You needed some television programme: *You Be the Judge*. The parent could sit on the podium – maybe, for sensitivity, safe in a soundproof box – and their offspring could set the scene. Doctors and physiotherapists could be called in as expert witnesses. ('I have examined Mrs Oakway here, and in my professional view, even with this impressive catalogue of ailments, she's more than capable of catching a train to her daughter-in-law's house in Preston. Why, I've seen patients far older and weaker than her who still manage to . . . bleh, bleh, bleh.') It would be most enlightening. And every week, Top of the Bill, they could have families in which the sons and daughters felt that even a bit of real neglect was in many ways reasonable. Again there would be a tearful, bitter prosecution, ranging (depending on the family concerned) from grumbles as trivial as, 'She never let me have a bike,' through commonplaces like, 'He never once, the whole time I was growing up, said something nice,' through horrors that would make the social workers in the wings reach for their notepads: 'And every time I stammered out of terror, he'd whip off his belt and thrash me till my freckles sang.' Clearly, the parent would be entitled to any defence they believed they could muster. 'If I seemed harsh, remember I had a mother who hanged herself with my own dressing-gown cord when I was three, I raised six crippled sisters all alone, and we lived on a flood plain.' That sort of thing. The studio audience would weigh up the evidence. Then, 'Take your old father home,' some pack of middle-aged whingers might be told. 'And be more kind to him, for, by his lights, he did try hard.' Or some iniquitous parent might be shipped instantly back to the Sunset Home from which he'd confidently smuggled out his *You Be the Judge* application, and his off-spring would stride from the studio clutching their much-prized Y.B.T.J. Certificate of Moral Exemption, secure in the knowledge that, during the nationwide phone-in, the vast majority of viewers had agreed they were guilty of nothing except, if you were being harsh, perhaps an oversized conscience.

No, till there were some sort of guidelines on this issue, the whole dispiriting business would be a mess of winners and losers. And, in that mess, there would always be hard-hats like Dilys.

And suckers like him.

Still, best to replace the toaster, any which way. 'I'm slipping out for a moment,' he warned Clarrie, who appeared to be doing nothing more pressing in the way of council business herself than gazing out of the window. 'Just along to the electrical shop. I shan't be away long.'

'But what if he phones *again*?'

'Who?'

She waved a hand towards the unwashed window, as if to invite the serried ranks of vehicles parked below to give witness to her patience. 'I *told* you. That horrible Mr *Braddle* man. I keep giving you *notes*. And he's *waiting*!'

He stared at the torn scraps of paper on his desk. It had been hard enough to get her in the habit of taking down messages in the first place. He'd better not give her any excuse for not bothering in future. 'Oh, yes. That. Well, I'll deal with it.'

He shovelled the pieces in his pocket, planning to fit them together and read them the minute she turned her attention back to her nails. But barely a moment passed before she swung round in panic from the window as the phone started blinking. 'That's him again. No point in pretending you're not here. And I'm not answering it!'

Fearing he'd pushed his luck too far already that morning with someone he knew from experience was skilled in a whole slew of subtle office revenges, he waved her away and picked up the phone on her desk. While Clarrie took the chance to untangle the strap of her handbag from round his ankles and slip off for coffee, Colin spoke into the mouthpiece. 'Mr Braddle, is it?'

'*Colin?*'

'Mother, is that *you*?'

'I take it you can hear how that noisy oyster next door is torturing me now?'

Behind the voice, crabbed with irritation, he could hear a familiar jangle. 'Is that the windchimes? They sound pretty close.'

'That's because that black-hearted goblin is standing there thwacking them.'

He quelled the response that echoed down from childhood – 'So what did you do to him first?' – and asked more tactfully, 'Have you the slightest idea what might have set him off this time?'

'How should *I* know? I'd like to take a rolled-up newspaper to him, really I would.'

'Would you like me to come round and speak to him?' (Perfect excuse! He could slip in a quick toaster swap while he was at it.)

'You'd be a lamb among goats. Last time I had words with the old bugger, I felt like a beanbag run over by a juggernaut.'

'I'll make it official,' he offered. 'Bring round one of our fancy new noise monitors and hand him a warning leaflet.'

He waited for the curt dismissal ('Oh, I can just see you standing on his doorstep like a tin of milk').

But no. The silence gathered like water slowly rising in a cistern, till suddenly it spilled over.

'Yes. If you would, dear.'

He sank down, hard, on Clarrie's swivel chair. His heart was thumping. Things were very bad. This was a pretty pass. For the first time in as long as he could remember, he wanted his dead father back. But not the way he'd wanted him in times long past – randomly, utterly, for something as stupid as showing him how to tie a bow tie or start up the lawnmower or choose his first car. No. More to complain. It wasn't *fair* that he'd been left to cope with this alone. What use was kindness, purely as a tender memory, to colour daydreams? Surely a bit of grit would have come in more useful. At this rate, the burnished crown he'd let his absent father wear for all these years would tarnish fast. Topping yourself was, after all, a choice. If you'd enough grip left to work your way through some sort of left-handed sheepshank for Dilys, then you could surely hang in one more day. And then another. It was a coward's trick, to drive yourself into a wall, and cop out for ever. Surely a decent father would have stayed around to give a tip or two about watching your mother go falling to pieces.

At least the office wasn't open-plan. Wiping his tears, Colin soothed himself by counting the years on his fingers. Fair's fair. In all probability the poor sod would have died quite naturally, years before now. And who was to say his parents would have been together still, in any case? These days it wasn't only sisters who waltzed away, sloughing off responsibility. It was spouses too. Look at Tubs Arnold, often heard in the canteen explaining in quite remarkably embittered detail just how he and Doreen felt each time they had to drive her crippled father past the Silver Age Dance Studio where Doreen's mother, a.k.a. the Merry Divorcée, was continually reported to be having a grand time.

And Mel had told him of a family she knew where—

Oh, God. Mel!

Flattening his palms on the desk top, he pushed himself to his feet. Important to get on top of things before they got on top of him. First, slip out and buy a toaster. Then go round to Mel's and explain how some stupid mistake of Tor Grand's might result in their sending a bit of his mail there. (He'd get to see his Tammy. Could he, perhaps, win back her heart with one of those colourful plastic windmills he'd seen in a bucket outside Woolworths?) Then he'd go round to Mother's. What else was on his list?

Oh, Mr Braddle.

Hastily spinning the torn squares round on the desk, Colin tried to form some kind of sensible message. Was that word *warm*? This was a *Mr*, certainly. But since the next letter was an *H*, not a *B*, then maybe . . .

And this looked like *see to it* . . .

See to *what*, for heaven's sake? Colin couldn't see to anything else at the moment. Why, he hadn't even got round to starting on his report on the dead chickens yet.

No. This bloody Braddle fellow would just have to wait.

Mel gave his glorious windmill a hostile stare and, in a tone that could not have been more at odds with the sentiment, said, 'Thanks very much.'

'What's the matter?' he asked, startled. 'Don't you think that she'll like it?'

141

Mel looked ready to shove it outside to get stolen. As though unwillingly reminding herself that, like the clothing with which he'd upset her so much last time, this windmill wasn't quite yet hers to lose, she strutted to the tiny kitchen area and ducked under the sink for one of those glossy rubbish bags his council dispersed in the haunts of the feckless.

'Bung it in this, for God's sake, before she wakes up and sees it. And don't for a moment think that you're leaving the damn thing here.'

So Tam was napping. Typical of his luck, and a waste of a visit. Frustrated, he handed over the unwelcome gift. 'But what's the *matter* with it?'

Mel's temper clearly hadn't improved since his last visit. 'You really don't *think*, do you, Colin? You're so bloody wrapped up in your own affairs, it never occurs to you to consider how things affect other people. What am I supposed to do with a windmill? Let her hang out of an unbarred window, waving it? Add it to all the other sodding things I have to carry down four flights of stairs each time we go out? She's not a *baby* any more. I can't just stick the damn thing at the end of her cot and expect her to *coo* at it.'

Stupid! And the sheer horror of raising his precious Tammy – any child – in this grim place struck him again. Surely Mel must be able to move out *somehow*. Anywhere would be better. Where was she before?

Resisting the urge to apologize for fear of irritating her even more, he made a massive effort. 'Mel, could I have a cup of coffee?'

She stared. If ever there were an inauspicious moment

to start to assert himself, this must have been it. 'Don't you have to get back to the office?' she asked him, adding with true spite, 'Since Tammy isn't up yet.'

This, he ignored. Trailing her over to the chipped grey cabinet that served for a kitchen, he pursued his objective. No doubt someone handier at conversation could have made a more subtle stab at raising the issue. But he at least did manage to spit it out.

'Mel, where were you living before this?'

Scrabbling a sight too near the uncovered rubbish bin for his professional ease of mind, she came up with a second mug. 'Nowhere. Everywhere.'

Well, fair enough. After a whole two years and more of taking no interest, he had no right to expect a sensible answer.

'It's all right. I was just wondering. It doesn't matter.'

'I wasn't not *answering*,' she snapped. 'That's where I was. Nowhere and everywhere. I was with a circus.'

'A *circus*?'

Seeing his sheer astonishment must have provoked her because, lifting her arms, she gave him a fast, faultless spin. 'Don't you believe me?'

Even through the drab jeans and very nasty woolly, the grace was evident. Had he been *blind*? She stretched out a hand and held the door behind her open so even in the dim light he saw the poster glowing on the wall: two magical figures, one hanging sinuously from his trapeze, the other in a spin. Everything fell into place – the pointy toes as he swung Tammy in her high-chair, the way she stretched her arms along the wall – even the mad prattle about red cottons made sense to him now. Not cottons.

143

Costumes. Through the half-light he peered at the faded lettering. 'What does that say? Is it "The Lavenders"?'

'Las Venturas.'

It was the flatness of her voice that so astonished him. What was it painted on the entrance to that little circus he'd had to cite for illegally drained Portaloos? He'd used it recently in a spell. *E pulvere, lux et vis*. Could Mel be proof of the reverse? Could that detached manner of hers, that strange, indifferent way of acting as if nothing ever really touched her, simply be evidence that, torn from light and life, even a spinning, shimmering aerial wonder can turn to dust?

Could she be simply *bored*?

'What does it mean?'

'*Ventura?*' She shrugged. 'Lots of things. Happiness. Chance. Luck. Risk. It can even mean danger.'

'Is that why you stopped when Tam was born? In case you fe—'

'Please!'

And he was glad to stifle it, not just because the child might have been half awake, listening; more in the hope of not stirring up further grim visions of the sort that had brought him to her flat in the first place. She spooned the coffee in the dingy mugs while he braved another question. 'So does he have another partner now?'

'Not like me.' Spreading her arms as if applause were swelling round her, she dropped in a curtsy. It was, he realized, the first real flash of theatricality he'd ever seen in her. Instantly, another thought struck. 'Why didn't you *tell* them? All those journalists who kept trailing you round asking questions? I read all of those papers.

You never said anything – anything at all – about being from a circus.'

'No,' she said sourly. 'Well, it's nobody's business but mine, really, is it?'

And he could understand that. If he had had to shelve a life of spangle and excitement to raise a child in this grim place, he wouldn't feed his glittering memories to any callow reporter, trawling for one more ingenious headline about a flying baby.

Still, she'd said, 'nobody's business'. Best to take the hint.

'I really dropped in to warn you a letter's coming.' On the way, he'd rehearsed a score of approaches, and all of them sounded stupid. 'By mistake.'

'Mistake?'

'Yes,' he ploughed on. 'It'll have your name on it, but it's actually for me. I was in a bit of a spot, you see, and had to think of something quickly.'

'What's *in* the letter?'

At least he could reassure her there. 'Nothing. Only a bit of rubbish from Tor Grand Insurance Company. You can just shove the whole thing straight in the bin.'

'Anything from Tor Whatsit? Straight in the bin?'

'That's right.'

'And it'll have my name on it?'

'Well, yes,' he admitted. 'It'll be addressed to Mel. Or Melchior.'

'Melchior?'

Her hoot of disbelief broke straight through Tammy's dreams. And even as he was leaving, he still assumed it was the child's fractious wake-up wail that had distracted

Mel from the lambasting he expected to follow. ('How *dare* you use my name?' 'Whatever makes you think——?') He drove on to his sister's, to get the clothes he'd salvaged safely off the back seat before driving on to Mother's. And only as he was pulling to a halt outside her door did it occur to him that Mel was more than capable of soothing Tammy while scolding him.

No, strange girl that she was, the hoot had been one of simple amusement. And she had not been the slightest bothered that he'd taken advantage of her name and home for a private, and possibly nefarious, purpose.

Truly, she did come from a different world.

7

THE FRIENDSHIP WITH MARJORIE CLEARLY WASN'T blossoming. His sister's relief at seeing him on her doorstep appeared for a moment even to outweigh her pleasure at spotting the sleeve of the Tavernier jacket trailing out of his bundle. And Marjorie, too, gave the impression of having a glint of interest in his arrival, going so far as to take her hand off the top of her tumbler. 'Well, perhaps a tiny top-up, just to be sociable. But then I really must be pushing off.'

'Not for me, Dil. I'm driving.'

But either his sister wasn't listening or the sheer joy of deliverance had made her skittish. 'No, Col. You must at least let me fetch you a ginger ale, if only to thank you.' She turned back to the heap he'd tipped onto the arm-chair. 'The Barolo shoes! And that grey Formani top! I'd forgotten all about them! Colin, you're a *gem.*'

Her warmth in no way spread itself across to the sofa. Marjorie gave him a couple of moments in which to feel particularly uncomfortable, then said, 'It's Colin, isn't it?' adding in a tone he thought rather more in keeping with an initial police interview, 'Do please explain how Miss Riley is fortunate enough to end up with all these clothes she's so obviously been coveting.'

Miss Riley? Christ! Things must be terminal. The question was, had he himself become a brother since that disastrous evening in the Stemple Street gallery? Desperate for a hint as to how to explain himself, he swivelled round to Dilys. But her attention was still on the treasures he had brought. Clearly, he'd have to work out for himself if this grim stiffness on Miss Whatsit's part was simply part of her firm rebuttal of further social advances from someone lowlier in the bank, or early curtain-down on some previously burgeoning friendship during which she might well have picked up the fact that he was Dilys's brother.

'Well, it was just a bit of a clear-out, really . . . ' was all he ended up daring to mutter. At times like these, his sister's habitual failure even to make the first gesture towards fetching the drinks she so airily offered could prove a real blessing. 'Well, I think I'll be off now.'

'Back to the family?'

Now he was skewered. Was this some fanciful detail from a new Colin Dilys had invented? Or simply the assumption that he was the husband of a friend. ('If you're driving past Dilys's, could you just drop off that bundle of clothes on the chair by the dresser?') How should he play it? Best – safer – not to lie outright. Perhaps some bland remark along the lines of some people thinking a clothes cupboard all the better for a regular weed-out would smack of that wifely shadow he usually found himself invoking only with shoddy workmen. ('Well, personally, of course, I probably wouldn't even have noticed it's not quite flush along the edge. But what it looks like won't be up to me . . .') Was this the moment to resurrect this pitiless imaginary judge of plumbing shortcuts and work-top surfaces out of true?

But Dilys put paid to that one. 'Colin? A wife and kiddies? That'll be the day.'

It was dropped like the bombshell it was supposed to be: 'Not according to Perdita Moran.'

It was that bloody 'wife and child' he'd claimed, come back to haunt him! He waited for his sister's foot to freeze halfway to the Barolo shoe as, satisfied, Marjorie leaned back against the sofa. Even her prim knees seemed to relax a little, and her forbidding look mellowed to some smug, churchy version of 'duty done'. She was happy now. Clearly his unheralded arrival had offered this stolid, dis-approving woman the chance, in the guise of a bit of leaden, if supposedly innocent, humour, to unburden her-self of the very nugget of information that had been making her so uncomfortable. 'According to our colleague Perdita, your twin here is a bit of a dark horse.'

A brother, then. And even the same age. It wasn't clear if Dilys's snort signalled contempt for Perdita for betray-ing this particular secret, or scorn for the notion of Colin having secrets of his own. But Marjorie read it as in-difference, and leaned forward earnestly. 'No, Dilys, really. Do listen. It seems your brother has been keeping one or two really very important matters from those around him.'

Rude bloody woman, he thought, speaking as if he were dead or unconscious. And how dare his sister keep paying more attention to a pair of shoes than to the idea that he might be leading a double life?

Marjorie tried again. 'Dilys—'

His sister finally dragged her attention back from the ill-fitting Italian courts. 'Oh, I think we all know how seriously to take anything Perdita tells us.'

Stung, Marjorie reverted to her churchy look. 'I must say, your mother wasn't quite so quick to dismiss the idea.'

'According to Perdita.'

'No, no. It was your mother who said as much.'

Dilys was baffled. 'You've never *met* my mother.'

Our mother, Colin felt like butting in. Excuse me. *Our* mother.

Marjorie's colour rose. And though, all his life, Colin had tended to sympathize with anyone caught in the sights of his sister, on this particular occasion he found his heart stone. Marjorie deserved to feel uncomfortable. The priggish bag. Happy enough to embarrass him with her overdelicate insistence on passing on gossip in front of people rather than behind their backs. But this sensitivity clearly hadn't been matched by any equally fine impulse to lay bare a compromising little detail about her own life. Relief at ridding herself of a disquieting confidence was ebbing fast. Her cheeks burned through their powder glaze. '*Surely* I must have mentioned that I met your mother.'

Dil's tone was glacial. 'No. You never did.'

'Really? Well, it was very briefly. After that gallery opening. We ended up sharing the back seat of the car when Perdita picked up her mother from Canasta Club.'

Paddling away from her own guilt, she steered the conversation back towards Colin's by turning to tell him, 'Do you know, your mother believes you're capable of keeping secrets from your own reflection.'

At least she'd finally had the courtesy to draw him into this assassination of his own character. He was about to speak when Dilys overrode him. 'Of course she doesn't think that. Mother's simply out to make mischief. Or pass the time cashing in on some of Perdita's.'

'That's not a very nice thing to say about your own mother.'

Colin waited for Dilys to point out that it was nowhere near as unpleasant as what Marjorie had just been saying about him. But Dilys didn't bother. 'Mother isn't very nice.'

'Personally, I found her charming.'

'Then she must have been clutching a fistful of winnings.'

Again Colin sensed in Marjorie that sudden upsurge of confidence that stemmed from feeling righteous. 'But what a horrid shock! To learn from the daughter of a friend that your own son's been hiding a wife and child.'

His sister burst out laughing. 'Colin? A wife and child?'

'No, really, Dilys. It isn't funny. To find out from a young woman who's simply offered you a lift home that you've been a grandmother for some time!'

'A *grandmother*? Do me a favour! Colin here couldn't blow a kiss over a hedge at a blind girl, let alone sneak away and get married. The whole idea's ridiculous. Utter tosh.'

Should he, he wondered, standing there scraping his feet on the fringe of the carpet, be trying to feel *gratitude* towards this brash sister of his for being so cast-iron certain she couldn't be hearing anything but nonsense? How could she be so sure he hadn't changed? Maybe in childhood he had been capable only of 'Colling it up' when he took to deception. But people's lives could alter. Look at Mel. Nobody ends up on the high trapeze after a six-week course. She must have trained for years and years to get on that poster. She'd made air her resting place, kept danger as her closest friend and thrilled a thousand upturned faces twice a day. She'd had a job that weaved her fragile, intimate, celestial magic into the bread and butter on her table.

Then she'd stepped down to earth to live the drabbest life he could imagine. But had he disbelieved her, half an hour ago, when she'd spun round for him? No, he had not. He'd known the truth of it: people could change. So he was furious with his sister, whose confidence that he was just the same old Colin she'd always known felt, not like supportiveness, but like contempt. How could she be so bloody sure he couldn't possibly have got a life?

And that was when it first fell on him like a shaft of light: how much he wanted one. Not just that feeble, drippy wish that he were different. He'd had that all his life. But something tougher, something more like cussedness, that even he might think could power him off his tracks into the sort of extraordinary derailment his sister had dismissed out of hand. At least his mother had been good enough to imply he was capable of telling whoppers. She hadn't meant it charitably, he was sure. God alone knew what she had meant. (Possibly she hadn't meant anything at all, except not to let that toe-rag Perdita feel that she was one up on her for one single moment.) She clearly couldn't have believed a word of it, or she'd have remembered to crucify him on his next visit. But he was grateful to her all the same. It was a vote of confidence – of a sort. And there was something so pathetic about the way he was living now – through a life no one cared about. If he fell in one of Turner's illegally overfilled slurry pits and drowned tomorrow, who'd cry their eyes out? Who would crow?

No one would even miss him.

Except his mother.

'I'm off now,' he told Dilys. 'Round to Holly House. Any messages?'

Did revelation bring some firm new tone? It seemed so, for clearly his sister was startled. And that in itself brought one advantage in that, even making for the door no more hastily than usual, he still found himself safely out in the hall before she could manage to bring out a crack along the lines of, 'Late for the wife?', or, 'Congratulations to Granny!'

His mother opened the door in a cloudburst of tissue paper. 'You took your time. I was about to give up on you and go round myself.'

'To do what? Remind him of recent variations of the Nuisance and Noise Abatement Order of 1985, whilst taking care to make no actual misrepresentations of his legal entitlement to fair use and benefit?'

'No. Stuff this up his windchimes.'

He took her flurry of tissue in return for the neat wad of newspapers under his own arm. 'Here. Why don't you go upstairs and start on these?'

'Don't bother bringing anything but a cup of weak tea. I've completely lost my appetite.'

Clocking the order, he went round the side of the house to stuff the tissue paper safely in the dustbin before going next door to do his imitation of a council warning. But once in sight of the windchimes, his mother's plan struck him as one of genius. He took his time, crouching behind the still mysteriously burgeoning hydrangea while he tore tissue paper into strips. Then, pulling her precious Chilean flame flower's support stick out of the ground, he leaned across the wooden slatted dividing fence and, making as little noise as possible, poked paper up as far as it would go inside each dangling metal tube. After, even when rattled together, the chimes barely pinged; and, thinking to celebrate with a few stolen minutes with Suzie in the woodshed, he was about to creep off further down the path when up shot a window and out poked a head he had known since his childhood.

'Are you the dustbins?'

'Yes,' he said, furious at not being recognized after forty years, but judging it safer, in the circumstances.

'Right,' said the livid face. 'Well, tell that mad old bat to put her lids on properly.'

'I will,' said Colin. Realizing it might raise even this singularly unneighbourly eyebrow if one of Priding's cleansing operatives were blatantly to make off in the wrong direction down the path, he abandoned his hopes of a few moments' carefree poolside frolicking, and, after a quick gnaw at the support stick so he could lay the blame for the flame flower's collapse onto Flossie, went back to the kitchen to make a snack his mother would enjoy refusing and some tea she could criticize.

He found her knee-deep in obituaries. 'The world goes none the lamer for this old bugger, that's for sure.'

All his attention was on stepping over Floss without dropping the tea tray. He asked the first question to spring to mind. 'So who was that, then?'

'George Henry Besterton.'

'Oh, I know him.'

His mother's disbelief was evident. He flushed as he put down the tray. But on reflection he reckoned that, not only did he have every right to take a leaf out of her own book and make use of the facilities in the nearby Chapel of Rest, but his snippet of gossip might actually prove as welcome as his news of the weeds in Mrs Deary's grass seed. So, as he sat down, he pressed on with his explanation. 'It's just that I happened to be in the funeral parlour when he was—'

What was the word for it? Surely not 'on display'. Could it possibly be 'resting'?

She hadn't waited for him to finish speaking anyway.

'Well, you won't have had to beat your way through the crowds to toss roses on his coffin, that's for sure. That man would boil potatoes in a widow's tears.'

And, having rendered his news flash otiose at a stroke, his mother went on to reel off all George Henry Besterton's sins, public and private, during which disquisition it became obvious that civic corruption and personal venery had had to spend their time vying for attention, in between culpable poisonings of Chaffer's factory employees.

'They put all *that* in the obituary?'

'Don't be a twerp. They claim he was a fine, upstanding member of the community, beloved by all.'

He had a vision of the weeping wraith. 'I met his widow.'

'Well, that's a pleasure you won't have again.' Rooting through her heap of discarded *Priding Herald*s, she showed him another obituary.

'Florence May Besterton?' For a moment he was thrown by her habit of going through the papers in reverse. And then he realized. 'What? She's died *since*?'

His mother pointed to the headline staring from the paper beneath. BROKEN-HEARTED WIDOW TAKES POISON. She sniffed. 'Broken-hearted, my fanny! More likely a fit of pique at realizing she won't get to trough at any more civic banquets at Joe Taxpayer's expense.'

'Come on, Mum! Poison!'

'Nonsense! I expect the frail sap just stood too near the old bugger's factory without her veil.'

He felt obliged to defend the gentle bag of bones whose hand touched his. 'She looked' – it was the only word – '*bereft*.'

'Only one woman couldn't get through,' his mother said sourly. 'And she got pushed.'

He put it down to memories of her own loss. Still, he sat shaken, listening to her black mutterings as she went back to her obituaries. '"*Only in the next room*," indeed! Can these people not rake up a forkful of brains between them? "*No flowers, by request*"? How they must have hated the poor soul, to give her such a drab send-off. "*Gather to celebrate the life of*"! Ha! I certainly hope, after I'm gone, that no one will ever think of celebrating *my* life. I've spent a deal too much of it on sorrow's path.' If she had stopped for an answer, he could, he realized, have reassured her easily. After all, do as you would be done by, and he would hate to think no one would bother to wear black for him, or let even one day be given over to tears and to sadness. At least Florence May Besterton—

But she'd stopped grumbling to her invisible familiar, and was speaking to him now.

'—parched as a summer's drain.'

'Would you like me to make more tea?'

Her mood lightened. 'Not if it's like the last lot, and tastes like sump oil.' Burying her rotting slippers deeper in Flossie's matted coat, she nodded at the window. 'So. Speaking of people I'd like to celebrate the life of, how did it go with Windchime Willie?'

To deter her from probing for detail, he put on his official council air. 'Oh, I don't think you'll have quite so much trouble from that direction in future. In fact, I think he took rather well to that notion of yours of stuffing them with tissue.' He made a brave stab at forestalling an early enlightenment. 'Though perhaps best not to crow – unless you're prepared to be a little more conciliatory about putting the lids of your dustbins on properly.'

That shut her up.

They sat in a companionable silence as she returned to lifting one paper after another off the pile, and he drank tea. From time to time, she offered a liverish mutter.

'*Bank error?* Ha! . . . *In self-defence?* Oh, yes, and I'm a Chinaman!'

Fearing she'd get bored and take to accusing him of making no effort, he had a go at turning her next outburst – '*Fell off*, indeed!' – into the start of both a civil conversation and a way of assuring her she wasn't a granny.

'Talking of "falling off", did I mention to you that I know a young trapeze artist?'

She glanced up. 'We're really diving in the waters of Lake Me today! "Oh, I knew George Henry Besterton." "I met his widow." And now, "I know a trapeze artist." What were you doing? Slapping an unsafe scaffolding order on the poor bugger's highwire?'

'*She* doesn't happen to be working at the moment.'

He saw the look. But all she said was, 'So you haven't actually seen this – *artiste* – of yours in action?'

How could he say he'd seen a curtsy?

'No.'

'But you *believed* her?'

He didn't bother answering. But after his recent glimpse into the tearful, nervy days to come, he found her cynicism rather cheering. This was the mother he preferred. The worst of the last few weeks had been that sense of his the two of them were on a see-saw: him going up, her going down. He wasn't used to things that way. It didn't seem fitting. It might be plain to both that this was the way their lives were headed now; that soon, this very unnerving state of affairs might even be permanent – well, at least till the end. But that didn't mean he couldn't still enjoy these soothing little moments of reprieve, flagged by odd scathing echoes of the cold comfort she'd offered so often after his childhood spats with Dilys. 'And you *believed* her?'

That was the comfort in his mother, he decided: her tough, old-fashioned realism. He found it bracing. As when he'd pleaded with her to phone the fire brigade so they could rescue poor mewling Tabby-kitten, and she'd said scornfully, 'Oh, grow up, Colin! How many cats' skeletons have you actually *seen* up trees?' Instantly, he had stopped fretting, and (if he had ever been able to master the skill) would have strolled away whistling. The trouble was, he thought, that gratitude for gifts of childhood came with timed release. And that might come too late. It might be only after someone's death that you first came to realize just what it was that they had given you. You could, he thought, solve the problem with an adaptation of his television programme *You Be the Judge*. This version, though, would be a lot more interesting. And more demanding. Perhaps it would work best as some sort of face-to-face thing along the lines of that old interview programme, *On the Psychiatrist's Couch*. (It might even be better on radio.) Those in the hot seat would be pushed into facing the truth about benefits they'd gained from their childhood. Not all that lightweight stuff like, 'Yes, we ate gravel, so now I'm satisfied with a good crust,' or, 'Without that big strap of hers chasing behind me, I never would have realized I had Olympic potential.' No. Things that ran very much deeper. This programme would examine all the qualities that people liked to think they'd forged themselves from their own character, and weren't too happy to accept might have been things gained from their family. And there'd be few enough who'd be exempt.

After all, wasn't it generally from watching their parents that most people learned that irreplaceable upside-down lesson: that to live badly is a kind of death? Even just living wrong. Who does the son of the workaholic have to thank, if not his father, for the fact that he's learned to take time to appreciate the glories of his garden? How would the child of the hippy get such a buzz out of paying the mortgage if it weren't for those years being dragged round by mother? As for himself, surely the reason he was now so good at getting through department meetings without argument was—

'Colin!'

He looked up, startled.

'I said, while you're at the shop, could you pick up that telly guide Mr Stastny's put aside for me?'

Shop? He'd said nothing about going shopping. Still, mad to look a gift-horse in the mouth, and he could always make a little detour on his way back via the wood-shed and Suzie. Stretching his foot towards the grey heap softly snoring on the rug, he said, 'I'll take Floss with me, shall I?'

'If she wants to go.'

How would one tell? Levering up Flossie's hind end with his foot, he watched with interest as it softly sank again, like a parachute settling. She didn't even waken. 'I don't know what's happening to this house,' he found himself saying suddenly.

'I'll tell you one thing. It'll be none the better for that tinny new toaster you're planning on leaving.'

Alerted, he warned her, 'I hope you're not thinking of digging that old one back out of the dustbin.' She sat with

160

the enigmatic half-smile that told him, plain as paint, that he'd soon find his gleaming, safety-checked appliance back in its box. And, once again, he had the strongest sense her loss of confidence was in remission. She was pert. Almost herself again. And, cheered as he knew she'd always been by the discomfort of others, his unease grew . . .

'Anything else, then? I mean, from the shop.'

'Well, if he has any nice tomatoes— Oh, and a spot of plant food, unless it's in one of those fiddly packets. And I wouldn't say no to a couple of apples, just so long as they're not French.'

Remember to peel the stickers off the apples.

'I'll leave Floss here, then, shall I?'

'No. Second thoughts. Take her with you.' Floss's new status as a barely living floor cover was borne out by his mother's next remark. 'The smelly thing never gets much of an airing.'

He stooped to jack the old dog to her feet. There was a bit of wobbling, but finally the eyes did open and Flossie started on the long, long totter towards the door. Colin put out his foot to steer her safely round the spindly side table, then picked up the lead, more to give himself the means to tether her neatly to somebody's gatepost than in any real hope of dragging her the whole way.

Outside, the light was failing, but still the gardening chat was filtering through hedges down the backs.

'Well, that's the trouble with potentillas, William. Like my late wife, they simply will not share a bed.'

'They're fierce atoms, these cotoneasters. They'll do anything to get through the fence at your saxifrage.'

The conversations stopped as he hauled Flossie past the first gap in the Al-Khatibs' privet. Unnerved, he glanced back through the next bare patch to see four separate pairs of eyes on him, all balefully staring.

For God's sake! No wonder his mother had been sitting there with that glint in her eye and a fresh charge of energy. She must have passed on Perdita's gossip. Now wasn't that typical! The bloody woman manifestly didn't believe a word of it herself, yet she'd still told them! He could practically hear the tut-tutting ricocheting, as it must have done all week, over fences and back gates: 'Lord knows, it was bad enough when he was simply tormenting her with worries about toasters and insurance. But now it turns out, all this time, behind her back . . .'

'Well, now you mention it, Ruby did happen to notice Colin only a while ago outside the Funeral Emporium. And he did have a small child in his car.'

The silence lasted down the backs. For the first time in living history, Mrs McKay failed to spring from her porch to add her list to Norah's. No one appeared to be in need of bread. Or milk. Or cigarettes. And it was obvious that Mr Stastny, too, had heard the news because, instead of serving everyone else who had come in as usual, he turned to Colin as soon as it was his turn, and his respect was unmistakable. First Rizla papers, and now this!

Right, Colin thought. That settles it. He'd tackle Mother the minute he got back. 'Listen,' he'd tell her, stabbing a finger on the tray on which she would have placed one lonely sandwich in order to remind him she still had no appetite. 'What are you playing at, telling the world I have a wife and a family? You know perfectly well

162

that, whatever I might have told that booty-hunter Perdita, the whole thing is nonsense. Pure nonsense!'

And that's exactly what he would have done, he realized afterwards, had he not been offered that second bag. For the tomatoes. On any other day they'd have been jammed in along with the apples and the leaking plant-food bottle. And this, Colin couldn't help thinking as Mr Stastny hurried round to pass him the television guide he'd left on the counter instead of carelessly tossing it over to him at the door, was what it must feel like not to be a Colin. Light-headed. Powerful. Utterly different. And if he hadn't already had to tether Flossie halfway along the backs when her poor little feet gave out, he might even have celebrated the transfiguration by breaking totally with tradition and strolling home the front way.

Inside the woodshed, it seemed mustier than usual. Across the work bench lay a few dry leaves, his candle stumps and one or two spent matches. All stuff of his, but still the little space seemed different somehow. Had she been in here, snooping? (Or even, to be fair, looking for paint?) Or was it him? Did things seem strange the way a room looks strange after bad news? As when that young policeman had to beg his mother, 'Oh, *please* sit down, Mrs Riley,' and, sensing what was coming, just like her, Colin had stared at that little painted jug on the sideboard and seen its colours glow more brightly than usual through air so still he could have touched it. Perhaps he was finished with the woodshed at last. Grown up. Grown out of it. Too old for spells.

Too old for Suzie, even? That would be a shame. He

tugged at the drawer to pull her out from underneath the chisels, and have a look. Old-fashioned little creature. A real back-number – worlds away from all those knowing girls round lifts and water coolers who drove his married colleagues wild and left him cold. *Should* he be moving on and moving out? Close up the shed, shift the bolt back to the other side in case of temptation, and go and get a proper girlfriend like Helen Letherington, but, this time, make an effort to make it work? Even get married?

Oh, should he hell! His whole damn life was one long wail of 'Colin this' and 'Colin that'. Damned if he wanted any more people of flesh and blood to drain him dry and send him whimpering in one direction after another to serve their own purposes. Suzie was *his*. That was the point of her. Over the years, he'd built the two of them a little world in which he pulled the cigarettes he'd never smoked from his lips, dropped them where no one dared frown at him for careless littering, and ground them beneath the heel of boots he'd feel a fool to wear. 'Come here,' he told her. And she came. And stood obediently while he peeled off her itsy-bitsy top and frilly skirt, and turned her round to that strange, featureless ledge that always materialized at just the right moment, just the right height, and took her – hard, successfully, and very fast.

Christ! Where were the tissues? Standing on tiptoes to scrabble behind the paint tins, he caught a glimpse of willie dangling and felt an idiot. The matches were so damp it took an age to start the bonfire in the tobacco tin. And by the time he'd prudently transferred the old toaster from the dustbin to the back of his car, and peeled the stickers off the apples, it was late enough to leave Mother to telly and one of her mysterious invisible suppers.

He found her sitting on the three-legged stool beneath the stairs. He found the sight of it oddly unnerving. In all the years they'd lived in Holly House, he'd never seen his mother on that seat (nor sat on it himself since the first time, in teenage, she'd told him sharply to go park his fat bum on something more his own size). It was disquieting to see her perched somewhere so strange, yet so familiar.

Wisps of her hair were lifting in the draught that he himself brought in with him.

'I'll see you upstairs, shall I?'

She opened her eyes with a start. 'No, no. I've one or two small things to do before I settle.'

She launched into her usual evening litany about turning down heaters and putting out bottles. It didn't ease his sense of deep disquiet. Somehow, not having seen her on that stool before, he saw her differently. Like someone else's mum. Frail, valiant, vulnerable. This was no time to scold her about toasters, or even tick her off for ruining his reputation along the backs. He'd end up having to explain how the whole story got started. She'd miss the start of her programme and get ratty. And he was starving.

It could wait a day.

'Right, then,' he said. 'I'll just pop in tomorrow, shall I?'

She shooed the idea away with her hand. 'You don't have to drag your carcass round here two nights in a row just because it's my birthday.'

Her *birthday*?

'No, no,' he said, without a flicker. 'I've got it planned. I'll be here.'

He pulled the door behind him, close to tears. Oh, things were very wrong. What was the *matter* with her? How could a woman who had spent her days so primed for self-pity, skilled at brewing rancour and brilliant at inspiring guilt, have handed over, seemingly without a thought, a chance like this? Could greed for victimhood, like any other human appetite, suddenly fail, to leave a nicer – but a different – person? No one he recognized, that was for sure. Why, that last little exchange could have been with a stranger. The mother he knew would never, ever, in all the years he could remember, have tossed away that quite extraordinary opportunity – almost a Martyr's Holy Grail – of letting her own son forget her birthday.

He brooded on it down the path, and through the long root in his pockets to find his keys. At least the car started. As he pulled out from the kerb, a dark van further down the street nosed out as well. He hated people on his tail – especially neighbours, who from his very first days behind the wheel had been anxious to report to his mother his most venial infraction. Tonight, after his supposed perfidy, the curtains would be twitching all down the street. Slamming the brakes on more out of prudence than from courtesy, he gave a little flash, and waited.

The van stayed put.

'Fine,' Colin murmured. 'Don't mind me. I've got all night.' And he did truly feel, for once, as if time didn't really matter. Tired by the endless fretting about his mother, already his mind was straying back to more seductive poolside matters. And such was his fondness for Suzie and her sheer trouble-free amenability, even in retrospect, that it was quite a while before he even noticed that the van was so close it was blocking his mirror.

And, even when he noticed, he didn't mind.

On the mat under his letterbox was one of those cheap, almost furry, brown envelopes into which Clarrie spent a large part of her day resentfully shovelling letters. He tore it open, hoping for one mad moment it was her resignation, and was put out to find a letter from his own council threatening him with legal action on the matter of a two-year-old bill for a gas fire.

He dropped it in his briefcase, wondering if he should phone up Dil to get a tip or two on how to sort out Arif in Accounts. At the same time he could fish for suggestions on what to get Mother for her birthday. Unlike the girls in the office, Dilys would understand the difficulty of finding the right thing – though, to be fair, their mother couldn't be the only old person in the world to make a virtue of not wanting anything. In this respect, the lofty-minded pensioner could be a real pain. It wasn't, after all, as if they didn't need things. But what they needed were the sorts of things you weren't allowed to get for birthdays. 'Oh, lovely, dear! I'd been thinking about getting a sturdier hand rail.' 'A brand-new panic button! And in my colour – silver-grey!' A tragic waste, especially with those who made a point of not appreciating proper presents. 'But, dear. There's nothing wrong with my old bath sponge.' 'What would I want with any mobile telephone? I'm barely mobile.'

Neither could Norah be alone in making a point of being grumpy on birthdays. 'Oh, don't remind me! I did at least have hopes of celebrating this one underground.' No, there were fortunes to be made in presents for the ageing citizen. The Old Folk's Anti-Birthday Hamper. It could include all those expensive luxuries they'd always thought so over-rated: champagne and caviare, *foie gras*, organic jams – maybe even a few exotic fruits they could leave ostentatiously rotting in the bowl. Sometimes it seemed to Colin that nothing brought greater pleasure to his mother and her neighbours than simple disapproval – unless it were being able to ram home with condolences the very worst of news. 'I'm told that Dora will be laid up for several months. And you with your bad back! How *awful* for you both. You'll be pretty well housebound now, the two of you. I *am* sorry.'

A way of offering that sort of birthday pleasure would take some detailed working out. No time to muse. To get advice from Dilys, he'd have to make the phone call now. He could begin with an apology for rushing away from her private little get-together – ask after Marjorie, that kind of thing.

It might seem natural. Other people did it.

Give it a try.

She picked up on the first ring. 'Colin! The very man! Have you only just got back? I've been ringing and ringing.'

'Me? Why?'

'Why? To apologize, of course.'

If he had ever heard the word from her before, he had no memory of it. 'Apologize?' Stifling the astonished, '*You?*', he managed to ask instead, 'What on earth for?'

'For letting that awful Marjorie fix her infected fangs into your leg and shake you about like that.'

That awful Marjorie?

'Oh, so she's gone, then?'

He heard her sip from what he guessed was one more little top-up, and with a rare stab of fraternal sympathy asked, 'Are you sorry?'

'Sorry? I was glad to see the back of her.' He heard ice tinkling. 'In fact I'm having a field day. Tara just rang—'

(Tara. Try to remember that.)

'—to tell me Perdita's been given the push.'

'Perdita's *sacked*?'

'Not sacked, exactly. But moved out of Sales back to Insurance.'

Thank Christ he'd swapped that toaster. 'I expect she'll enjoy it back there,' he said bitterly. 'Poking through Mum's insurance for irregularities.'

'No.' Dil's voice was mellow with gin and satisfaction. 'Not even that bit. They've shunted her into a little sideline called Policy Promotions.' She waited for his gasp, then, realizing he wasn't informed enough to offer one, told him, 'It's where they shove all the board members' work-experience children for the summer, and anyone they're scared will sue them if they're sacked outright.' She snorted. 'I'm afraid that the rest of us tend to refer to it as "The Tor Pit"!'

Clearly the news had brought her unadulterated pleasure. And that was good, since, in her merry state, she for once might manage to advise him without delivering a lecture.

'Dil, any ideas for something for Mother's birthday?'

Out it came, pat. 'A snowstorm.'

How drunk was she, for God's sake? 'Sorry?'

'Not a *real* one, silly. One of those glass domes you pick up and shake.'

He had a sudden memory of perfect happiness – of sitting drenched in moonlight, safe out of sight between the winter curtains and cold panes, shaking his precious glass ball and watching trapped flecks of snow swirl round and round some jovial Santa in another world.

'Colin?'

'Sorry. Miles away.'

'I saw the most fabulous one only today in "Gifts from the Gods". A man in a blue cloak striding through snow. Could he have been Good King Wenceslas? It struck me the moment I saw it as the sort of thing I would have bought as a present for Mother.'

Was Norah so much in her mind, after five years? He trod as carefully as he could. 'Well, if you happened to be thinking of getting her something yourself . . .'

'Don't be so silly, Colin.'

It was worth trying. 'But you could.'

'Why should I?'

He was astonished not to hear himself saying hastily, 'No reason,' but rather, 'Well, *someone* has to start up again.'

She sounded more puzzled than hostile. 'Why?'

'Well,' he said, somewhat desperately. 'For one thing, she'd be pleased.'

Out came the snort. 'Pleased? Do me a favour, Colin! A bit intrigued, perhaps. Suspicious, definitely. But never pleased.'

Spot on, as usual. She couldn't have drunk that much since Marjorie walked out the door. So why did he persist in arguing? 'No, I think it would mean a lot.' Why was he lying? What was this drive in him to make her think about putting things right between herself and Mother before they reached the state where nothing mattered any more? 'I think she'd care. *Really*.'

'Colin, we've talked about this before. You can't be nasty to people all your life, then expect them to come round again just because you're old.'

He could tell from her tone that she thought what she said would wrap up the whole matter. She wasn't expecting him to bounce back as he did. 'She hasn't been that bad.'

That lit the fuse. 'Oh yes, she has. You *know* she bloody has. Don't get forgetful on me now, Col. You shared it. You were *there*.'

He couldn't stop. It was exhilarating. (And possibly unprecedented, unless you counted that feverish spat the day he came down with the chicken pox.) 'But maybe she was trying. By her lights.'

Clearly his sister would take a very tough line on *You Be the Judge*. 'Not bloody hard enough.'

'And we're not children any more.'

'No. But she still puts the boot in when she's bored. See how she fell on that crap about you marrying behind her back because it gave her the chance to blacken you in front of her friends and the neighbours.'

He felt light-hearted, just from the business of holding his corner. 'Be fair. Perdita probably made it sound pretty convincing.'

'Oh, really, Col! Do try not to be more of a dim bulb than the good Lord made you. People like Mother, they're like witches stirring trouble. The truth means nothing. Nothing! And nor does anyone else's reputation. They're so wrapped up in their own little ways of burning up their twisted energies that they forget other people actually *exist*.'

'You're making her sound practically psychotic.'

'All right, then. Other people *exist*. But their feelings don't matter – well, certainly not enough to stop her snaring them in her horrible, mean-minded little pursuits whenever it suits her.'

And she was right. His mother knew that she'd been spreading lies. And lies did matter. He had a sudden memory of Val curled at the very end of the sofa, explaining why they had to tell even their youngest patients they were going to die. 'We have to,' she'd said simply. 'Lies and deception just can't be reconciled with trust and respect.' Or with love, he had thought since. And now his sister was only saying the same thing in a different way. 'People like her, they spread their own sort of immoral ooze that poisons everything between people.' But Val's line had been born from caring. And Dilys's was different, because it stemmed from old resentments, ancient hates. And it was always easier to be a moralist where it most suited. So he pressed on. 'But things are different now.'

'How, different?'

'Mother's changing.'

'Because it suits her! Colin, you're such a fool to let her get away with it! It's so damn *brazen* – like that loophole for Catholics in that poem Mrs Barker made you learn

172

when you brought all those maggots into the lunch hall.'

'*I* didn't bring them in. Somebody in that foul gang of yours tipped out my sandwiches and filled—'

'Something about "mercy this" and "mercy that".'

It flooded back, to startle him. '*Betwixt the stirrup and the ground, Mercy I asked, mercy I found.*'

'Well, I remember Mother being scathing. And now look. She acts mean and nasty all her life, then cops out at the end. No, it's despicable.' Again, he heard ice tinkling. 'And whatever you're up to, Colin, I don't want anything to do with it. She's like a sort of moral syphilis. I'm staying away.'

And who could blame her, he wondered, putting down the phone. Who could say she was wrong? Like so many other things to do with Mother, this was nothing to do with 'good' or 'right'. It was a matter of temperament, and if his sister had been born with a leaning to *fatwa*, then bloody good luck to her. It must save a fortune in greetings cards. No Mum. No Val. No Perdita. And now no Marjorie. No doubt it was important to have both sorts of person in the world. With judgement strewn all over, there'd be no room for charity or mercy. And if the forgiving ruled, there'd be no judgement (and, as Mrs Barker used to say when she marked down his messy work after Tess had been kicking his chair back all morning, 'To spare the bad, Colin Riley, is tantamount to injuring the good'). Neither could sinners like Mother be excused on grounds of ignorance, or 'Things were different then'. That sort of line might wash with trespasses like doctors not washing their hands before germs were discovered, or Clarrie's teachers leaving her pretty well totally to her own benighted devices in the misguided hope she might still learn things. But how could it be that someone of Norah's quick intelligence could ever truly have believed her children must take on the chin whatever she, in her frustrated miseries, had simply felt like dishing out?

So, yes. Good luck to Dilys. Stay away. Don't come back now. Don't lend a hand. Hold firm, as things get worse and more and more visits have to be made, and toasters confiscated and windchimes stuffed with paper. But how come he didn't feel, as usual, that he was being dealt the poorer hand? Because he didn't. He couldn't help it. Usually at times like these, a little wallow in self-pity had been his compensation. This time it didn't come. He sat there waiting, but he just felt chirpy. Somehow he was sure in his bones that, right as his sister might be in principle — and she had justice on her side, no doubt of that — not only was he utterly incapable of slamming the door between himself and his mother, but there was something in it for him over and above more bloody drudgery.

It's just he wasn't yet sure what it was. Or how he'd recognize it when it came.

8

CLARRIE WAS ON HIM BEFORE HE'D EVEN GOT THROUGH the door. 'No point in taking your jacket off. The police rang. You're to go down Sperivale Road.'

'Sperivale Road?' His heart flipped. 'Why? Is it the restaurants?'

She gave her little how-should-I-know? shrug before swivelling back to whatever it was she'd just lost on the computer. No need to ask. It had to be the restaurants. And what with it still being early enough for the snarl-up at Hammer Road not to have cleared yet, it was quite possible that, by the time he arrived, the police would have sorted the matter out nicely. It was a cheerful Colin who walked down the stairs and found that, even after the slightly unpleasant stand-off with Herbert in the Mice'n'Maggots van in the narrow car-park entrance, it was his gears, and not his spirits, that had slid hastily in reverse.

After a satisfactorily long wait at the Sperivale lights, he pulled round the corner. The narrow strip of pavement outside the restaurants was bright with condiments. Mr Haksar stood flanked by brothers, uncles and sons, watching his sister-in-law shriek from an upstairs window. All the Lees stood in a line, alternately jeering and looking bored. And the pair of police officers appeared to have parked their buttocks so very comfortably on the wall as to practically invite accusations of idling. 'Waiting for you,' they explained when Colin pulled up the van outside New China Heaven and stepped out, crunching on a sea of coriander.

Colin said hopefully, 'I suppose it's a police matter now,' and then, disquieted by two blank looks, added firmly and hastily, 'What with the public disturbance.'

One of the officers lifted an eyebrow.

'All this palaver,' insisted Colin, taking care not to step in a pile of boiled noodles.

The younger of the policemen jerked a thumb. 'Well, when that tin of yellow stuff hit the side door, Geoffrey here did think we might have an "intentional or reckless" on our hands . . .'

Colin gazed at the sunny drifts of turmeric. 'Yes?'

But the officer offered only a Clarrie-style shrug. Colin said desperately, 'But what about all the rest of it? Harassment! Damage to property! Threatening behaviour! Invasion of privacy! Not to mention interference with means of employment, and presumed loss of earnings!'

'Well, there you are,' said Geoffrey comfortably. 'You've clearly got it all off pat. Best left to you, I reckon.'

'I can't do anything. I'm not police!'

'More up your street than ours, though, isn't it? Restaurants and such . . .'

Colin surprised himself. 'This isn't restaurants! This is

176

an endless mindless bloody squabble over a wall! This is phone calls all day every day, till I can't concentrate on anything else, let alone leave the office. This is my voice-mail bunged up every morning and my secretary in tears! This is me at the end of my tether. This is *impossible*.' He really felt it. 'Quite impossible!' He saw them staring at him. 'No! No, no. I'm sorry. I've struggled on by myself quite long enough. Look at the state of this pavement! Dumplings all over! Those prawns will be stinking by lunchtime if someone doesn't clear them up. And I sus-pect that's chilli on that meter. If anybody parking should end up touching that by accident and not wash their hands very thoroughly indeed, they could end up with seriously inflamed eyes. Or *worse*,' he added darkly on reflection. 'No. This is the limit, I'm afraid. I have to insist. You are the long arm of the law. Well, stick it out and do something!'

Astonished at himself, he stepped back into bean curd.

Then, did he hear it? Did he really hear it?

'Or—?'

'*Or*,' Colin said, with equally quiet menace, 'I'll feel obliged to get in touch with County Hall and take it higher.'

What he of course meant was, I'll go straight back and hand my notice in. I'll walk away from the whole boiling rather than cope with this lot a single day longer. I'd rather lose my pension and start again doing something as poorly paid but a bloody sight easier. But it just came out in the way it did, and after a good long stare the officer called Geoffrey must have decided to take him at his word because, turning to his companion, he muttered equably enough, 'All right, then, Jamie-boy?'

'All right,' said James. And slipping on authority with more ease than most men put on a sock, the two strolled through little piles of stir-fried cucumber towards the families waiting on the pavement. There followed a welter of shrieking from the upstairs window, and some long grinding argument in which the only element of agreement between the two camps was indicated by a series of matching black looks in the direction of Colin. But one, at least, of the officers must have been blessed with the mediator's gift, because after a few more threatening glances and shaken fists, the ranting on both sides diminished to receding tides of sullen grumbling. Colin's relief was palpable as, one by one, the Lees vanished through the door into the shadows of Old China Heaven. And, stooping only to pick up the huge pans they'd clearly brought outside to serve as weapons, the Haksars slid silently into their own restaurant, with only the youngest reappearing a few moments later to stroll to the side door, whistling, with a dustpan and brush.

Jamie-boy ambled back. 'Happy?'

Colin considered. He hadn't cared for the dark looks. But perhaps it was to be expected that, as the one who'd failed to stop things getting out of hand, he'd find himself absorbing the blame for this little street battle. He couldn't resist shooting a warning 'I-hope-your-father's-not-thinking-of-using-that-turmeric-again' look up the alley at the Haksar boy before admitting to the officer, 'Well, perhaps it'll put a stop to some of the trouble.'

'Any time,' said the officer, giving Colin cause to wonder what possible reason, apart from simple sloth, had caused the two of them to be so reluctant to intervene in the first place. Another squall of temper from the window above reminded him he'd be wise not to linger; and, crunching his way back over coriander seeds, he slid in his own van and followed the police car down Sperivale Road, peeling off only when it occurred to him that, with a quick detour, he could pick up his mother's glass snowstorm – and one for Tam, if they looked suitable – and still gain a bit of sympathy at work for an irritating start to a long, tiring morning.

Mel's face was dark with disappointment. 'Oh, it's *you*.'

Even for a man accustomed to tepid welcomes, this was discouraging. If the warm clamp of Tammy's arms around his legs had not made turning round impossible, he would have thrust the box at her and simply fled. Instead, he stood his ground as best he could. 'I've brought a present.'

Rolling her eyes, she stooped to prise him free. 'For Christ's sake, Tam! Let the poor bugger through the door.'

He stepped in, wincing. But it was better not to disapprove in case she took revenge. Anyone who could fuss about a plastic windmill could slap a safety embargo on a large glass ball. If she was in this bad a mood, he would be wise to clear the contents of the box with her before even letting Tam know there was anything in it, apart from fresh fruit and a bottle of vitamins.

Neatly avoiding the upraised, grasping little fingers, he passed it over.

Mel raised the flaps. 'I've got a toaster, thank you. And mine is newer.'

Oh, God. Wrong box. Mumbling idiocies, he fled to the lift, then down the four flights of stairs. The occupants of the vehicle parked beside his seemed to take an inordinate interest in his rootings in the back of the van. Were they planning a robbery? He could leave out some of the freezer food he'd taken off Betta-Shoppa's shelves for being past its date stamp. (That might teach them a lesson about other people's property.)

Or he could take the coward's way, and as good as buy them off by abandoning on the tarmac the box of hideously unattractive Monsters-From-The-Deep fridge magnets he'd had to impound for their overly high lead levels. They could resell those fast and well. But suppose they dropped some as they fled? Fearing that Tam might find one lying on the car park later and finger it, or, worse, put it in her mouth, he ended up locking even these unwanted horrors back firmly in the van before starting on the long urine-stained climb up the stairwell.

His second appearance in her doorway brought no more pleasure than the first. This time, so there'd be no mistake, he handed over only the glossy 'Gifts from the Gods' bag he'd put on top of the apples. 'That's what I meant to give you.'

The transformation was astonishing. 'Colin! How did you *know*?'

'Know?'

She hadn't even tweaked the bag to peep inside. And even if she'd felt the hard round lump through its stiff sides, she couldn't possibly have guessed what it might be. Hunting for meaning, his gaze fell, just in time, on two lonely birthday cards propped on the gas fire. 'Oh,' he said, almost lightheaded from the sense of disaster averted. 'We in the council have our methods.'

She lifted the softly rustling sphere out of the bag.

'It feels so *heavy*.'

Thank God he hadn't chosen Pluto trailing that mangy slipper through the snow. Or Snow White, looking wistful. He would have walked through fire rather than let her know this present hadn't been for her. Never had he seen anyone take such an age to unwrap anything. She spun it out till Tam went crazy with frustration, giving him the excuse to pick up his darling and hold her closer to the gathering excitement as, layer by layer, her mother reverently pulled off the trademark rainbow tissue from Priding's most expensive shop.

'Oh, Colin!'

Inside the perfect glassy dome, the pearly figure with upraised arms spun on her shimmering lake. The snowflakes swirled around, settling on tiny fir trees and distant hills, and her own upswept hair. He told Mel truthfully, 'I thought it looked a lot like you when you did that pirouette thing by the stove,' then, to his own astonishment, heard himself tacking on, quite un-necessarily, a glib, kind lie. 'I thought you'd really like it.'

'*Like* it? Oh, Colin! It's—'

Tears sheeted down.

'Oh, Christ!' he said, and kicked the door shut behind him. After the statutory few seconds of frozen staring, Tam started wailing worse than Mel. He shifted her to the other arm. 'Mummy's all right,' he said firmly. 'All that she needs is for you to show me how to make her a cup of tea. Can you do that?' On the way over to the kitchen area, he took the chance to sweep her so close to the gas fire that the draught from her leg sent the greetings cards flying. 'Whoops!' he said cheerily, taking the risk of putting his back out by stooping with her still in his arms to retrieve them and put them on top of the telly.

'They'll be much safer here, Mel. You really shouldn't ever put anything inflamm—'

Shut up! he ordered himself. Give it a break.

Pushing aside the unwashed crockery, he dumped Tam on the small space that served for a counter and pointed at the sugar tin. 'Is that the tea?'

Tam shook her head. He pointed to the coffee jar. 'Is *that* the tea?' Tam used the flat of her hands to wipe tears sideways into tangled hair, then made a face and pointed.

'Oh, there!' said Colin, switching on the kettle. 'And how many bags do you think I should put in the cup?'

Tam raised one grubby finger.

'You're good at this.' He kept her busy, pointing at spoons and sugar and putting him right over and over, till Mel's tea was ready and her weeping had quietened principally to sniffs. She sat, still clutching the snowstorm, while he continued to distract her daughter and put himself a little more at ease by rerouting the dangerously long lead to her kettle.

Once it was safely tucked away behind the microwave he'd been longing to take away to get tested for leakage, he took a chance and dared look Mel's way again. 'Ready?'

She nodded. 'Ready.'

He said to Tam, 'Now take it easy, sweetheart. Mum's feeling—'

Stumped for a way of putting it, he finished with the

word his mother always used to drain the last of what little confidence he had before school matches. 'Peaky.'

'Peaky?' She tested the new word, and in her state of barely soothed anxiety, repeated it louder and louder. 'Peaky, peaky, *peaky*!'

'Hush, sweetpea. Mum's upset.'

Was it his mere tone of concern that sent Mel back in floods? Instantly, Tam's shrieks shot into an hysterical crescendo. '*Peaky! Peaky! Peaky!*'

Someone upstairs banged on the floor.

'Oh, Christ!' Mel screamed at the ceiling. 'Didn't your bloody children ever make a sound, you dried-up ratbag!'

Tammy shrieked louder. To try to calm things, Colin gave her a warning frown. 'Sssh, Tam! Be quiet!'

Failing to stem her yells that way, he tried putting his finger on her lips. At once, she lurched forward to bite him. Terrified she'd topple off the counter, he seized her elbows, and, as she struggled to push him away, her screams went into orbit. She drummed her bare heels as hard as she could against the flimsy door of the cabinet.

'Oh, thanks a million, Colin! Trying to help her drive me nuts?'

'Nuts!' Tammy took to screaming. '*Nuts! Nuts! Nuts!*'

Defeated, Colin swung the child down from the counter. Hurtling across the room, she grabbed at the snowstorm. 'I want to hold it! Let me hold it! My turn!'

Colin rushed over to pull her away. Holding her by the shoulders, he told her firmly, 'Not till you're sitting safely and sensibly right back on the sofa.'

A clever move. At once she stopped struggling and, turning her back on her frazzled, tear-stained mother, dived headlong into the leaking cushions. Swivelling around, she held out both hands, imperiously wriggling her fingers. He prised the snowstorm from Mel's trembling fingers, and carried it over. 'There's a rule,' he warned, holding it just out of reach. 'You have to *whisper*.'

Tammy nodded gravely.

'You see, she's so small and delicate and dainty that she can't hear you unless you whisper,' he said, to reinforce the point. Then he turned back to Mel. Lowering himself to his heels, he asked her softly, 'Isn't there *someone* who could help? What about your family?'

She took the tissue he was offering and roused herself enough to say, 'If I had any sort of family, do you suppose I'd be mouldering away in this dump?'

'Well, what about——?' Tactfully he nodded towards Tam, absorbed in whispering to the spinning nymph. 'You know,' he said. 'The other Lavender.'

She stared.

'I mean, *Ventura*.'

She twisted the tissue to shreds. 'Him? All he's interested in is getting me back.' She pointed. 'See?'

Taking it for permission, he picked up the nearer of the cards.

' *"With all good wishes for a better year, from Hermione"*?'

'Not that one. That's the bloody social worker.'

He felt a stab of nausea. On his last birthday he'd had no cards at all. But that was only because Dilys had been away at a conference, and his mother had forgotten. If any had arrived, they would at least have been from family.

Desperate to find some means to cheer her, he peered in the other.

' "*Come back! Alexi.*" Well, that's good.'

'Good?'

'Nice this Alexi bloke loves you enough to tell you he wants you back.'

'*Loves* me?' It was more of a bark than a laugh. 'He doesn't love me. I expect all that's happened is that his foul moods and bad temper have finally driven away my rotten, untalented replacement. I bet the only reason he's sent that is because he's desperate to get a halfway decent act back on the road before the circus management give him the heave-ho.'

Knowing a Tam-sized chunk of his own loving, beating heart was now in hazard, he forced the words out.

'It can't be that, or he'd just advertise for another partner.'

And now he'd done it. She was furious. 'Oh, yes? A lot you know about it! Just advertise!' Words failed her, and had she, he sensed, not feared a fresh batch of howling from Tammy, she might very easily have slapped him.

Instead, she turned her back. To be conciliatory, he reminded her, 'He did at least remember that it was your birthday. And you must *matter* to him. You are Tammy's mother, after all.'

She couldn't have looked blanker. 'So? Tam's the bloody *problem*, isn't she?'

'But if this bloke's her father—'

'Which he's *not*!'

My God! The hours that he'd wasted envying him! How stupid could you get? But no more stupid than the man himself, this oiled, muscled idiot who, offered a choice of Mel and Tam together, or neither, would seem to

185

be sailing very near the option of ending up with an empty life.

'I just don't understand.' He watched her rubbing at her tear-streaked face, and, like some soft-hearted hunter loosing a wire to let some desperate trapped creature go, felt obliged to add the words he knew might cause all his own happiness to fly from his grasp. 'Most of the circuses I've inspected have had plenty of small children. If everyone's strictly careful to adhere to the rules, then, with a very few added precautions, there's no reason to think—'

Seeing her lip curl, he wrapped up hastily. 'And there are nets.'

Again, that fierce hauteur. 'Nets? Oh, yes! Thanks to you meddlers there are nets all over. But you can still fuck up. You can still make a fool of your partner.' Tipping her head, she launched into what even Colin could tell from a meeting of moments was the poorest of imitations of Alexi: '"Is no good, Mel. Having child around will take the mind off."'

She let out an almost equally abrasive snarl of contempt in her own right. 'But really the bastard's just deadly jealous I had a fling, and Tam's not his.'

Even allowing for nameless foreign influences, the response seemed old-fashioned.

'But if you're *that* good—'

'I *am* that bloody good!'

'It seems so odd, then. To send you away.'

'Send me away?' The dark eyes blazed. 'That arsehole wouldn't work a proper set with me, and so I *left*.'

My God, he thought. Look at her. So alive. Alight. Could he have got it wrong? Could everything he'd so

186

unthinkingly taken for a mother's self-sacrifice – trading the glitter and danger of the highwire for down-to-earth safety nets for her young daughter: a nearby health clinic, regular nursery attendance, and even the freedom from watching the only parent she knew miss a man's grasp by a hair's breadth and spiral down through air – could all of it prove to be something quite different? Something in which the child herself was incidental – almost an accident, like her own birth? All this depression, all these whey-faced looks, the unwashed dishes and the dismal, unimaginative diet on which no growing creature ought to live . . .

Could it be possible they all boiled down to one enormous Artiste's Sulk?

So hard to judge. And hard to judge her harshly. Who, after all, would choose to live on a planet bulging with fudgers and shrinkers like him? The world cried out for passion. That is why people queued for circuses: *Ex pulvere, lux et vis.* Put a trapeze artist and a council officer in the same show, and there'd be no bets which way the audience would be looking at the moment the lights dimmed.

No, he thought, staring. It was unfair to think that someone from a circus should share priorities from a drabber world. Souls who could fly through air, despising nets strung under them by bureaucratic little fusspots like him, should be offered some leeway. No one would buy a ticket to watch him test seals on a canteen fridge. Hundreds would sit on chilly benches, risking piles, to see the soaring wizardry of her glimmering spirals.

Give the poor girl a chance. Instead of standing there

watching her spirits fade, he should stretch out a hand. She was only a fish out of water. If she'd gone belly-up downstream from some foul overflow or some unauthorized industrial drain, he'd be out of his van in a moment to help her. Getting her away from this dump for a day or two might lift her spirits.

Though, with someone so prickly, it was best to tread carefully . . .

'So where's this circus of yours now?'

Close to mind, that was quite obvious. 'Bridlington this week. Then up towards Whitby.'

'Not too far to go for a few days.'

She gave him a very sour look.

He panicked. 'During the refurbishment.'

'The *what*?'

Oh, why not? If it helped.

'The refurbishment. Did you not get your letter? Some of these flats are being redecorated very soon.' Oh, there'd be hell to pay with Hetherley and his workforce. And out-of-order billing going on for years. But it was worth it. Just the excitement of telling so many whoppers in a row made him feel a foot higher. 'I'm afraid I was rather naughty when the order came round, and put you and Tammy right at the top of the list.'

'I'm being painted? Soon? You mean, like next week or something?'

Next week? Christ! Forget Hetherley's workmen. But he could chase up that little old fellow of Perdita's. Pay him the earth to drop whatever he was doing, and smarten up the flat a bit. Maybe get in a cleaner. Anything to help the poor fettered creature through a few more grounded months.

'It could well be as soon as that. And you should really think about getting away for a few days. It's never wise to have a child around when there are workmen in a property. All those tools lying about. And nasty paint fumes.'

She didn't look convinced.

'He did invite you,' he reminded her.

'He didn't mean for the *weekend*.'

God, she was touchy.

'Maybe not. But you could see other friends. And I'm sure even Alexi can put up with seeing someone else's child around for one or two days. She's very winning, after all.' He jerked a thumb towards Tam, who'd done his argument the good favour of falling angelically asleep on the sofa. 'And she'd enjoy a circus. Look how she loves her poster. No, you'd be far better off away.'

Choosing the phrase 'better off' was a mistake. Mel asked him sourly, 'Oh, yes? And how am I supposed to get Tam all the way to Bridlington? Carry her?'

'No problem.' He fished out phrases from a thousand mind-numbing council memoranda. 'Your extra-domiciliary expense docket' – that sounded good – 'will have to be ratified anyway by our department. So if you planned to be away, I could give you the cash instead and deduct it at source. There'd be no problem.'

Diving into his wallet, he counted out notes on the table. 'That's thirty, forty—'

'Bridlington . . .'

He raised his head. She was gazing across at Tammy, shifting in sleep. Between the chubby fingers, the magic flakes swirled. The pearly skater was defying gravity, still in her effortless pirouette, as the tiny world settled again sideways around her.

Then Mel, too, suddenly was in full spin. 'I know. *You* take her.'

'*Me?*'

'Why not? She thinks you're wonderful. And you are good with her.'

He shook his head. 'Impossible.'

'Please, Colin! Only for a night or two. It would make everything so much easier.'

She didn't mean the travelling, he could tell.

'No, really, Mel. I'm sorry.'

She was begging now. 'She could still go to nursery. And, if you got stuck, your sister could help you. Didn't she even share a house with some sort of nurse person?'

'I'm afraid they're not very friendly any more.'

She was already looking round, as if to decide what to take. 'But you could still phone her for advice if anything went wrong. And nothing would.'

Dizzy with fright, he told her, 'My mother's not well. I have to go round every night, and stay quite late.'

Even to him, it sounded so lame and unconvincing that he was shocked, a moment after saying it, to realize that it was the truth.

'Well, take her with you! You could both stay there, and I could—'

'No!'

He felt as if he'd pushed her over.

The sullen mask of discontent dropped back on her face. 'Oh, sorry I even *asked*.'

'No, honestly. It's me who's sorry.'

'Oh, *please!*'

Embarrassed, he made for the door. 'In fact, I'd better be getting round to my mother's now. Today happens to be her birthday as well.'

It was clear just how much credence Mel attached to this. 'Of course it is. Goodbye. Thank you for coming.'

Her eyes fell on the money on the table, but, furious, she neither offered it back nor turned away, so he could easily step forward to fetch it.

'That's quite all right,' he burbled, shuffling backwards till he tripped on the box with the toaster. 'I had to come by. We had a couple of reports about vandals taking pot shots at some of the hall sprinklers.'

It was another glib excuse that, once out, struck him as the truth.

'I'll take a look at them on my way out.'

'Yes, you do that.'

And, inasmuch as it is possible to check a sprinkler as you hurry past, blind with embarrassment, that is what he did.

This time, he found his mother on the wicker seat beside the shower. Again he had the sense of confronting a stranger. 'Hello,' he said, frightened he'd startle her. Skipping the lecture on not leaving the doors unlocked so anyone who happened to be passing could step in and murder her, he held out his present. 'Happy birthday.'

She took the fat wrapped lump. 'It feels so *heavy.*'

The words might have been an echo, but whereas Mel's were bubbling with excitement, his mother simply sounded critical. Giving him one of her tired, watery smiles, she peeled off one layer of rustling rainbow tissue, and then the next. Uncovering yet another, she rolled her eyes up in that gods-give-me-patience way she'd used to squeeze discomfort out of him all his life. He didn't flicker, knowing from long experience how all these little drives to petty cruelty were nourished, rather than allayed, by any signs of his weakness. To his surprise, for once it proved no effort. Seeing her yet again so very differently, in this strange place, on this strange chair, he found himself, too, feeling oddly detached, capable of interpreting these almost involuntary flashes of contempt and disapproval as nothing personal, just her own greedy victim's way of acting as if each chance she missed to make a meal of upset or of disappointment would, like a dropped stitch, mar the overall design of the long tapestry of her life.

'By the time I get down to this present, I'm going to be far too exhausted to enjoy it.'

Strange thing to do, though, when you came to think. To poison everything. Force yourself, as Dante put it in that chunk of the *Inferno* that Mr Ashcroft made him learn when he got so mad at him for forever being bullied, to be 'sullen in the sweet air'. Dante hurled those who wilfully lived in sadness into a mud pool. He, Colin, would be kinder. 'Don't you fret,' he wanted to console his mother. 'I understand at last. All these past years, you've never really been at war with me and Dilys. All these attacks on others have really been digs at yourself, and we've only been stand-ins.' Could he explain to Dilys? Would she understand? For suddenly it seemed to Colin that, after a lifetime of guilt that stemmed from neither his sister nor himself having the faintest inkling of what it was their mother had been needing, at last they could change things. Surely there must be time. And the sooner the better, because bad character was its own worst punishment, and old age judgement on the life you'd lived.

So was it said as comfort or as warning? 'I think you're nearly at the end.'

The last few layers of tissue fluttered down. She blinked. 'Oh, Colin!' His heart swelled as her thin hands shook. He cupped his own strong palms beneath, for fear she'd drop the small glass world.

'Is it Good King Whosit?'

'Wenceslas.'

She shook the snowflakes into blizzard to watch them swirl. He would have given half a world to read her mind. Should he tell her that Dilys had chosen it? Better not take the risk. 'I thought you'd like him.'

'He's a treat and a half. Look at him, striding along with his beard like a rhododendron!'

Taking advantage of her distraction, he took her gently by the elbows and prised her stiff bones up from the wicker seat. 'Why are you sitting in here, anyway?'

'I'm hiding from that doolally young pest who flings her mascara on with a tablespoon.'

'Perdita? Has she been round again?'

'Only crooning through my letter box! "Remember what I was saying, Mrs Riley? About selling the house? Well, we're working a little differently now. So here's my new number, if you'd like to call." ' Scrabbling around in a pocket, she drew out a business card on which Tor

Bank's number had been blackened out, and another written over it. His mother's venom lent her imitation a verisimilitude that poor Mel's of Alexi had lacked. '"Oh, and if you're there, Mrs Riley, happy birthday!"' The pursed lips tightened. 'I tell you, if that young lady comes battering on my door again, I won't be leaving her hair with so much fight in it. How come the nosy baggage knows it's my birthday anyway?'

Oh, he could guess. From one last peek at a policy she guessed was void last time she'd had to clear a desk? But this was no day to worry his mother with talk of a property vulture. He stood there, steeped in pity. All of his life he'd hated these frantic spasms of dislike for all things unexpected and unplanned. But now, still bathed in that peculiar sense of seeing his mother for the first time as someone utterly removed, almost a stranger, he saw her horror of spontaneity for what it always must have been: the terror of a damaged soul at even the slightest slippage in control.

Knowing her lifelong loathing of uninvited visitors would draw the fire from any limp response of his, he steered her away from the threat he saw looming. 'I expect it was her mother who sent her round – maybe even with a present.'

'I'll send her back to Dolly with another – a necklace made from her own teeth.'

And might yet, Colin reckoned, unless he stepped in smartish. For that percentage-grubbing little witch was bound to be back. What had his sister said when she'd been prophesying Perdita's banishment to one of the departments in Tor Bank where she'd be less likely to offend? 'No fat commissions there!' If Perdita would have felt hard done by in drab old Home Loans or Arrears, think how determined she'd be to cash in one last time on all that determined, sweet-talking, bouquet-thrusting groundwork, before sliding in a sulk into the depths of the Tor Pit.

But it was shameful. Shameful! And gave the lie to all that tosh about old people getting only what they deserved. Maybe, about emotional matters, that was true. Everyone said it, after all: 'Be careful what you give a child, for, in the end, you'll get it back.' But that was *feelings*. This was different. This was *behaviour*. And how you treated people was a choice. It was outrageous to sneak up to try to take advantage of someone like Mother, whose powers were failing. It was like coshing someone in a wheelchair, or tripping the blind, or taking bets from the simple.

It was despicable. *Despicable*.

'I'm going to get you a proper working answerphone. And fix you up with one of those outside mirrors, so you can see who's coming up the path.'

'You? Mr Ten Thumbs? No, thank you. I prefer my walls standing.'

Again he wondered at his own tranquillity. Instead of trawling round for some excuse to rush from the kitchen, hurry to the woodshed, take Flossie down the backs, he simply dug into his huge box of shopping to pull out supper.

'Do you want fish or chicken? I bought both.'

'The way I feel, I'd just as soon throw up as eat.'

Should he heat neither? Or both? Conundrums that

would have put him in a tizzy yesterday left him un-ruffled. 'I'll do both.'

'Oh, make yourself at home! Then I'll come round to your house and mess your oven in return.'

'You'd be most welcome.'

The red-rimmed eyes inspected him for signs of sarcasm. After all, how many years was it since curiosity about his life had last assailed her with sufficient force to cause her to visit? Was it to the flat before this one? Or the one before that? But suddenly what Dilys had main-tained for years was simply another sign of her indifference now seemed an important, even, perhaps, a necessary bulwark against insecurity: the desperate need of someone fragile, someone vulnerable, to stay, poised for battle, on the ground she knew best.

And she was vulnerable indeed now. Perdita would soon be back, out to intimidate her into selling up with talk of hideous rebuilding or repair costs, and policies rendered instantly void by one small fraudulent response.

All stuff heard first at Dilys's table.

And from his lips.

'How about a little salad, then, Mother?'

'No, not for me.'

'Well, perhaps some soup . . . ?'

He inched towards the larder. Yes, there on the shelf behind the jars of beetroot gathering dust lay the spare key he'd begged for a score of times on the grounds of his convenience and, more recently, her safety. He might have spread the chicken's entrails on the table top, so strong his hunch the moment was auspicious, the time had come. With the sense of a Rubicon resolutely crossed – no fuss, no guilt, not even any doubt – he picked the old key off the sticky shelf and dropped it in his pocket, content to trust to luck that he could get a copy cut and sneak it back before she noticed. Safer than asking again, in case, sensing the way the seesaw of their lives had finally, irrecoverably, risen on his side, she petulantly shifted it to some other hiding place where he couldn't even find it.

Still steeped in calm, he emerged from between the shelves holding a bag of ancient pasta. 'Macaroni cheese?'

She didn't even hear. Shaking the dome into another fierce storm, she'd jammed her sunken face as close to the glass as Tam had earlier. What could it be about these self-sufficient little blizzard worlds that they should have the power to send all who peered into them into a trance? Some, like Tam, simply dreaming; some, like his mother, seeing worlds they'd been denied from twists of temperament; and some, like Mel, gazing at dreams they'd worn as close as cotton to the skin, and only had to shelve because some precious little accident of fate had—

Mel!

He must get back to her as soon as possible! Tell her that he'd been wrong, and she must, after all, leave Tam with him to go and kick sense any way she could into this tiresome Alexi. Surely if she showed up, free of the sweet encumbrance whose birth had done so much to prick the man's pride, he'd have to crack. Tam could be slid in later. What was important was getting Mel back to the circus. All very well to come to this new, charitable understanding of his own mother. But how could he live with himself, how could he watch his mother sink, still so unsatisfied, towards her death, if he could not forget that, through his craven shrinking from responsibility, he'd been a part of letting someone else fetch up on that sour path to pinched lips and a bitter life, where the sole pleasure came from taking revenge on yourself and everyone round you for what life had denied you.

Now it was his turn not to be even listening. 'Sorry?'

'I said, perhaps the tiniest sliver of chicken, then. I might just force it down. Since it's my birthday.' She sniffed. 'So long as it's not one of those nasty Fifine's Fancy Truffle Maribou Whatsits.'

He'd learned that lesson. 'No, no. It's just plain frozen chicken from Betta-Shoppa.'

And if he hadn't already moved on from worrying about her life to worrying about two others almost equally dear, he might have heard, over and above his own impatient assurances, a warning louder than the oven's ping.

9

ALL THE CALLS CAME IN AT ONCE: ARIF FROM ACCOUNTS, mystified at receiving a personal cheque from Colin for some two-year-old gas fire; Val, phoning from Priding General to say she'd just spotted his mother's name on a list of Emergency Admissions; and Shirley, ringing up from Reception. 'I have someone waiting for you here.'

'Who?'

'I'm afraid she's refusing to give her name.'

That sounded ominous. Could it be the ubiquitous Mrs Moloney? 'What does she look like?'

'Striking. She has the most astonishing eyes – though I have to say her hair is a bit of a bird's nest.'

Perdita!

But first things first. His heart already thumping, he phoned the hospital, only to find that, at the first mention of a 'suspect chicken supper', blood charged between his ears with such a surf-like roar that he took in little more than that food poisoning in someone his mother's age was a serious matter, and in all likelihood she'd be in hospital for several days. Should he avenge himself on Betta-Shoppa by dropping the details of their freezer department's malefactions straight in the tray marked 'forced to decide to prosecute'? Or face his own guilt? How many unmarked boxes in the back of a van could one man muddle? Offered the quite unprecedented chance to do away with half of the villains round Chatterton Court without the trouble or expense of trial, he had instead managed to poison only his poor old mother – oh, and of course, if there'd been leftovers, poor Flossie as well. (He'd have to put that high up on his morning's list – check Holly House for corpses.) Sweating, he dug in his pockets for a tissue, and ended up scattering a shower of paper scraps studded with Clarrie's laborious handwriting on the floor round his desk.

He picked them up and inspected them one by one. 'Phone Mr H.' 'That Mr H. rang.' 'Mr H. *again*.'

Taking it as a sign, he sat and stared.

Then, like a miner knocked half insensible as the supports around him began to topple, he found himself dragging his weakened, battered self towards the only chink of light that he could see by picking up the phone book and turning to the Hs.

Tammy was sitting on the desk, helping Shirley sort out the mess in her handbag.

'I'm glad you're here. I run a switchboard, not a crèche.'

Alerted, Tam raised her head, and, spotting Colin, peremptorily stretched out her arms. Obediently, he scooped her into his own. 'So where's her mum, then? In the Ladies'?'

'Gone.'

'*Gone?*'

Shirley handed him the key to the lock he'd insisted on changing himself, the day some passing drunk fetched up sprawled on Mel's carpet. 'She said she was sorry to dash off, but you knew all about it, and it turned out the train left earlier than expected.'

Slyboots! Small wonder that she hadn't been there earlier, when he went knocking.

'So she just dumped Tam and ran?'

Colin surveyed his options. If he asked Clarrie to babysit, she'd have him in front of an industrial tribunal faster than you could say 'inappropriate request'. If he took Tam with him to hospital, he would quite possibly be adding a heart attack to the inflictions he'd already unleashed on his mother. And, now that his council insisted, for safety reasons, that each 'child care facility' provided a countersigned list of 'parent-approved emancipators', he couldn't even dump her at nursery for fear they wouldn't give her back at the end of the morning.

Perhaps the hospital had a crèche. Or Val! If she was still round there, perhaps he could—

A wagging finger fetched his attention back. 'So, young lady! Tam's the name you were hiding, is it?'

He owed Shirley a touch of civility. She must have held the fort for a good twenty minutes while he made his phone calls. 'Her name's Tamina, really.' He gave her chubby legs a little squeeze. 'She's Miss Tamina Poppy Gould.'

'Really?' Shirley looked startled. 'Then we had someone in here yesterday, trying to find her.'

'Find Tam?'

'Tamina Poppy Gould. Not a name you'd forget, is it?

201

He was a courier with one of those envelopes. I don't think he'd realized that we mostly go by street addresses. In the end I just lent him my phone book and he spent half an hour copying down Goulds.' Clearly the topic of surnames had set Shirley's mind working, for now she turned to ask, with studied innocence, 'So where are you off to now, Tamina? Up to the office with Daddy?'

It was a smart trick but it didn't work.

'*Not* Daddy. *Col*.'

He bore her off on his shoulders, taking the service lift to avoid any gauntlet of comment or query. His list was getting longer by the minute. What was it now? First, track down Perdita's little man to see if he could take advantage of Mel's being away to whip into her flat and brighten it up a bit. Then buy the child a car seat. Take her with him to do a quick dead dog check at Holly House. (How would one tell?) Cake somewhere other than the Little Bakery. Then off to the hospital via Bellamy's children's knickerwear department, since it was obvious that Mel had had even less time for the niceties than usual, and from the rather disquieting odour clinging around his collar, had clearly left him – the agent for her revivified hopes of a glittering future – not only with no choice in the matter of babysitting, but also, manifestly, with an unbathed child.

It was as if his sister took no interest at all.

'Any day,' he was telling her. 'But after eleven. Before that they're all busy with doctors and stuff.'

Did that faint tapping mean she hadn't even stopped on her keyboard? 'I can't think why you're telling me all this, Col. I shan't be going.'

'But she's *ill*.'

'*So?*'

'If you'd seen her—'

As he had, only an hour earlier, unrecognizably swamped in some bright, white, frilly-necked hospital gown, her wispy hair afloat round the pink scalp, her fingers picking at the coverlet as she asked him anxiously, 'Have you been round to the house?'

She'd sounded very odd. Was she having trouble breathing? 'Don't worry. Floss is fine.'

The pinched face had fallen back, less anguished, against the pillows. 'How did you get in?'

He'd taken a stab in the dark — 'Went round to Ruby's' — and waited, fearing he might have to take off rather promptly on some other tack about Ruby recommending a locksmith, or something. But, no. He'd guessed right. Ruby had a key, because, brushing the matter of the house aside with a feverish twitch of her fingers, his mother had reverted to her worries about its only other occupant. 'So Flossie was at least smart enough not to clear the dish?'

Colin shrugged off the picture of Tam, only an hour before, sitting merrily on the kitchen table, swinging her chubby legs in and out of the mop's path as he gave the floor one last disinfecting swill after cleaning up dozens of revolting little messes. Let Mother worry only about herself. 'No. Floss is fine.'

And now, it seemed, his sister, too, was only interested in the dog. 'I certainly hope you aren't planning to ask me to look after that mangy old mutt of hers.'

'No, no. The ambulance men dumped her with Ruby.'

'I thought Ruby hated animals.'

'Well, that's how it goes,' snapped Colin. 'When someone old gets sick, most people put a little human kindness ahead of their own convenience.'

His sister took snapping lessons from no one. 'Don't lecture me on how to deal with family! If you'd ever had the guts to stand up to her, maybe she would have made the effort to be nicer, and a bit more worth visiting.'

' "Worth visiting"?'

'Oh, sneer away, Col! But don't forget it's wimps like you who let her get away with it all her life.' He held the phone a little further from his ear, and, as Dilys hectored, leaned across the desk to draw a really rather passable upside-down Flossie under the tree with sticky-out branches that Tam was busily dotting with bright red leaves. No point in interrupting. If Dilys wanted his views on anything, she could always take the opportunity of stopping talking to ask him.

And he felt sorry for her. She was about to be the loser, after all. One of the things that had struck him so forcibly that morning was how much easier it was to feel warmth for his mother now he had seen her in this different guise. Maybe the reason old people were so tiresome was because all they generally offered was The Recipe As Before: their austere childhoods, endless fussing about teaspoons, or moans about health. That, after all, was why he had invented *Swap-a-Wrinkly*, his brilliant game show in which frustrated carers could put their old folk up for swaps, and get to take home someone whose ailments and confusions and obsessions might at least bear the stamp of novelty. Like all his other inspirations, it hadn't ended up on television; but he was getting to play it now, as solitaire. Over the past few weeks, he had been privileged to watch a woman in whose harsh, battling nature bitter self-pity had always been uppermost soften and – oh, say it fearlessly – get nicer and *nicer*, until today, with the stuffing so comprehensively – almost literally – knocked out of her, there'd even been a touch of acceptance in her character, and, if you chose to interpret her silences charitably, a hint of gratitude. It would be good to stand at her grave's edge and think on that while Dilys had to stand, cold and unfeeling. For it was always better, surely, to miss at least some part of the departed – regret their passing in some way, however small, however fleeting. Or what had been the point of all that time spent sitting reading the papers together, or listening to their grumbles as you dumped your spurned groceries out on the table? No doubt Dilys was technically in the right. No doubt, viewed as a moral conundrum, he was being as spineless and irrational as she claimed. He could even see the force of her argument. After all, looked at in one way, it was unassailable. If, all your life, you'd had a selfless, loving parent who in their last years turned cantankerous and mean, pretty well anyone would agree that you should try to look on these startling new traits of character as nothing more than disfiguring twists to do with a steady softening of the brain, and press on as kindly and determinedly as you could, right to the end. So why shouldn't the reverse hold? Why shouldn't Dilys have the right to judge their mother by her long, willed past? And, having found her wanting, why shouldn't Dilys stick to judgements made? What he was offering her was not the person she had known. So why should she waver in her response? Unless, of course—

A nudge at his fingers forced him back to the moment. Tammy was shoving at his hand. 'I don't want that!' Startled, he looked down. Under her brightly spotted tree, he'd drawn a grave with unkept grass, and he was halfway through the careful lettering of his mother's name.

In his left ear, the hectoring voice took on an even sharper edge. 'Who's that?'

'Who?'

'Talking.'

He laid his fingers on his lips and grinned at Tam. 'Just someone in the office.'

'Sounds like a *child*.'

He drew a huge smile on his drawing of Flossie, to make Tam giggle.

His sister sounded even tenser now. Had Marjorie's talk of secret lives sprung back to mind? 'It *is* a child. Col, how come you have a child there?'

He drew a little pile of dog poo next to Floss, to remind Tam of the mop game. 'Oh, you know council offices. Short-staffed in the crèche? Clarrie doing someone a favour? Who's to say?' He winked at Tam. 'But I can tell you this. The little lady concerned is not only very charming and an excellent artist, but I just happen to know that she's wearing a brand-new pair of knickers with spotty yellow cats on.'

And for reasons he would have been hard pressed to explain, it gave him the most enormous satisfaction to hear Tam snigger loudly inches from his own phone just seconds before his sister, exasperated, slammed down her own.

* * *

Colin watched anxiously as Perdita's ancient little handy-man let drop the last of the boxes and wrinkled his nose. 'Bit of a rabbit hutch, isn't it?'

Was he referring to the dimensions? Or the smell from Chaffer's Bonemeal? Attempting to ride both horses, Colin pulled shut the window while admitting apolo-getically, 'Well, yes. It is compact. But all the woodwork could be brightened up as well. And it will need to be back to rights by the time the tenant gets home tomorrow.'

Mr Walter tugged open a cupboard, then closed it fast, to stem the avalanche. 'Won't take that long.' Perhaps at the thought of having asked Colin to carry so much gear up so many flights of stairs for such a small area of paint-work, he suddenly felt the need to offer his own version of an energy-sensitive suggestion. 'Unless we take the opportunity to go for the works, in which case this window frame is going to need a proper—'

'No, no,' said Colin, taking fright at the thought of how much he'd committed himself to already that morn-ing. 'A lick and a promise. Just bright and cheery by tomorrow night. If you could do the woodwork more or less the same white as before.' He twisted the larger of his paint cans round in its box to peer at the label and refresh his memory. 'And the walls in this Warm Spanish Ivory.'

'That's just pink.'

From a host of conversations overheard at the water cooler, Colin knew this to be nonsense. 'Well, I'm not exactly sure—'

But Mr Walter was clearly climbing into his professional

stride along with his overalls. '*Pink*. You can call it whatever fancy name you like. But if you'd only had the sense to come to me, I could have tipped some red into a can of cheap white, and Bob's your uncle. You and the young lady would have walked away a whole lot better off.' He sounded so like Tubs Arnold that Colin suddenly felt at ease, willingly picking his way between buckets and boxes to give a hand shifting Mel's table into the middle of the room, and stacking clutter beneath it. Mr Walter pushed open the door to Tam's sleeping space. 'This bit as well? Not much of it, is there? Shame about the kid having no window. Still, makes you grateful.' Without stopping to explain quite for what, he tugged the tiny bed away from the wall and started hurling Tam's toys onto the coverlet. Hastily, Colin reached over to snatch up the snowstorm which had presumably been set on the shelf by the bed in the hope of enticing her into it quicker. Then he slid past to rescue the precious Las Venturas poster, before Mr Walter mistook its value from the crumbling corners.

Even when rolled, it looked vulnerable. 'Safe in there, maybe?' suggested Mr Walter, pointing to the box in which Colin had carried up the paint cans. Colin glanced round. If things went badly with the proud Alexi, Mel would come home so tetchy that, notwithstanding any nice new gleaming woodwork, she'd still give him a roasting if anything was damaged. So, lifting off the arm of the sofa some floppy red garment he'd often seen on Tam when she was playing 'Lavenders', he wrapped it carefully around the snowstorm and jammed the bundle between the padded paws of Tam's teddy. He wedged the whole lot in the box. The rolled-up poster fitted snugly between the bear's sturdy upright legs. That should be safe. Colin looked round again. There were a few tatty photos. Prudently he added those. And all the bits and pieces of paperwork behind the clock. Some of those might be to do with Mel's benefits. Best not let any of that get mislaid, even for a day or two, or she might starve. While Mr Walter unsystematically shunted his paint pails and boxes around in the search for his sanding brick, Colin strolled round the flat on one last trawl, shocked, after a lifetime of watching his sister lay up little treasures, to find scarcely enough of value to fill up one carton.

Saved by the bell. (Except that, being broken, it was a rapping on the door.)

'Sign for this, please.'

Still on his knees, he leaned across the boxes to take the proffered envelope and scribble his name on the courier's worksheet. It formed a perfect layer of padding for the top.

And he was done.

Mr Walter was eyeing him hopefully. 'So you'll fetch up those dust sheets for me, will you, on your way down again?'

He had no choice. The fellow looked as frail as Mother. Making a mental note to send yet another memorandum to Hetherley about finding some way to fix vandal-proof grilles in front of the lift control panels, he accepted the car keys and picked his way once again through the jumble of paint stuff. This would make four trips, once he had lugged the floor sheets up again. At least he could clear some space, taking down that box with his mother's old toaster. Oh, God! His mother! Should he phone the hospital again? Or visit after work? Oh, Christ! Work! Only an hour earlier Clarrie had warned him of yet another message from that awful Braddle man; after a quiet week, Mrs Moloney had sprung out of the wood-work; and Arif was still acting little short of half-witted about that cheque for the gas fire. Not only that, but in the canteen yesterday he'd overheard a rumour that some-one called Lee had upset Shirley mightily by precipitately giving to her, rather than to the voicemail she was offer-ing, an all too graphic description of what he was hoping to do to some Haksar. So clearly Colin couldn't even chalk the Battle of Sperivale Road up as a victory. Partly from prudence, partly from despair, he gazed around before unlocking Mr Walter's vehicle. What sort of world was this for Tammy to grow up in? Grim enough for her now as a child, stuck in this place of the damned, ringed by cars with flat tyres and smashed windows, and menacing-looking vans like that one he kept seeing by the gates, behind whose blacked-out windows God knows what ghastly urban hell-hole practices were taking place.

And, when she was older, ready to face her share of obligations, just like him?

Just worse. Yes, that described it. Worse, worse, worse.

At least his mother had picked up a bit.

'Who's this, then?'

'Tammy.' (Brazen it out.) 'I was supposed to drop her off at nursery for a friend.' He lifted Tam onto the only available chair – a high-backed, somewhat thinly cushioned commode – and watched her stare at his mother as though at a witch in a pantomime. 'But somehow we never quite seemed to get round to going, and then it wasn't worth bothering.'

His mother laid a hand proprietorially on the magazines he'd dropped on her bed. 'Don't think I'm letting her loose on my Shinies.'

'No, no. She's fine.' And indeed Tam sat riveted, till her attention shifted to a stray hairgrip floating strangely from an invisible strand of his mother's hair. She tugged at him, wanting to share this mystery. His mother peered back with a wicked squint. 'Bit of a fidget, isn't she? She had better behave or they'll shove her in the broth pot.'

Tam's rapt face froze. Colin dropped a hand onto her shoulder. He might have been hoping his mother would intimidate her just enough to keep her on her best behaviour around all these sick ladies. He hadn't wanted her to be traumatized for life.

'She's all right. And we won't be stopping long.'

'Good thing. I've already been savaged half to death by one surprise visitor.'

A feeling of the most enormous relief swept over Colin. So Dilys had come! He was no longer solely responsible for every decision. He could phone Dil tonight, and they could put their heads together. Between the two of them, brother and sister, they could—

'Yatter, yatter! I could have grown a beard down to my feet by the time she took breath.'

Tammy looked fascinated. 'Well, there you go,' said Colin diplomatically. 'Lots to catch up on.'

'I honestly thought the woman would never go!'

It was, he told himself, quite understandable. To pick up even the most casual of friendships after so long would

211

have been tiring. To see a daughter after five whole years—

'Nosy, fat cow! Sat in that chair, proud as a bump on a log, and still wearing that nasty green bogey.'

'Oh, you mean *Elsie*!'

'Who did you *think* I meant? I don't think that black-hearted goblin on the other side is likely to visit – unless it's to bring me a bowl of poisoned soup.'

Tam's eyes were huge. Ladies with beards down to their feet. Fat cows and bogies. And now goblins bringing poisoned soup! She clutched at Colin's fingers – a solid comfort as his spirits sank.

His mother didn't miss the tiny gesture. 'I see Miss Kitty Knickers thinks you're something special.'

Again, Tam's face went rigid.

'Yes,' Colin said, suddenly certain from the shape of a long dark absence just what a father ought to be. Exactly what he'd been wanting all those years he sat like Tammy with his lip trembling and his eyes too bright. What Tammy needed now. Simple as that.

'Yes,' he said, scooping her up again. 'She thinks I'm the bee's knees. And I think she's pretty special. And you're just jealous because you don't have beautiful new knickers with spotty yellow kittens.'

That easy. You'd think he could have done it years ago, just for himself.

Dismissing him for a madman, his mother went back, unruffled, to the subject in hand. 'Ghastly woman, sat in that chair there, so fat she looked practically upholstered, turning the neighbours' whispers into shouts. The way she has it, even Ruby is complaining.'

'What? About Flossie?'

'I suppose so. I couldn't bring myself to listen. She wittered on and on. I thought Christians were supposed to bring comfort to the sick, not simply drone on interminably about dirt and mess and noise.'

His heart stopped. Dirt and mess and noise?

Oh, this could be disastrous. This could upset the applecart and have her out of bed a day too early.

'*Noise?*'

His mother reached for the topmost magazine and flicked through the pages. 'Noise, indeed! Why, the poor lambkin has barely the strength to whimper these days, let alone bark.' She settled on a double page, and, suiting her actions to the last words she bothered to bestow on him, said rather distantly, 'Well, naturally, as you'd expect, I just stopped listening.'

And thank God for that.

They had their first real spat on the steps to the nursery. 'I want to come with *you.*'

'No,' he said, strapping Val's advice over his anguished heart like a breastplate. 'You have to stay here. I have to go to work.'

The face went pouty and the voice resentful. 'I want my *mummy* and I want to go *home.*'

What had Val said? 'Try not to argue. Just tell her firmly how things are. She'll feel much safer.' Then she'd let fall that last small droplet of advice that kept him staring at the ceiling almost till dawn. 'And don't, for God's sake, tell her her mum's coming home today, in case she doesn't.'

Now Tam was setting off purposefully back down the steps. Catching her sleeve, he asked her, 'Don't you want to show everyone at nursery your nice new frock?'

'No.'

'Or your nice new hairslides?'

'No.'

'Or your nice new knickers?'

For just a moment, she was torn. Then, with an equally petulant, 'No!', she pushed him away, to carry on stomping down the steps. Val had warned him to use bribery only *in extremis*. Was this *extremis* yet? He hurried to get further down, to stop Tam in her tracks, eyeball to eyeball. 'What say we make a deal? I'll give you something nice, and you go into nursery like a good girl.' A wave of shame swept over him. Could Mel herself have cracked any faster or acted more craven? 'Sweeties? How about sweeties?'

She could have been some mafiosa spitting out her last offer. '*Chocolate.*'

Chocolate? Anything chocolate in the back of the van would be courtesy of Betta-Shoppa and months past its date stamp. But Clarrie would kill him if he was late again. Sighing, he led Tam to the back of the van. How could good intentions take a dive so fast? Was this what dragged Mel down – her pristine, hopeful mornings dissolving into threats and bribery before the two of them had even made it up the nursery steps? Decanted with such swift ease onto the path to sloppy parenting, he made a massive effort to change course. 'Right, then,' he backtracked. 'You let me take you into nursery where you'll have a really good time. And when I come to pick you up, I'll bring you an apple.'

He might have said he was about to boil her in oil. Outrage pumped through her. Out of her scarlet face came a screech that would have incapacitated even his department's impressive new noise monitor. A passing car braked in alarm, and heads turned down the street. What should he do? Clap his hand over her mouth? Give an urbane fatherly chuckle? Or simply flee? '*Sssh!*' he hissed desperately. 'Sssh, Tam! All *right*! I give in. You can have chocolate. *Lots* of it. *Now*.'

The cheeks were still sheeted with tears, the lip a petulant shelf and the look chillingly baleful.

But she'd at least gone quiet.

Trembling, he flung open the van doors. Which were the boxes impounded from Betta-Shoppa? That one? No. That was the one with the toaster, surely. But, shoving it aside, he had doubts. It seemed far too heavy. Raising a flap, he caught sight of a furred paw and leaped back, startled, before realizing one of his mix-ups for once had proved lucky. Rather than poison his darling with gangrenous chocolate, he would be able to let her take her teddy to nursery.

'Look, Tam – Tam?'

The patter of footsteps stopped his heart. The world bleached round him. '*Tam!*'

Oh, Christ! Oh, Christ Almighty! Had she slipped round the van doors? Was he about to hear the sickening screech, the skull-splitting crunch of all his old nightmares? Where in God's name had—?

'No point in *calling*.'

He spun to face a woman struggling backwards up the steps, dragging a pushchair. 'Sorry?'

'They've both gone.'

'*Gone?*'

The woman nodded upwards. Sure enough, round the fluted pillars two little figures weaved a complicated skipping path towards the door. How could a child's mood switch so fast from murderous to merry? And what was that wafting back so cheerily? Was it *singing*?

He could have cried himself into a pulp from sheer relief. My God. Did poor Mel have to ride this roller-coaster every day? Small wonder she preferred the terrors of mere gravity.

'Bugger!' The woman was still struggling to tug the chubby pushchair wheels up the steep steps. 'I have to go in anyhow. Do you want me to take up Tam's lunchbox for you?'

Lunchbox?

'Save you a couple of moments . . .'

His senses returned and he sprang up the steps to grasp the foot bar under the shoe of the sleeping toddler and help her to the summit. Lunchbox? Another bloody mystery of life! And yet another half an hour gone, chasing up foodstuffs. Would it be totally out of line to arrange for delivery of a pizza? And he'd been so proud of himself, following all Val's advice to the letter. Now look at him. *Shattered*. In the last sixty seconds he had sailed close to being responsible for his small charge's death by apoplexy, street collision, chocolate poisoning, and now, it seemed, lunchtime starvation. Oh, it was very much a chastened Colin who crept past Clarrie's desk nearly half an hour later – over an hour late – vowing that he would never again think ill of any pre-schooler's mother for profanity, carelessness or alimentary dereliction.

Clarrie was standing admiring her nails in the light from the window.

'I see you're still being followed by that horrid Braddle man.'

'Followed?' Had all the fiends from hell been offered some day out to torture him? He hurried over. 'Where?'

'Inside that van.'

She pointed. Just the other side of the gates, a perfectly normal dark van was parked on the double yellow line. It was the sort of van seen fifty times a day, in front, behind, parked on a side street, swinging round a corner.

'*Following* me?'

Like the one that had pulled out behind him when he was leaving his mother's . . . Like the one he'd suspected of harbouring robbers . . . Like the one that housed perverts in Chatterton Court car park . . . The sort he'd seen only that morning when he was dropping Tam at nursery, and again as he drove round the Stannard Street roundabout.

'Are you *sure*?' He was terrified. 'For Christ's sake, Clarrie! Why on earth didn't you *tell* me?'

'I like that! I told you for about the millionth time only yesterday morning!'

'You did not! If you had mentioned I had a thug on my tail, I think I'd have remembered!'

'I *told* you,' she insisted. 'I was standing here at the window when he rang, and I distinctly remember saying, "No point in your pretending you're not here."'

'You didn't tell me that was because you could see

the bloody man phoning from some van outside!'

'What difference did that make? He's been phoning you from everywhere else in the world for *weeks*.'

'My God!' For a moment he stared down at the van in a paralysis of terror. Then he made shift to save his own bacon. 'Well, whatever it is the man wants, we had better get on with it right this minute.'

'Don't drag me into this. I'm not working through my coffee break. I've done my bit. I've taken all his nasty phone calls and put dozens of notes in your in-tray. It's not my fault that all you've ever done is push them away or tear them into pieces.'

He felt a worrying stir of memory. Fishing in his jacket pocket, he fetched out a handful of torn scraps. Ignoring Clarrie's self-righteous look, he pushed the papers on his desk aside to spread them out, only to stare at them helplessly till Clarrie softened and came over to help him. 'Well, that bit obviously goes there. And that joins up with this bit. And though you've lost a corner here, I reckon—'

Fright turned him snappy. 'You *wrote* the bloody things! Can't you *remember*?'

'Well, this one was something about warning you, I do remember that.'

'*Warn?*' He stared down. 'I thought that word was "*warm*".'

'No, *warn*. I definitely remember that.' Her fingers whipped the scraps round on the desk. 'That bit here, and that there. There's a patch missing, but that's sort of what it looked like.'

He peered at the little he could read of his fate.

Something deeply disquieting about '*seeing to it*'. And could that bit say '*fired*'?

'I shouldn't worry,' she consoled him. 'No one will fire you. After all, you've spent enough time trying to sort it out.'

Desperate for comfort, he asked her, 'Have I?'

'Of course you have! Only last Monday you were gone for hours.'

'Was I?'

'Of course you were. Don't you remember? After the police rang.'

'That was the *restaurants*. This is Mr *Braddle*.'

'No, *Haksar*,' she corrected, pointing. 'See? "Phone Mr H."'

'You just said "Braddle".'

'No, I didn't.'

'You did. I *heard* you. You've been saying "Braddle" all along.'

'No need to *snap*. It's just I always mix up things like that a bit.'

'For Christ's sake! Things like *what*?'

'You know. Spanners and braddles and haksars and stuff.'

Could she mean *bradawls*? And *hacksaws*?

The coldest of lights dawned. 'Clarrie! Are you trying to tell me that ever since this row between the restaurants blew up, it has been Mr *Haksar* who has been phoning to threaten me?'

Clarrie was back to inspecting her fingers. 'Well, to be fair, not *openly*. Not till he said what he did by accident while Shirley was still listening.'

He stabbed his finger along the scraps of paper, making the closest he could come to sense of them. ' "I *warn* you . . ." "*see to it* . . ." "*fired*". That's bloody open enough, isn't it?'

She gave him one of her baleful don't-you-get-ratty-with-me looks. 'What I mean *is*, he never actually lets on it's him. It's just I recognize his voice from when you sent me there to steal those poppadoms.'

'Not "steal",' he reproved her automatically. ' "Legitimately purchase for the purpose of testing" . . .'

But she'd turned sullen now. 'It's not as if cumin seeds even *look* like mouse turds.'

'If someone makes a complaint, then I'm obliged—' He broke off. 'For God's sake, what's *this* got to do with any of it?'

'It's just I'm not surprised the man's fed up with you, that's all.'

The icy fingers of terror slid back round his heart. '*How* fed up?'

Embarrassed, Clarrie went back to scratching at an invisible blemish on her top coat of varnish. 'Do you mean, what's he been *saying*?'

He kept his temper. 'Yes, Clarrie. Exactly that.'

'Well . . .' She turned her attention to her perfect thumbnails. 'I try not to listen for more than a moment. But once there was something rather nasty about hanging you upside down by—'

Delicately, she broke off and went down another track. 'Oh, and he thinks people like you should—'

Again, tact stopped her finishing. 'And when he phoned this morning, he said that now he's finally worked out where you live—'

'The man said that? This *morning*? *When*?'

She gave one of those careless little shrugs of hers that drove him mad. 'I'm not s—'

'Think! It's *important*. Think!'

She did a little brain search. 'I think it was just after I came out of the Ladies'.'

Eight forty, if the coven was on form.

Just after he had yet again given up on Mel answering her door, and had hurried down the stairs and out of Chatterton Court, back to his car.

'Oh, yes. And *once* I remember that he said to me—'

But Colin was no longer listening. He had pushed past her and was gone.

10

COLIN CAME UP BEHIND THE POLICEMAN AND THE TWO FIRE officers just as the building's innards were collapsing. Professional interest was intense. 'Look at the way those walls are coming down – a textbook infill! I certainly hope all the trainees are paying attention.' The uniformed trio continued to gaze with satisfaction on the blaze. 'No, the only possible disappointment has been the absence of Crispies.'

Even in Colin, curiosity could triumph. 'What's a Crispy?'

The officer who'd spoken turned. It turned out to be Jamie-boy, from the Battle of Sperivale.

'Back behind the rope line there at once, if you wouldn't mind, sir,' he ordered, failing to recognize Colin in his new roseate, firelit hue.

'You know me. I'm from Environmental Health.'

'Oh, right.' And Jamie stepped aside to make a space for Colin in the favoured front row for the rest of the spectacle. Though he didn't go so far as to explain the word Crispy, its meaning clearly informed his next glum utterance: 'Not a single fatality. Everyone safely out, tickety boo, on the tarmac.'

One of the fire officers obviously shared his disappointment. 'Well, for that, of course, you have only the lifts to blame.' Catching his colleague's warning eye, he corrected himself hastily. 'I mean, to thank.'

In the face of this burning vista of destruction, Colin's intense anxiety about the performance of council fittings would not, he hoped, sound out of place or excessive. 'What's that about the lifts?'

Jamie went back to watching coils of water being spilled from a great height. 'All broken, weren't they? Every last one. Doors wouldn't even close. So no one, not even the absolute thickies, could manage to get stuck in them.'

Again, the fire officer beside him unguardedly added his own note of regret. 'Ergo, no Crispies.'

'Still,' Jamie insisted, nodding at the throngs of rosy-flushed faces behind, absorbed in the blaze. 'Bit odd that they *all* got out.'

He said it almost as though it offered grounds for suspicion.

'Train of events,' explained the fire officer. 'It seems that someone on the fifth floor still had an active battery in a smoke alarm. So it went off.' He turned to Colin. 'It was a dicky toaster that started it all, apparently.'

The sudden flaring of the nearside ground floor went some way to disguising the rush of blood to Colin's cheeks. 'A dicky toaster, did you say?'

'That's right. This ancient little painter guy felt a bit peckish, lifted his dust sheet to notice some old toaster in a box, and didn't think twice until he smelled burning. Even then, he says, he could have had the little bonfire out in a trice, but for the fact that he tripped on a pile of boxes cluttering up the place and sent a bottle of white spirit flying.'

It was, Colin upbraided himself, nobody's fault but his own. The black miasma that was Perdita seeped far and wide. He should have known that, just as a sorcerer needs only the slightest of fingernail parings to wreak the worst of voodoo witcheries, so asking Perdita's little painter man to slosh a bit of emulsion around Mel's walls would be enough to bring a curse on all their heads.

'But what about the sprinklers?'

Everyone turned to stare.

'On the stairs,' persisted Colin. 'Were they not working?'

They looked at him as if he were a man unhinged.

This time, the flickering firelight disguised a face from which all colour drained. 'What, *none* of them?'

Out of sheer pity at his innocence, they all turned back to watching the blaze. But the subject of sprinklers had rekindled the interest of the firemen. 'Be fair, mind. Even with half the sprinklers shot out and the rest bunged up with gum, you'd never usually get a fire as good as this.'

'Absolutely not. No, for that you must give credit to the person who dumped all those piles of old clothes in the basement.' The fireman held out a singed scrap of chequered brown tweed that Colin distinctly recalled his mother wearing to Aunt Ida's divorce hearing. 'Look! Textbook, that is. A quality material, soaked in cheap alcohol – possibly even meths – and dried off nicely in the boiler house.' He turned to the man beside him. 'I ask you, could you find a better form of tinder if you went searching?'

His colleague's tired shaking of the head implied he was a man of far more sense and experience than to bother to try.

'Not only that,' persisted the first fire officer, 'but it must have been a fair long while before anyone living here bothered to ring in and mention the building was alight.'

Colin flinched as a roar of flame shot up the last stair-well. His ears cleared to the sound of a carillon of agreement.

'No, can't get a blaze like this up without a good deal of local co-operation.'

'Still a close-run thing.'

'True. One single responsible citizen taking the trouble to phone 999, and it would never have got this far.'

Still, not even the thought of this unhappy possibility could take the edge off their good cheer. And as the last wall fell and the fire burned lower so they could finally see their colleagues on the other side playing their hoses in gorgeous glistening loops over the flaring rubble, Colin found his own spirits rising to match. Praise be to Mother! If she'd done nothing else in her long life, she had at least achieved what eighteen councils in a row had failed to do – get rid of Chatterton Court for once and for ever.

And, on this score, a party atmosphere seemed to be developing all round now. None of the flats' inhabitants appeared in the slightest bothered by this dramatic and colourful destruction of their habitat. Slipping back under the rope, Colin strolled between clusters of cheery people, some clutching a few possessions, one or two even guarding piles of plastic bags. After a while, he realized most of the conversations were centred round the happy coincidence of Tor Grand Insurance's recent Special Promotion: a taster offer of one month's free contents insurance, prior to checks or inspection. It seemed that, gamblers to a man, and furnished with prepaid envelopes and the chance to win a speedboat, pretty well everyone in Chatterton Court had, in the past week, whiled away a few unemployed minutes filling in an application form with some wildly inflated opinions of the value of their property. Indeed, the general view appeared to be that Mel's altruistic gesture of bribing her painter to set fire to the building had simply anticipated by a few days the plans of a slightly more dilatory gang of professional arsonists.

But, lest this thought seemed churlish, Mel was the happy toast of all. Some smouldering embers had been borrowed to start a small, informal baked-potato franchise. Much of the burning of the boiler house provided the flash and excitement of any reasonably colourful firework display. And, Colin noticed, the former denizens of Chatterton Court appeared to have every confidence that their council would provide, not simply adequate emergency accommodation overnight, but somewhere more permanent to live in the morning. Indeed, he heard the words, 'Nowhere they put us could be worse,' spoken so many times, and with such confidence, that it was a man on the verge of proud to call himself a council officer who wandered back towards the firemen as they reluctantly prepared to admit to themselves that, regretfully, the best of the show was now over.

'Still, *classic* while it lasted. Couldn't be faulted. And

if I'd had the sense to take a video of how that boiler blew, I'd have the great bulk of my men through their practical examinations first time.'

'Nice little run here, too, if you recall.'

'Splendid. Possibly even a record-breaker.' The fireman turned to Jamie-boy. 'You were on our tail all the way, weren't you? What do you reckon? Mount Oval down to here in under three minutes?'

'Two forty at the most. And if I'm being anything, I'm being hard.'

'Between here and Mount Oval?' Colin was filled with admiration, till he remembered they were allowed to speed through all his council's brooding lights.

Jamie-boy sighed. 'Would have been a sight faster, but for that idiot who shot ahead of us into the roundabout.' He turned to Colin. 'You know the bloke. You're always tangling with him.'

'*Me?*'

'Yes. What's his name? Stanley? Jemmy? You know! That nutter with the pods.'

'Pods?'

'All over the pavement. Crunch-crunch. Crunch-crunch. Outside his restaurant.'

'Do you mean *Haksar*?'

'That's the one. I hope he cooks a whole lot better than he drives. He was spinning round that roundabout like a nut in a blender.'

To a man less absorbed in a last pretty flare-up of the embers, Colin's distress might have been evident. 'Where was he headed, for God's sake?'

'Sorry?'

227

'When he came off the roundabout! Which way was he going?'

'Up towards West Priding – luckily for him, or we might just have stopped to book him for driving like a bloody astronaut on wh—'

But Colin wasn't listening. He'd already gone.

Mr Herbert could not have apologized more graciously or more often.

'I simply don't know what to say to you, Colin. My workmen know the rules about smoking on other people's property, and they're usually most careful.'

'Be fair,' the fire officer said. He was still panting from the second run. 'Your bloke was standing outside, after all. He was hardly to know those windchimes had been stuffed with tissue paper.' He shook his head admiringly. 'Nasty, floaty stuff, tissue. It catches all too easily. In my experience, it's part and parcel of a lot more fires than people are prepared to give it credit.' He gave Colin's mother's scorched buddleia one final going over with the last of the hose dribbles. 'Mind you, it was only luck that the wind happened to be in the direction of the woodshed.'

'*Bad* luck,' corrected Colin, since the man's more sensitive colleague had not yet managed to arrive in time to do so.

'And then there was that stripper in there – practically uncovered, if you please!'

Christ! Had he spotted Suzie?

'Paint's bad enough. But stripper! Well, you might as well drop matches in a tank of kerosene.'

They all gazed at the dripping, roofless ruin that had been Colin's hideaway. Then at the blackened walls of Holly House. 'It's only the back, really,' said the fireman, reeling in his emptied hose. His voice had taken on that tone of glum wistfulness with which Colin was becoming all too rapidly familiar. 'And a lot of that's nothing but smoke damage.'

'Still,' Mr Herbert said to Colin, 'I can't see your mother being very pleased.'

Colin gazed up at the windows, each with its brand-new sooty eyebrow. 'I could ask them to keep her in hospital another day or two. Till I've cleaned up a bit.'

He waited for Mr Herbert to offer to lend him a couple of men to give him a hand. But there was an uncomfortable silence, till Mr Herbert suddenly thought to dig in his breast pocket. 'Well, I can at least give you this.'

'What's that?'

'It's what you said you wanted when you rang in all that hurry.' Sensing there might be a moment of stickiness when he sent in the bill, Mr Herbert made a point of repeating in front of the fireman as an uncommitted witness, ' "Mr H.," ' you said. ' "Double time for your men if you can get that sodding Certificate of Approved Electrical Installation fixed up and watertight before my mother's out of hospital." '

'Really? Did I say "sodding"?'

Holy Joe Herbert shot him a look of reproof. 'Indeed you did. And as I said to Mrs H. at supper afterwards, that's not like Mrs Riley's Colin. In fact, frankly, after that sort of language, if it hadn't been for thinking of your poor dear saintly mother, I wouldn't have leaned on my men as hard as I did to get the job finished.'

Through phantom drifts of bills for restoration and repair, Colin sensed, rather than saw, his first real glimmer of hope since, skidding round Mount Oval, he'd seen the wreaths of smoke rising from beyond the end of Green Lane. Maybe his world was brightening. This fire, after all, had been an accident. Maybe, charged with some sense of inner satisfaction that came from presuming he had successfully reduced Colin's home to a heap of charred rubble, Mr Haksar had simply been shooting off with such verve to lay in a fresh supply of uncontaminated turmeric. Perhaps, when Mr Herbert so casually let drop the little word 'finished'—

'Finished? Did you say *finished*?'

Mr Herbert looked smug. 'Oh, yes. We had the cabling buried by last night. It was only trying to get that massive overgrown hydrangea back upright that fetched us back this morning.' He gazed round. 'Still, the garden looks nice again, doesn't it? I think the men have done a lovely job of stamping things back in. And just so long as anything that decides to die has the sense to take long enough, she might not even cotton it was your fault, Colin.'

Having sloughed off responsibility so stylishly, Mr Herbert turned back to the paperwork he was signing.

'You realize this form's dated back from months ago, when we first started working in the house. Will your mother mind that?'

'No,' Colin told him. 'She won't mind at all.'

And he practically had to force himself not to reach out and snatch it.

The fire officer snapped the catch on his portable hose reel. 'Well, that's me finished. Except, of course, for filling out your "dangerous structure" warning.'

'Dangerous structure?'

The fireman nodded at the only bit of woodshed that was still standing. 'That wall behind the mangle could come down in a puff of wind.'

'I could fetch it down now,' Mr Herbert offered, as if his conscience had been rather troubling him. The two professionals stepped with impunity through the permanent spell Colin kept laid across the threshold. He heard them chattering to one another. 'Look at this rubbish!' 'It is *astonishing*, isn't it, what people keep?' They were speaking, thought Colin, as though he were dead or unconscious, or nothing to do with the place he had spent half his life in. And then he realized it seemed an age since he'd been here. Running his fingers through the charred silt across the workbench, he wondered what he ought to save. Should he, for example, rescue his poor neglected Suzie, for old time's sake? He peered in the drawer, awash with hose water, and tugged it open, trying to pretend his only concern was for chisels. The magazine came out in a sodden lump. What were you supposed to do with books and papers that were soaking wet? Freeze them, then brush off water crystals, page by page?

Could he be bothered?

No.

The fireman rooted in the filth on the floor. 'Now that's worth saving.' He tipped the worst of the water out of the spell box and handed it to Colin. Inside was clutter from another lifetime. Some greasy stumps of candle. A few scummy mirror shards. The hawkmoth chrysalis was none the better for a proper soaking. The fox's tooth looked even dingier and more pathetic than usual. And there seemed far more stupid bleached chicken wishbones in the casket than he could imagine anyone ever wanting or needing.

Oh, and a photo of his father. He pulled it out, still sodden wet, and stared at it while the thoughts sprang. I'll be the opposite of you. Where you stayed silent, I'll speak up for her. Where you played blind, I'll see. But, most of all, when you were gone, I will be there. Always. *Whatever.*

It was a pretty box, though. She'd like that. She could keep something *nice* in it. Jewellery, or beads or hairbands. Something like that.

Turning it over, he emptied his warped childhood on the floor without regret, and glanced at his watch. My God! What with there being no word yet from Mel, he had only a moment to nip along and order more dog food before it was time to play safe and fetch Tammy.

How strange it felt – how very comforting – to have a deadline nothing to do with work. Or Mother.

'I have to go now,' he informed the two of them. 'I have to pick someone up from nursery.'

Nobody snorted. Nobody made a face. The fireman only asked him, 'What about this shed? Will you be taking Mr Herbert here up on his offer?'

'Yes,' Mr Herbert said, pleased to have come to terms with conscience so easily. 'Just say the word, Col.'

He looked from one to the other as they stood waiting. And then he simply said it. 'Yes. If you would, please. Take the whole lot down.'

* * *

The wail of sirens had brought the gardeners out in force along the backs.

'I see you're finally making a success of getting rid of that horsetail, Edmund.'

'Indeed yes, William. You see I'm working to a brand-new principle. "One in, three out".'

Colin found himself, as usual, spotted through a bare patch. 'Is that you, Colin? How is your poor, dear mother? Back amongst us soon?'

'Tomorrow,' Colin assured her. 'Failing that, Saturday.'

Today, nosiness was clearly taking precedence over disapproval. 'And things in the house? It wasn't your place, I hope, that all those noisy sirens were headed for earlier?'

Colin put on a burst of speed in the hope that the Mansons' thick beech hedge would screen the deceit in his headshake. But self-interest, as usual, had triumphed over general curiosity. 'You wouldn't happen to be off to the shop, would you, Colin? Would my asking a tiny little favour be in order? Just a packet of pins and a couple of bananas?'

'And twenty Kensitas, if you're that way anyway.'

'And if Mr Stastny should happen to have any more of those little jars of horseradish—'

Turning, he spoke up so everyone could hear first time. 'Happy to help. But I'm afraid that, this time, you'll all have to give me the money first, because I've left my wallet in the car.'

Could they have slid away faster, with less fuss? He stood entranced. How *easy* things were when you dared step out of half-light. It was like growing muscles, or getting wings. It was like—

That's right. It was like *living*.

Next time, he'd miss out that excuse about the wallet. Oh, yes, it was a sturdy and determined Colin who strode past the Emporium, whistling, to step in the shop and give Mr Stastny his order. Fearlessly he ambled back past the sprinkling of frost-tops still busy in their gardens, most of whom made great play of affecting not to notice him. Giddy with power, he slid in his car and made the vehicle coming up behind slam on its brakes as he pulled out. Driving back into town, he sped across two separate sets of amber lights. No sirens followed him. The world went on. He even dared leave the car up at the top end of Stemple Street without a ticket, gambling on getting back safely with Tammy before any warden dared slap on a fine. And it was only after he'd cut through the little alley beyond Market Square and, still humming cheerily, was taking the stone steps up to the nursery two at a time, that Colin even realized he'd just walked down Bridge Row without a thought.

What sort of personal landslide was going on here? What else could change?

His charmed life, in a blink, one step through the doors. 'Gone? *Where?* Who *took* her?'

The nursery helper was practically backing away from his panic. 'Nobody *took* her, Mr Riley. She went off early, with her mum.'

His world came back to rights. 'With Mel? Where?'

'I don't know. Home, I suppose.'

Best not to mention Mel no longer had one. Best just

to catch up, and then break the news. Would they be on the bus? Or walking back through Abbey Shopping Centre? Either way, if he drove fast he'd probably make it. Again his sense of purpose lent him wings. And over-keen sight. A half a dozen times he must have thought he'd spotted them, their heads together on some bus, or reflected in windows, only to realize he was staring at strangers. So by the time he finally overtook them, walking past Chaffer's Bonemeal Factory, his expectations had fallen so flat it was Mel who waved crazily, seeing the car slow.

'Col! Hope you didn't think Tam had been snatched. It's just I came home early.'

Early? In his book, she was already a day late.

She caught his look. 'Didn't you get my message?'

'Message?' He scrambled from the car in time to counter Tammy's suicidal charge into the street to greet him. 'Col! Col! We did *painting*.'

Mel sounded more peeved on her own behalf than his. 'Honestly! I couldn't have made it clearer if I'd tried. Your stupid switchboard put me through to the wrong place. But the man said he had to get in touch with you anyway about the bill for some gas fire. And since I only had a couple of—'

'It doesn't matter.' He had his Tammy in his arms, and nothing mattered. Though Mel did still have to be told. And, preferably, before she reached the end of the road and turned into Tanner Street.

'I'm afraid there's been just a little bit of trouble at the flats.'

'I thought you'd take her to spend the night at your own place. Or at your mother's.'

'And so I did. But—'

Too late. With some new elasticity in her stride, she'd covered the last steps and, turning the corner, seen in front of her, instead of the unfêted architectural bin-end of Priding's least-favoured civic son, just a vista of clear skies and sunlight.

'Col?'

Embarrassed, he shifted Tammy onto one arm, and slid the other through hers. 'Bit of a shock?'

She took another step forward. 'Where's it *gone*? What *happened*?'

Tam hadn't even noticed. All she was doing was poking sticky fingers in his hair, and twisting it tightly while she chattered about nursery.

'Bit of a chapter of accidents, I'm afraid. Too long a story to go into now.'

Even charred rubble could take a moment to make its point. But things were sinking in. 'Did it burn *down*? For God's sake! Is it *gone*?'

She sank on the kerb. After a moment's doubt, he lowered himself beside her, with Tam still clinging round his neck, smelling of poster paints and chocolate. They were sitting in a different street: sunlit, and shadow-swept. He could see all the way to Abbey Towers, and the sycamores beyond. He could see traffic shooting cheerfully over the hump of the West Bridge, and even the arch of the entrance to Vane Park. It was like being in another world. And suddenly the thought struck. After his mother died, would he sit with the stuffing this knocked out of him, as shocked as Mel, finding it almost as difficult to believe that such an overpowering presence had vanished from his life? Would he be sad, or glad? Or just amazed? And would he, afterwards, be at a loss, like some poor actor locked in a telly series for years and years, who, when the show was axed, found that he'd lost, not just the part he'd played, but the one thread that held his life together, and seemed more real than any of the roles he faced in all his involuntarily salvaged hours?

Best not to brood. Shifting Tam on his knee, he slid his arm round Mel, to comfort her. 'The general view, I think, is that, in the long run, it may all prove a bit of a blessing.'

Mel was indifferent to the long run and the general view. She shook him off. 'All right for you! My *things* were in there! What about my *stuff*?'

'Oh, well,' he said. 'I managed to save some of that.'

Tipping Tam off, he stumbled to his feet and led her and her mother back round the corner to point out the box he'd been ferrying about for a couple of days now.

The sharp-eyed Tammy spotted the paw first. 'Teddy!' Hurling herself headlong into the boot of his vehicle, she dug for her precious soft toy.

Mel wasn't far behind. 'Is that my benefit book? Thank God for that!' Pushing aside the envelope he'd dumped on top, Mel rooted deeper. 'Brilliant! You saved the photos!' She tugged out the poster he'd rolled so carefully. 'Is this——?' Unravelling an inch or two, just to be sure, she spun round to hug him – 'Oh, Colin! You're a gem!' – before turning back to her digging. 'And look! You even thought to save my first *ever* costume – my absolutely best lucky one. The one I love most in the whole world!'

She fell on the rag he'd taken for some dress-up.

He shot out a hand. 'Careful! I used that to wrap—'

'Lavender!' squawked Tammy, spotting her precious glass snowstorm. Fast learner that she was, she scrambled instantly into her car seat and held out her hands, already whispering. By the time he turned back, Mel had spread the glistening red costume against her body and, resting a hand on his wing mirror, lifted a leg to flex an ankle. Only two days away, and yet she looked so different. Had she grown taller? Stretching each foot in turn, she raised her legs both higher and more gracefully than he'd have thought possible. Her skirt fell away, exposing all too much leg for Colin, who dragged her attention back by flapping the envelope.

Mel tilted her head in the middle of a leg bend to glance at the sender's name, richly embossed in steel-grey letters across the top. 'Taw, Grant and Sorlence? Fine. Toss it out.'

All of the bureaucrat in him came to the fore. 'You have to read it, Mel,' he told her sternly. 'This isn't simply junk mail. I had to *sign* for it.'

'I like that! You were the one who told me I was to throw them away without bothering to read them.'

He stared at her. 'Sorry?'

She was far too absorbed in her stretching to notice his face. 'And a bloody good thing, too, or I'd be knee-deep in them. This must be the fourth, at least.' She took a moment from arching gracefully over backwards to chortle, 'Though none of them have been addressed to Melchior.'

'Melchior?'

The penny dropped.

'Not Taw, Grant and Sorlence, Mel! Tor Grand Insurance!'

Can someone bending like a lily shrug?

'Mel. *Read* it. *Now*. It might well be *important*.'

She raised her leg so high, his heart thumped. 'But they still sound like bailiffs or solicitors or something. And I've had quite enough bad news today. If you're so bothered, *you* read it.'

Bothered, he certainly was. What madness had come over him, to give instructions to someone so careless to toss post of any description away? What had he brought down on their heads? Imminent arrest for a failure to show up for jury service? A final summons for that gas fire?

Ripping open the envelope, he flattened the contents on his car roof and, ignoring her leg-lifts, began on the letter.

'Mel, I do think you really ought to listen to this. Mel—'

It was like trying to talk to human origami. Each time he glanced at her, she was a different shape. Who would have thought a body could slide with such ease from swallow to shepherd's crook, from sickle to gazelle?

'Mel, really. I was right. This is *important*.'

Now she was spinning like a top.

'Mel, stop that! Please! This *matters*. It's a letter to Tamina Poppy—'

'Who can't even read!'

'That's not the point. These people want to give her something.'

Now she was spinning the other way. 'She could do

with a new roof over her head. We both could. That's what you ought to be thinking about, Colin. Not—'

In his excitement, he had interrupted her. '. . . *in the absence of any indication of the invalidity of . . . and pending further and thorough investigation . . .*'

She was back on her body bends, resting each leg in turn on his car wing and stretching along it. 'It doesn't *sound* as if they want to give Tam anything. I'd say the bits you're reading out sound rather nasty.'

What were those raw red patches? Hastily, he looked away.

'That doesn't mean a thing. Frampton Commercial send round a circular that manages to make their annual fire extinguisher inspections sound like a favour. The fact remains' – he worked his way down through the dense unpleasantness of formal language – 'I'm almost sure these people want to give Tam money.'

'Oh, yes? How much?'

His eyes fell on the sum. 'My Christ! I don't believe it!'

Mel froze in the middle of a back bend.

'It's all In Trust,' he told her hastily. 'Until Tam's twenty-one.'

Mel snorted. 'Twenty-one!' Clearly the notion that this small creature in the car seat still cheerfully gabbling away to a tiny plastic girl in a glass ball might ever reach school age, let alone adulthood, was, to her, almost entirely unimaginable, and made the whole boiling seem even more fanciful. 'And what does "In Trust" mean?'

'That you can't spend it. Only the bits you'd need to send her to a good school and buy her uniform and—'

Losing interest at once, she went back to her stretching.

'I don't believe it anyway. It's all some stupid mistake. We don't know anybody who has any money – certainly not enough to hire some posh lot like this to dish it out. And if it really was us they meant, they'd be writing to me, wouldn't they? Not to Miss T. P. Gould who's only *three*.'

He wasn't listening for, in his mystification, he'd flicked over the page yet again to notice, this time, clipped to the back, a flimsy half sheet of handwriting beached in a sea of darkly speckled paper. It spoke of copies of copies, and was presumably part of a letter, trimmed to excise bits deemed irrelevant to Miss T. P. There were only a couple of paragraphs, and even these were written in a hand so crabbed and shaky they were hard to decipher. But some parts were clear:

'. . . *time of great grief and sorrow . . . learn who your true friends are . . . the only two people in the world to bother to sign my dear late husband's Book of Condolence . . . this thoughtful tribute to my beloved George Henry . . . moved to the quick . . . revoke all previous codicils . . . this little bequest . . .*'

Little?

He wasn't going to tell her now. They hadn't time – not till he'd visited Mother. Still, he couldn't help but mutter over the sharp little intakes of breath born of her stretchings. 'Not *that* bloody little!'

She wasn't listening. 'So who is this old bag who was so fond of her dear hubby?'

He flipped back to read Taw, Grant & Sorlence's letter reference aloud. '*Estate of the late Florence May Besterton.*'

Clearly her lack of curiosity about the money stemmed not from indifference but from disbelief. 'See? A mistake. I don't know anyone called Florence Whatsit.'

'Get in the car,' he ordered. 'I'll take you round to my place. You can stay there at least till I find out where they've rehoused you.'

She bent, just like a lily, one last time. And, as the breeze lifted the blouse from the back of her neck, he saw the bright raw graze. 'Mel! Have you been back on the trapeze?'

'Just making sure I could still—'

Wincing, he broke in on all her chatter about pikes, and back balances, and something distressingly referred to as 'skinning the cat'. 'Mel! For one thing it's *dangerous*. Especially if you're out of practice. And for another, you're a *mother* now. With serious responsibilities. You simply can't—'

'Oh, do shut up, Col.'

At least his fussing had driven her into the car. He turned to strap in Tam. Before they'd reached Mount Oval, Mel had abandoned her sulk and was rattling on cheerfully about the train ride and the look on Alexi's face when he slid down the rope at the end of his practice set, practically into her arms. She was still telling him all about the welcome in the caravans, and the parties that followed, when Tam started squawking about sweeties 'for Lavender!'.

'Oh, God!'

Unbuckling her safety belt, Mel turned and draped the top half of her body over the back of her seat to reach for the lemon drops Colin's speedy skirting of Mount Oval had sent skidding out of the child's reach.

'There! Happy?'

She twisted back and buckled up again, still filling him

in on things about which he hoped he'd never have to hear again: *corde lisse*, and roll-ups, and something she kept vertiginously referring to as the one-toe cross-over hang. But not before he'd spotted the angry red rope burn right across the very top of her leg. And the look of pure triumph that had utterly transformed her.

Absorbed as he was in the sight of the flames roaring upwards, he still noticed the police undercover agent taking his photo.

'Problem?' he asked her, proffering his card.

The woman looked shifty. 'It's just that you seem to have been to an awful lot of fires this morning.'

'Statutory duty,' lied Colin. 'Toxins pouring forth, and such. I'm afraid my department had been getting rather slack over the past few months and years. But a new government directive came round recently, so we've been trying to pull our socks up.'

God! Was this him? From barely articulate, he'd turned into as glib a liar as a poorly paid salesman on a used car lot forecourt.

'Still, three in one morning . . .' She shook her head and said, a trifle sarcastically, 'You'll be quite the world's expert now. Any idea how this one got started?'

'None at all, I'm afraid.'

'Know anyone who lives here?'

'Me.'

'Really?'

Embarrassed, she slid off. He watched a shower of sparks fly from his bathroom window. What could that be? His aftershave exploding? He was losing the whole lot. Anything he cared about? Not really, no. Guiltily his thoughts crept upwards, like the flames, to Mrs Singer's cosy flat above. She had been dazed and weeping as she'd been helped past. But, on the other hand, for some years now that very pleasant daughter-in-law of hers had been saying she'd be far better off in some form of sheltered accommodation. So maybe, even for Mrs Singer, this fire was a blessing in disguise. After all—

No! he recanted, remembering Val pointing out how very easily people managed to assure themselves that whatever suits them will suit the elderly. Like ghouls, she'd said, itching to nail down the coffin lids on the still undead. 'This car of yours is really just cluttering up the garage now, isn't it, Grandpa? Would you like me to—?' 'Bit hard to garden all this lot now you're on your own, isn't it, Doris? Would it help to sell me and Linda just enough of a strip at the back to build a—?' 'Mum, don't you ever worry about burglars spotting these valuable old pieces through the window? Would you feel a bit safer if—?'

The police nark was back at his elbow now. 'Have a quick word?'

He turned to see if Mel or Tam were getting restless. But Tam was still dead to the world in her comfy new car seat, and Mel was back to doing her ballerinery bits and bobs with her hand on his car wing.

Still. Three fires in one day. The sooner he was away from here, the better.

'I really should be getting along. My mother's coming out of hospital today, and—'

She brushed off her fleeting pretence of taking an interest. 'Young Jamie over there was just saying you'd

244

been having a few run-ins recently with some fellow called Hacksaw.'

'Haksar,' corrected Colin. He gazed, entranced, as, in a spilling, shimmering haze of colours, the inner floors fell. 'No. I'm quite certain that's all settled now.'

And bloody well ought to be. Haksar had done a good job. Everything he owned was gone. His sterile flat. His squeaky-clean appliances. The pictures he had never even glanced at. Odd bits of pottery abandoned by Helen. One or two personal documents a man of the desk like himself could get replaced in no time. And, most miraculous of all, the ghastly family sideboard his mother had decided she couldn't stand but wouldn't sell. 'I can't bear looking at it. *You* take it, Colin.'

All gone. All burned to ashes, unsought, undeserved. The last dregs of his boring life.

And, in his hands, the generous wherewithal to start another.

Nodding apologies, Colin turned back to his car, carrying only the envelope that the courier, bewitched by the sight that presented itself as he turned the last corner, had finally thought to tug from his saddle-pack, and, after a bit of discussion with the other onlookers, most of whom were neighbours, put in the hands of Colin Aloysius Riley, Esq.

Tracked down at last.

The minute he'd tipped the still-sleeping Tam out of his arms onto the sofa, his sister signalled him to follow her into the kitchen.

'For God's sake, Col! I'm having someone round. Is

there absolutely nowhere else you could think of leaving them?'

'Like where, for instance?'

'Well, your place, for starters.'

'I only just finished telling you. It's burned down.'

'I thought you said that was *her* place.'

'Yes, it was. First hers, then mine.'

'This is *insane*. Why can't you drop her off at some hotel? Or Holly House?'

'Oh, yes? Fetch Mother out of hospital to meet a stranger and a bouncy child?' He gave a shudder.

'Well, it's no more convenient for me.'

Edging past him, his sister made one small concession to hospitality by peering back through the doorway to check Mel wasn't listening. He saw her eyes widen. 'What on earth is she doing?'

He didn't even bother to look. 'Practising.'

'Practising what?'

'Her high-trapeze stuff.'

'Really?' Clearly, the romance of the circus had never seeped through to his sister's soul. 'Well, she can't stay here. I don't think Tara would get on with her at all.'

'What sort of person can't get on for one evening with a mother and child who've just been made homeless?'

'Someone like Tara. She's one of the top-flight solicitors from our insurance arm.'

'From Tor Grand?' His sister's stunningly selfish lack of interest in the fires made him bite back. 'Then I doubt that she'll come. She'll be far too busy sorting out this Chatterton Court mess.'

Though she was almost through the door, she stopped. 'Which Chatterton Court mess?'

'You know. The Special Promotion. A month's free contents insurance.'

'No, no. Perdita has already been carpeted for that.' His sister snorted. 'As if it wasn't absolutely typical of her arrogance, to walk into a new department in the morning and take it upon herself to turn a simple intra-office design and marketing exercise into a full-bodied outside mailing without even checking with anyone above her.'

He stared. 'You mean they weren't even supposed to be posted.'

'God, no! And Tara heard Marjorie saying that if there should actually be a fire—'

'Which there has been.'

'A fire?'

'I *told* you. I *kept* telling you.'

'I thought you told me that was *your* place.'

Would they go round in circles all afternoon? 'And so it was. Hers first' – best leave out Mother's for the moment, so as not to confuse things – 'and mine straight after.'

'Chatterton Court. Gone up in flames?' He'd never seen a person's mood change quite so fast. You'd think he'd waved a wand to turn her from ratty to radiant. 'The whole lot? Are you serious? You never told me.'

He felt like Clarrie. 'I like that! I've been telling you for the past *ten minutes*.'

His sister was ecstatic. 'Well, isn't that bloody Perdita in the soup?' He hadn't seen her so enchanted since the first time her trick of stringing dental floss between the magnolia and the laurel fetched him off his bike into the lupins.

A moment's thought and her smile became even more radiant. 'And this is going to cause a heap of shit to fall on Marjorie as well! In fact, I wouldn't be at all surprised if—'

Snatching the tray from him, she rushed from the kitchen to fall on Mel just like a proper hostess. 'Is tea all right? I'd be delighted to fix you a drink, if that's what you need more after all your horrors. Though we will be drinking later, when my guest comes. I hope you don't mind. You're *terribly* welcome.'

Her eye fell on Mel's grubby and travelworn clothing.

'Though perhaps you'd be happier tucked away with the telly. You think about it. But, right now, you must tell me exactly when you last had a bite to eat. There's supper coming. But right now I could offer soup. Or a sandwich. And, while I'm getting it, you must come through with me into the kitchen to tell me all about this dreadful, *dreadful* fire . . .'

She was still chuntering merrily when he left.

A pity his mother hadn't thought to close the larder window before embarking on her pestilent chicken supper. Smuts had flown in with the smoke and left dark splatters over everything. Should he toss all the food out, or could he simply wipe down jars and packets? Tugging things out one by one, he caught sight of something tiny and still and black behind the semolina. Talk about shoemakers' children being the worst shod. Could this all-too-large speck be the corpse of a cockroach in his own mother's pantry?

So hard to see. The smoke-filmed lightbulb dangling overhead was practically no help at all. He'd get that wiped off first. He tested his weight on the breadbin into which he'd just slid Mr Herbert's pre-dated certificate, ready for any battles to come ('Not with the rest of the paperwork? Good heavens! Let me send you a certified copy of the original') then, guessing the breadbin's lid wouldn't bear his weight without denting, went off for a chair he could climb on.

Now that his eyes were level with the highest shelf, he could see everything she kept up here. Perhaps, he thought, suddenly reminded of his detritus in the wood-shed, she was versed in her own form of medical wizardry. There was that stuff she used to make him gargle with when he had mouth boils. A sticky-lidded jar of glycerine of thymol. Some ancient Friar's Balsam. One or two linseed poultices. A package of grubby-looking thermo-gene wool. And an old nasal douche bag.

And, behind that, a long thick envelope. Presumably private. And recent, too, or it would surely share that yellowed look of the instructions for the poultices and the label on the glycerine. He stretched out his fingers to prise it from its little hiding place behind the medicines. And it was a hiding place, he was sure of that. She, being shorter, would think the envelope pretty well invisible, tucked behind there. It wasn't sealed, though it had clearly been so once. Had she come back, time and again, to read and reread the contents, until the self-adhesive strip along the envelope gave up the ghost? He checked his fingers for tell-tale Friar's Balsam, then, coolly, and pushing all qualms aside, fished out her secret.

Her new will.

Of spite unparalleled. Blinking, he tackled it a second time. And then, in disbelief, the covering letter in all its unsheathed malevolence.

Knowing just how much trouble comes about when twins are not treated with scrupulous fairness . . .

(What was the self-righteous old bat on about? She had let Dilys be top dog since the Year Dot.)

. . . and since, with my death, my son and daughter will only have one another left . . . would hate to come between them . . . matter of principle, given our estrangement, not to leave anything at all to my daughter . . . sadly leaves me with no alternative . . . nothing for Colin either . . .

Giddy with shock, he sank on the chair. Old people were *amazing*. First, the embittered Widow Besterton, spiting her friends and acquaintances by leaving her not inconsiderable Chaffer fortune to strangers on the strength of two ill-written signatures on a blank page. And now his mother, heaving everything into some charity skip – which was it, for God's sake? Bloody Help the Aged? – on the strength of a principle in which she'd never before shown a smidgen of interest.

Still, credit where it was due. It can't have been easy. Not the business of giving away his inheritance – that would have been a breeze. But it must have been hard for someone who so delighted in taking sides to treat the two of them fairly. (Though, there again, there'd be the splendid consolation of thinking she'd more than likely introduced a canker that would spoil what little sense of kinship remained.)

Not bad – even for someone who had spent the larger

part of her life making malice an art form. Small wonder she'd had so little time for jobs or hobbies. She'd put her heart and energies into this business of growing grievances and fomenting ill-will. In these two areas, at least, you had to hand it to her. She had taken pains. Indeed, you had to admire her. Such was her level of commitment to her vocation that, like some martyred saint of old, she was prepared to turn even her very own death and funeral to account, as proof she wouldn't miss a trick.

So look at him now. Off the hook, and *free*. That ghastly miasma of guilt that hung around him like bad breath – all gone, gone, *gone*. And he would never even have to tell her why. In those sharp tortoise eyes, the same old dark contempt would burn. He wouldn't care. He had stopped feeling grimed with guilt the moment he'd grasped the gist of the letter. No longer would he have to squirm when she went on about the cruelties life had dealt to her. He would remind himself that some people go through life gathering roses, and others thorns. Instead of peevishly tolerating one another through what might come, he could, like Tammy, sit bewitched. She'd look at him as if he were the usual old smell on the landing. And he'd be able to look levelly back, and stroll off whistling with her will in mind. Admiring her, even. And feeling close to lucky. After all, how many other people had a parent so committed they would devote, not just their whole life but their death as well, to dealing their off-spring one last astonishing, hurtful black card?

Talk about black. His hands were filthy as her heart. It would be nice to get the place cleaned up a bit before his guests came. For, yes. Now that he knew that he could face his mother down, he could go back for Mel and Tam. Herding the little flock of gruesome medicaments back into place in front of the envelope, he picked up the cloth and started wiping off particles from the fire. What better place to start his new life than here in Holly House, grave of the old? He could nip up and find some sheets and stack them on top of the boiler. By the time Tam was sleepy again they would be aired enough. And that back room in which his father seemed to spend the night so often in the months before the accident was cosy and warm – and out of the way. Mother would barely even notice a small child pattering around. Best to choose somewhere sensible, after all, since it was clearly going to be a matter of weeks – not till Mel started slipping away on trips back to the circus: that, from the driven level of the practising, was clearly going to start almost at once. But till the money came through, and he'd had time to look for a nice house close to an excellent school – and, of course, near to the station so Mel wouldn't ever have to bother with taxis. And pretty soon, of course, he'd have to face the fact that—

On with the cleaning, Colin. First things first.

The hospital escalators faced one another crosswise between the mirrored walls in which Tammy was com-placently admiring her smart new pigtails and her brand-new frock.

'Col! Colin!'

Val had shot past.

Hastily, he started to walk backwards down the rising

steps, with Tam still on his shoulders. Val took the same tack, dragging the blonde woman standing at her side up backwards in step. 'Off to see Mum,' explained Colin across the twin handrails that had become his only point of reference in a dizzying universe. Was this the sort of exercise Clarrie and her keep-fit friends did for hours at step class? If so, they must be mad. The back of his thighs were aflame, and Tam felt like a boulder.

Val was insistent. 'Wait at the top. I need a word.' As he sailed on and up, he heard her adding, 'It's professional.' But, frankly, she could have been planning to sting him for a tenner and he'd still have fallen in with her, rather than face the physical strain any longer. 'You're a giant great lump,' he told Tam almost crossly, lifting her off at the top and dumping her down firmly.

'And you're a big farty mole!'

She fell into hysterical giggles at her own wit, and he stood panting till Val and her colleague had sailed up to join them.

'Not here,' said Val. 'Private. Come round the corner.'

Not that private, Colin thought somewhat sourly, as the other woman followed. But he said nothing, merely giving her the briefest of nods as Val whipped out her notebook.

'Now, Col. About your mother . . .'

'Still in Ward Four,' he told her, jerking a thumb upwards. 'Passing the lonely hours sharpening her fangs.'

Tam squeezed his fingers in that flutter of delicious terror he'd come to recognize. Val sighed. 'I mean, what's going to happen when we sign her out today? Where is she going?'

He couldn't help asking hopefully, 'Why? Will she be on *your* list?'

'Of a fashion. Just till she's a little less shaky.'

'She'll be all right,' said Colin. 'She'll have us looking after her for a while.' He leaned down, testing the water with his beloved. 'Isn't that right, Tam?'

'Tam?'

Val's colleague stepped back to take a better look at the neat pigtails and the spanking clean frock. 'This can't be Tammy Gould!' She switched on her professional voice. 'Well, well! Remember me?'

'No.' Tammy scowled.

'Oh yes, you do,' the woman told her calmly. 'I'm Hermione, and I come to visit.'

'Say hello,' Colin ordered, more out of prudence than any desire to mend fences between Tam and her mother's despised social worker.

'No,' Tam said, making a face. 'And you can't come to see us any more.'

Hermione ignored the rude tone. 'That's right. You're all burned down, aren't you?' She turned to Colin. 'Is that why they're moving to your house?'

'Not my house,' fended Colin cheerfully. 'Never my house.'

'See? You can't come,' Tammy informed her firmly.

Val looked up, grinning, from the discharge form on which she'd been filling in sections. 'And you won't need to, either, Hermione, if I know this man. He is obsessed with fitting safety rails to balconies, and tacking down wires, and not eating stuff past its date stamp.' She ripped her completed form off the pad. 'Well, that's your mum ticked off. I think it's a brilliant idea, having someone to live with her. And this young lady here will obviously bring a bit of light and life into the house.'

Light and life?

His wish for his mother! How many ways did magic have to work its mysteries? And he could tell, just from the conspiratorially merry way Val and Hermione were exchanging glances, that what he wanted for himself was on its way as well. Neither of these two would step in to veto his glorious, burgeoning plan. After all, as even Mel had grumpily admitted, people of his sort spread safety nets all over. What better way of making sure everyone got what they needed than leave it to him?

He was still standing, lost in astonishment, when Hermione turned back to Tam. 'So you won't be too pleased to have me visit you at Colin's mother's?'

But Tam had changed her mind. Winsomely tipping her head to one side, she said sweetly to Hermione, 'Oh, yes. You can come. And Norah will give you some of her special *soup*.'

And knowing disquietingly well just what sort of special soup his small charge probably had in mind, Colin took her by the hand and hastily ushered her onwards and upwards.

His mother sat bolt upright on the bed, ramming the hat that sat on her head like a shiny black slug through with a hairpin.

'I see you've brought Little Miss Smartypants along with you.'

'She insisted on coming. I think she must like you.'

Even to him in his new mood, this came out sounding rather rude. But his mother just snorted. 'You really have made her top billing, haven't you? I expect, when she asks, you'll be giving her the eyes out of your head to play marbles.'

Already Tam was sitting starry-eyed. What was it about children, that one could thrive on acid that had eaten away at the soul of another?

'Actually, she's coming back with us to Holly House.'

'Really?' His mother gave Tam a very beady look indeed. 'Well, just so long as she behaves. Otherwise she'll go in the broth pot.'

'Mustn't tell lies,' Tam told her gravely.

'Don't talk back to Old Bones.'

Hastily, Colin distracted the two of them by asking his mother, 'So how are you feeling now, anyway?'

'Like a wobbly foal. But ready to come home.'

And he, he realized, was ready to take her. After all, what was so wrong with doing right by her? He wouldn't be doing it just for his mother. It was for him, too. He'd face his deepest fear – the fear that, one day, she'd be at his mercy and he could pay her back for all the wrongs that he and Dilys still believed she'd done to them.

And he would not. He would be good to her. There she sat, dressed up and ready to go, halfway between what she was and what she thought she was, just like everyone else on this crummy, flawed planet.

And he'd do right by her. Survive. And live to tell the tale.

As good a son as anyone could hope for.

'Let's go home.'

THE END